The
Shy Tulip Murders

Also by Rebecca Rothenberg

The Dandelion Murders
The Bulrush Murders

The
Shy Tulip Murders

• • •

Rebecca Rothenberg

THE MYSTERIOUS PRESS

Published by Warner Books

A Time Warner Company

Excerpt fron   DEC 9 6   ʃ
Handbook, k
1963 by the University of California Press, used by permis-
sion of the publisher.

 Mysterious Press books are published by Warner
Books, Inc.,
1271 Avenue of the Americas, New York, NY 10020.

A Time Warner Company

The Mysterious Press name and logo are registered
trademarks of Warner Books, Inc.

Printed in the United States of America

First printing: May 1996

10 9 8 7 6 5 4 3 2 1

Library of Congress Cataloging-in-Publication Data
Rothenberg, Rebecca.
    The shy tulip murders / Rebecca Rothenberg.
      p.   cm.
    ISBN 0-89296-607-6
    1. Women scientists—California—San Joaquin—Fiction.
  2. Microbiologists—California—San Joaquin Valley—Fiction.
  3. Environmentalists—California—San Joaquin—Fiction.
  4. Endangered plants— California—San Joaquin—Fiction.
  5. San Joaquin Valley (Calif.)—Fiction.   I. Title.
PS3568.0862S59   1996
813'.54—dc20   95-46447
                                                      CIP

To
Linda, Dan, Ray, Mickey, Carla, Martin,
and the Tule River Conservancy

The
Shy Tulip Murders

Chapter 1

Almost certainly it was the two guys from the restaurant who nailed the owl to Marcy's door.

But to get to the guys in the restaurant we have to back up a bit—about, say, ten million years, to the late Cenozoic, when the great batholith of the Sierra Nevada began to uplift along faults on its eastern side, up and up, until sheer scarps rose thousands of feet from the desert floor. Meanwhile, out in the Pacific the plates slid east, nudging the edge of the continent and leaving behind parts of themselves in a coastal ridge that became a Coastal Range. So that by the late Pleistocene, California was much as it is today: two parallel ranges of mountains separated by a long groove of flat valley.

As the Sierras rose, their open oak woodlands became thick conifer forests. Rivers notched the granite peaks, pouring west toward the sea but spending themselves in the vast landlocked slough of the Central Valley. Sometime later it was toward the tall conifers—the pines and firs—that Sierra Wood Products turned an avid eye, and it was down the narrow canyon of one of the rivers, a minor one, that Claire Sharples drove to work every day.

She was a young woman lucky in work and unlucky in love, a pattern that never registered on the geologic time line but that seemed to her every bit as significant and inexorable as the stately drift and bump of continents across the aeons. And on Tuesday morning she was also late—again, not by the cosmic clock but by her boss's watch—and she needed her morning coffee, and the water was taking ages to heat. So she lifted the kettle and cautiously held a palm six inches over the burner. Gradually her hand descended until it rested peacefully on the stone-cold coil.

Damn! Not again!

The electrical system in her place seemed to be afflicted with a wasting disease: one by one outlets had shut down, and now the condition was spreading to major appliances. Were you supposed to have an electrician check the wiring before you bought a house? How should she know? She had never done this before.

And never again, because she was nothing if not loyal, unlike some people. A one-house woman. She loved her little witch's house, with the tall pines and the tall oaks and the not-so-tall manzanitas . . .

And the dying wiring. Still in her underwear despite the high-altitude chill, she stomped out to the front deck, opened the fuse box, and wiggled a circuit breaker up and down, a voodoo routine that had worked yesterday.

Magic, however, is even more fickle than science, and this time there was a sizzle and an arc of blue flame. She yelped, jumped straight backwards, and stared at the blackened smudge above the switch.

Well, now she could call the contractor. Surely if she

did everything else herself, no one would consider her a useless female for not making electrical repairs—no one, for example, like Sam, who had probably laughed himself silly when he heard about her fixer-upper mountain cabin. If he had heard. She didn't know; she hadn't talked to him in almost a month, not since that last conversation in the lab. I'm sorry, he'd said, maybe fifteen times—surely the feeblest phrase in the English language. Not even a decent verb, just that weak, ambiguous adjective, as in *you sorry bastard.* Spanish and French were more eloquent. *Lo siento,* I feel it. *Je suis désolée,* I am desolate, I cannot be consoled. . . .

Ow! Her right shin collided with the knife edge of a flimsy sheet of paneling stacked in the dark hallway—dark because the hall light had blown the day before yesterday—and she hopped into the (dark) bedroom, tears of pain streaming from her eyes. Okay, she would also hire someone to help finish the paneling. That was reasonable, right? She pulled on jeans that concealed her scraped and bleeding leg, which she didn't want to take the time to tend. She had been late for work every day for weeks; luckily she was in a honeymoon phase with *someone,* even if it was only her boss. Ray was still giddy over the fact that she, a genuine MIT-trained Ph.D., had taken his extension expert job, so for the moment she could do no wrong.

Up to the main highway she drove in her zippy new lipstick-red Toyota, and then left, west, toward the Central Valley. The road sashayed out toward the river and back into the mountain in such tight curves that it seemed she steered her nifty car simply by shifting her weight.

Her tires crunched across the flattened fragments of an animal—and then another. And another, and the highway began to seem like one long avenue of roadkill, as if a steamroller crawling downhill had met with a herd of lemmings racing up.

Four miles: she had wound down a thousand feet, the pine and cedar had given way to oak and manzanita, and the trail of carnage continued.

"Who would have thought the old stegosaurus had so much blood in him?" she muttered, though by now she had figured that whatever was smeared across the road was neither dinosaur nor rodent. It was too dry. And flaky . . .

Bark! she thought suddenly. It was the color that had fooled her, that shocking raw red, but that's what it was: the sluffed-off skin of fresh ponderosa pine being hauled down this mountain. She slowed in anticipation of coming up on the logging truck around the next blind curve.

But she didn't. So at three thousand feet, where the chaparral opened up and she could see the steep granite cliffs at the mouth of the canyon, she took her foot off the brake. And when she hit Riverdale, where the road finally leveled and straightened on its way westward to the San Joaquin Valley, she had made such good time that she was hardly going to be late at all.

Rather than set an unfortunate precedent, she decided to stop and eat breakfast.

In the old days, that is, six months ago, before her life blew up in her face like a mail bomb, this would have meant Katy's Koffee Kup, but Sam and Sam's friends hung out at Katy's. Instead she slowed just east of town, where the north and middle forks of the river converged, and took a hard right. So did the trail of bark.

In fact, it led right into the parking lot of Ma's Donuts and ended at a logging truck stacked with fresh-cut sections of ponderosa. She squeezed her car between it and a dirty white pickup. She knew that pickup. This should be an interesting breakfast.

Two guys who must have belonged to the truck—one blond and clean-cut, the other with a greasy black pony-tail hanging limp between his shoulder blades—sat at the counter. Wedged into a corner booth was the entire environmental community of Riverdale, all six of them. And at their center, as always, was Marcy Hobbes.

Marcy had defiantly placed herself directly under the placard that said "We Support Loggers—They Support Us." Here in the southern Sierras, where very few people actually made their living off timber, this sign was ideological rather than literal, a declaration of which side of the Great Divide the proprietors came down on, and it wasn't the side of the lily-livered, soft-handed, government-loving environmentalists. No, sirree, they were rugged! Cowboys! Trappers! Loggers! (Actually most people in Riverdale and up on the hill lived on Social Security.)

"Good morning," Marcy said when Claire walked in, and smiled brilliantly. Marcy was a very pretty woman—glamorous, even, a rare quality in this part of the world. At forty-four, eight years older than Claire, she still had the cloud of soft brown hair, the glowing skin, the doe-like eyes, and the girlish manner of Mary Pickford in her prime. And the clothing allowance. Surreptitiously Claire checked out her wardrobe—four-hundred-dollar silk-and-suede Ralph Lauren Country Girl, as usual—and received a precious cup of coffee.

"Hi," Claire said to the table at large, but it was Marcy who answered, saying, "You know everybody here, Claire?" and leaning back against the arm of a young man as she looked up. Claire registered the two bits of data simultaneously: he's cute; he's hers.

Did she know everybody? She scanned the assembled heads of the Friends of the Redwoods, or the Redwooded League, as she thought of them. Halo of sepia curls: that was Naomi Weissberg, and the sleek dark hair next to her, her husband, Paul (they were the white pickup). Bad perm: Marie Martelli. Claire often wondered what Tom Martelli, the local police chief, thought about his wife's sedition. Iron-gray hair in merciless Doris Lessing knot and fluffy blonde: Hazel Batts, Cheryl Preuss.

And the new head, Marcy's friend: small gold hoop in left ear, straight, sun-bleached hair, blue eyes. Interesting color—kind of a high-altitude blue, a wide open blue.

"Oh, this is Will, Will Brecker," Marcy said in a voice uncharacteristically breathless. That's for him, thought Claire, indulging in a moment of cattiness as she ripped her eyes away. Then she chastised herself; she was a little breathless too.

The blond logger spoke from the counter. "I'll have me two eggs over easy, biscuits, and some fried spotted owl," he announced loudly for the benefit of the other patrons.

"Same for me," said the other logger. "Only make mine owl *hash*. Damn things is tougher'n a mother-in-law's tit!" He looked over his shoulder at the corner table and grinned. He was missing a few teeth. The corner table glared back, but nobody moved.

Nobody but Marcy, who stood and approached the pair, having decided that this was an opportunity for dialogue and mutual education.

Sit down! The fervent, silent plea from her friends was palpable, but Marcy was oblivious. She had a mission. ("Don't let the girlishness and the clothes fool you," Marie Martelli had told Claire. "Marcy's about as sweet as a chain saw when she wants something.")

"You folks working around here?" she asked.

They ignored her.

"Salvage over on Black Mountain?"

They gulped coffee.

"Taking out a lot of beetle-damaged trees up there, I bet."

"Some," Over Easy admitted, responding to her soft voice and pretty face.

"If they ain't damaged when we git there they're damaged when we leave," said the other, but Claire thought this was braggadocio. The loggers weren't supposed to take anything but dead or dying trees out of a salvage area. It was only from what was called "green sales" that they could cut healthy timber.

"Just wondered," said Marcy, "because your load out there looks pretty healthy." Uninvited, she perched on a stool. "You know, if you folks would cut a little slower, you could log for years up here without destroying these forests. At this rate you're going to work yourselves out of a job."

"No, *you're* going to work us out of a job, *Miz* Hobbes," Owl Hash snarled. "You and them," he added, nodding at the table, "with your lawsuits and injunctions and regulations! All you care about is the view through your fucking tinted windshield." (Marcy did drive a Jaguar.) "You don't give a shit about the people who got to live and work and raise their families up here!"

"I care a lot about your families!" Marcy shot back. "I'm a mother too, and I want there to be forests for my kids when they grow up."

"Yeah, well, I ain't sure my kids is going to grow up. I ain't sure I can feed them!" By now his voice was high and his face red.

"Marcy," Paul Weissberg called, "this isn't the time. Let's go."

She slid calmly down from the counter. "I hope you both come to the forest service's public hearing next Thursday," she called over her shoulder. "We want to hear all sides of the issue." And she slipped out the door, followed by the rest of the group.

Claire had maintained a certain neutrality during this by retreating to her own table, but she paid her check and left, too. A postmortem was in progress in the parking lot, inevitable in this group of basically shy people who had doomed themselves to constantly confront their neighbors and then feel upset about it.

"That was a gutsy thing to do, Marcy," said Naomi.

"It was pointless," her husband said sharply, voicing Claire's feelings. "You just made them angry."

"They made themselves angry." That was what's-his-name, Will. His voice was husky and boyish. "People choose to create that space in themselves. And you never know, these guys might have been tired of their old tapes and ready for some new ones. It was worth a try."

Claire stared at him, searching for some irony behind this speech and finding none. What she did see was that he wasn't as young as she had thought. His sun-streaked hair, pulled back into a ponytail, was just beginning to thin on top: his years as Golden Boy were numbered.

But not over. In fact, to Claire the evidence of wear, the fine vertical lines from cheekbone to jaw, made him all the more attractive.

But Marcy shrugged away both men. "Are you going into Parkerville?" she demanded of Claire.

"Past there. Why?"

"I need a ride to the Riverdale Forest Service headquarters. Somebody smashed the windshield of my Jag, and

it's still out of commission," she said, shooting a reproachful look at Will.

"Still waiting for the part, Marce," he said.

"When they cut the brake lines you fixed it right
away."

"That was standard quarter-inch line. This is custom—"

"Wait a minute," Claire interrupted. "Somebody cut
your *brakes?*" For a sick moment she imagined careening
down that hill without a way to stop.

"Oh, yeah." Marcy shrugged, as if this were just a cost
of doing business. "Nothing happened; I noticed it before
I even got out of the driveway. Anyway"—she turned
back to Will—"they've had it for three weeks! Why don't
you be a little more aggressive?"

"Why don't you drive a reasonable car? This isn't Bev-
erly Hills!"

So he *could* speak the language of normal human irri-
tation, thought Claire, and said, "I'd be happy to give you
a ride, Marcy."

". . . pick up the Environmental Assessments for the
Red Cloud and Bear Mountain cuts," Marcy was saying.
"Right in my viewshed. Anyway the forest service has no
business issuing permits for green cuts with all this beetle-and drought-damaged timber around."

They had passed through the two-street tourist town of
Riverdale and were just about to come to Lake Prosperity, local testament to the motto of the Army Corps of Engineers: No River Too Puny, No Dam Too Big. It was
only late June and already the water was receding, leaving bathtub rings around the shore. By September Lake
Prosperity was a blue puddle in the middle of a good-
sized mudflat.

"Their science is lousy. In fact it's not science that

drives these national forest sales at all, it's money—the Genes' money."

"What are the genes?" Claire managed to interject. The same thing was happening with Marcy that had happened every other time they had met: Claire, hoping for friendship, extending fragile rhizomes that were stopped cold at Marcy's impervious wall of sound; Claire, feeling like nothing but a big ear. A big anonymous ear. Marcy could have been talking to anybody; it was a nervous, almost hysterical kind of chatter, interesting in content but distancing in affect.

"Not what, who," said Marcy, slowed for a moment. "Gene Doughty Sr. is Sierra Wood Products. He owns the sawmill in Tierra Buena, he and his son Gene Junior. Everybody calls them the Genes. They're the only show in town—the only sawmill I mean—and they retooled a few years ago and geared up to a twenty-four-hour a day operation and now that place is a bottomless pit. They can't keep it filled with salvage so they pressure the forest service for green sales even though those sales are always a net loss to the public, I mean, they would be anyway, what with subsidized roads and the fact that they throw away all the fir and the cedar, just stack everything but the ponderosa in slash piles and burn it, but around here there isn't even any competitive bidding, like I said, the Genes are the only show in town, it's typical of these agencies that get captured by the businesses they're supposed to regulate. . . ."

She was up to speed again, and in a minute had segued seamlessly from the corruption of the forest service and government in general to the BIA to the mistreatment, historical and contemporary, of Native Americans. Claire snuck a look to see if she was practicing circular breathing like a jazz flutist: in through the nose, out through the mouth.

Marcy saw Claire looking at her and actually stopped. Abruptly. "I'm talking too much, aren't I?" she said, in one of her disarming, charming about-faces. "I'm sorry."

"Oh," said Claire, disarmed and charmed. She had begun to nurture bad thoughts about Marcy. "It's fascinating—"

"Up to a point. I know. Will says the way I talk is a form of aggression. But really, I think I'm just angry. I'm so angry about this forest stuff that I get wound up and can't stop and drive myself and everybody else crazy." She halted again. "Will's helped me learn to relax." (I bet, thought Claire; I bet he's a good relaxer. But she softened toward Marcy.) "Anyway, let's talk about something else. You're a biologist at the field station, aren't you?"

The first question Marcy had ever asked her. "Microbiologist, used to be," Claire said. "But now my position is extension expert in plant pathology." Marcy looked blank, and Claire added, "Like a farm adviser."

"Farm adviser!" Marcy was amused. "Drive around in a UC pickup?"

"Yup."

"Tell people what to spray for scale and thrips?"

"Yup," she said again. "Well, blight and wilt and rot are more my line—diseases rather then pests. And mostly I tell people what *not* to spray. At least, that's the official policy of the extension. Biological control and all that."

"Good," said Marcy. "Clamp down on some of these nozzle-heads."

Claire laughed; she'd have to take "nozzle-heads" back to work with her. Or maybe everyone else had heard it. She was still out of the loop of station subculture.

"Still," Marcy was saying, "what these agencies say they

support and what they actually do don't always coincide. Take the forest service. . . ." She trailed off, and Claire prepared for another installment of Marcy's obsession. But what Marcy said was "Ever do any research that could help us?"

"Help you?"

"Well, after all, trees are just another crop, right?" she said acidly. "A 'fiber crop.' I mean, that's why the forest service is under USDA."

"I don't work for USDA," Claire said, not sure if she was being attacked. "And that's not how I see the forest."

"I know. I'm just kidding. I was thinking you could provide expert testimony for some of our lawsuits. Or comment on Environmental Assessments, especially the two I'm picking up today, the two new green sales."

"I'd be happy to help if I can," Claire said. "But off-hand I can't think of any expertise I have that might be relevant to you all." Had she always said "you all"? she wondered. Or was that an Okieism she had picked up from the second-generation Dust Bowlers of Kaweah County?

"How about botany? Like rare plants, you any good on them?"

"Not great. But I know a . . . a first-rate botanist." Sam. First-rate botanist, second-rate human.

"Wonderful! Listen, why don't you come over for dinner tonight and we'll talk about it? You know where my place is? Good. Will's a great cook, even if he is a strict vegetarian. I'm not, though I avoid red meat, and veal of course, you know how veal is raised—"

"I'd love to," Claire said firmly, stanching the hemorrhage. "Seven-thirty?"

*   *   *

Claire dropped Marcy at the forest service office just beyond the lake, then turned south through the orchards and Sierra foothills, hills whose sweet, deceiving green had enchanted her when she visited two years ago from Boston. "You might not like it so much in six months," everyone had said, and in fact six months later the green hills were parched and brown and the thermometer was topping off at well over a hundred every day. But at least she had been falling in love. This summer would be every bit as hot and bleak as the last two, without that mitigation.

The office—that is the University of California Agricultural Field Research Station at Citrus Cove—was a low brick bunker crammed up against the foothills. As she had for the last month, Claire made her way crabwise down the corridor, looking out for Sam's narrow silhouette so she could have an instant to compose herself. Shit, there he was. She tried to demystify him, to see him as the gawky guy with thick glasses he was, instead of as omnipotent Rejecting Lover.

They nodded to each other with every appearance of cordiality; she was an old hand at this, passing ex-lovers in the hall. He would never have known that she had spent the wee hours dreaming of pummeling his new lover, of savagely driving her fists into Linda's plump, blue-veined breasts. She had awakened ashamed of her own political incorrectness. Why direct her rage at Linda? It was Sam she was angry at.

And not angry enough, according to her therapist-wanna-be friend Sara. "He lied to you!" she had said. "Let it out!" she had said. Anger at deception was Okay.

But in truth if Sam had been a braver person, if he had come to her and explained in reasonable tones that he missed his old girlfriend, Linda, and thought she'd make a better stepmother for his boys than Claire, it might have benefited *his* immortal soul, but Claire wouldn't have felt much better. What she was angry about was simply that he had chosen someone else. She was jealous.

Definitely Not Okay, but there it was.

She scrambled down to the lab, taking stairs two at a time, called Don, her contractor, and left a message about the stove, appending it to her catalog of malfunctions. The hall light, the bedroom light, the socket in the living room, the stove. It was like a children's memory game: "I went to the store and bought apples, bananas, cherries, Demerol. . . ."

Then she drove out to Alma to look at some walnuts with incipient hull rot, then to Poplar for some plums, and ate lunch in the car on the way up to the big Kearney field station. She was collaborating on a field trial of possible substitutes for methyl bromide, MBr, an incredibly versatile soil and post-harvest fumigant that was also toxic and ozone-eating. Its imminent ban had growers scrambling for replacements, and Claire was looking at a couple of biological alternatives.

Then home.

Claire sat cross-legged on the warm deck, letting her mind empty of hull rot and methyl bromide and fill with the sound of the river and the steep green-textured canyon wall across from her.

A huge manzanita reached above the deck, its dull red branches braiding one another with shadow so that two trees seemed to coexist in intricate space. A sherbet-colored bird alighted on the stiff gray-green leaves, emitted a call between a whoop and a whistle, and zinged off toward the far side of the canyon. Birds constantly darted or glided like schools of tropical fish across the narrow gorge—a short flight and a hell of a walk; the canyon was so steep that from her deck she looked down on the birds as they flew. Crows spread their wings and tails like open hands, and their glossy backs gleamed.

To the west, over the Dusty Valley, the sky glowed like orange Jell-O, suspending a banana slice of a setting sun. Jell-O . . . banana . . . she was late for dinner with Marcy!

Chapter 2

"They lie." Marcy poured herself more Chardonnay. "They can't help it. It's the Y chromosome."

"It rhymes," Claire pointed out. " 'Y,' 'lie.' "

"Who lies?" Will poked his head out from the kitchen, where he was making coffee. "The forest service?"

"Yeah, the forest service." Marcy lifted an eyebrow at Claire, making her snicker.

Will returned to the kitchen. "Now, my first husband," Marcy went on, in what was surely the modern equivalent of "Once upon a time," "was . . . I don't know, it's like he was wired backwards. He'd have a vanilla ice-cream cone and tell you it was chocolate; I mean, he'd lie for no reason, he'd lie just so he knew something you didn't. So when he *did* have a reason, forget it. The whole time we were married he was seeing other women and I don't even think it was for the sex. I think he just enjoyed making up the stories and keeping them straight. It was exciting, you know? Like being a spy."

She topped off her glass, and Claire covered her own with her palm; she'd already lost count. But she seemed to have discovered the nutrient medium for friendship with Marcy: a nice little dry white wine. The more Marcy drank—at least, the more *somebody* drank—the more personal, and the funnier, she became.

"When I found out about the first one—my next-door neighbor," Marcy was saying, "he swore there were no more. Swore up and down."

"This was up here?"

"Bakersfield. I'm originally from Alton, over near . . . near . . . well, I guess it's not near anything."

"I know where it is," Claire said. West of Bakersfield, middle of the Valley. Cotton country. Not her responsibility, cotton; she worked with specialty crops: citrus, stone fruit, nuts.

"Anyway, when I found out about the bank teller, that was it, I left him. And then afterward I kept discovering there had been *more* women, and I kept putting things together . . . like the Thanksgiving he had to leave dinner early, because he had to meet a client. I felt so sorry for him. Come to find out he'd actually gone to my neighbor's house and had *another* Thanksgiving dinner with her—and then *another* one with the bank teller! Sucker had to eat three dinners in one afternoon! Turkey, stuffing, the works! 'Course he was probably working up an appetite every time," she added thoughtfully, and cracked up.

Claire was now laughing as hard as Marcy, who filled their glasses again.

Will reappeared with coffee in blue-and-white cups

that matched the Mexican tile on the kitchen counter. He looked at the two helplessly hysterical women, mystified.

"Gilbert," Marcy gasped. "We were talking about Gilbert."

"Oh," he said, face clearing. "Now there was a guy with some serious issues around intimacy."

"There was a guy who was an asshole," said Marcy. It wasn't that funny, but following on the heels of Will's solemn psychobabble it made them both laugh again. "But a good-looking asshole." She raised her glass in mock toast. "Gilbert Hobbes," she said solemnly, "you left me a decent last name and a new respect for prenuptial agreements. And Laurie, of course," she added in a different voice. "That's my daughter."

Claire was only half listening now, watching the candlelight flicker across the fine bones of Will's face, like shallow water over stones, and studying his arms as he distributed the cups. One brown wrist was encircled by a strand of what looked like barbed wire but was probably braided elephant hair. She gave a mental shrug. Too bad about Will. He was nice to look at, and a wonderful cook, and presumably gave Marcy what she wanted: adoration, sensitivity up the wazoo, an antidote to the perfidious and thoroughly Old Age Gilbert. And relaxation workshops. Too bad he . . . well, too bad he talked like a Stepford husband.

Too bad he loved Marcy, was her first unworthy thought.

"Let's move out to the deck," said Marcy.

Her "cabin" was about a mile up the road from Claire's, but had essentially the same view. To the left, the east, was Slate Mountain, its nine-thousand-foot peak still stippled with white; straight ahead to the south the river's steep gorge; to the west, the pink haze of a Valley sunset. They watched while the last of the alpenglow dimmed to shadow on the mountain. Venus bloomed in the southern sky. The river roared below them as it ran down into the Valley, fast and deep with snowmelt. The night air smelled of cedar.

For a long time none of them moved. Then Marcy's chair scraped on the wooden deck. "Thank you, Granny."

"Granny?" repeated Claire.

"This place was my grandmother's. I used to come up here when I was a kid—spent all my summers here, in fact. That's why I love this forest so much."

"You're really grounded here, Marce," Will, inevitably, agreed, and Claire thought, Oh, that explains the money; she's from a wealthy farming family.

"Was your family in cotton, Marcy?" she asked.

"Uh-uh"—taking a swallow of Will's excellent coffee— "ducks."

"Ducks?"

"Yeah. We ran a duck club when I was growing up— you know, guys would pay to shoot the poor little things—"

"I used to do that," Will interrupted. "I can't believe the macho crap I was into!"

"Our land was marshy," Marcy said, ignoring him, "and not much good for anything else. God, I couldn't wait to get up here in the summer!"

Well, so much for the wealthy old Valley family, thought Claire. There couldn't have been much money in ducks. " 'Course, this place was just a ramshackle old cabin then," Marcy was saying. "Just a shell, really. No plumbing or electricity. I had to fix it up some."

Some! Claire thought of the Mexican tile and thick carpets and art on the walls and smooth-gliding windows and Italian pitchers full of wildflowers. Marcy's house was, like Marcy, an artful and expensive blend of the rustic and the classy. She tried another tack. "Have you ever lived anywhere else?"

"Oh, sure. After Gilbert, I moved down to L.A. I was there for seven years. But I couldn't take it."

L.A., then. There was lots of money in L.A. Marcy must have tapped into it somehow.

"I moved back here for the forest," Marcy was saying. "That's why I'm so concerned with saving it. Obsessed, like I said. But how can I not be? The people who are supposed to protect it, the forest service, are selling it off as fast as they can! And lying about it! That's what really makes me crazy. They just flat-out lie, to your face."

"Really?" Watergate and Contragate and the October Surprise and just generally getting older had convinced Claire that every branch of her duly elected representative government might lie to her at any time. But not the forest service. Not the forest rangers, with their doughboy hats and their Smokey the Bear Sutra (Drown Their Butts, Crush Their Butts). Anyway, Marcy's history with men might have made her somewhat paranoid. Claire knew this because her history with men had made her somewhat paranoid. "Like what? What's an example?"

"Look," Marcy said, "right up there," pointing toward Slate Mountain. "It's too dark to see right now, of course, but just north of the peak there's a saddle, and running down from that saddle is a big old clear-cut, like somebody came along and shaved the mountain. And what happened was this. First," ticking off a point on her fingers, "by some miracle we heard about the sale before it went through. So we all marched into the district office, and Nelson Pringle, he's the supervisor, he said," ticking off another point, "oh, no, it wasn't going to be a clear-cut, it was going to be selective cutting. 'Grove enhancement,' they call it. It's like the military, you know . . ." She was fishing for a phrase.

"Collateral damage," supplied Claire.

" 'Zactly!" Marcy had continued to toss back Chardonnay along with the coffee, and while her mind didn't seem to be slowing, she was knocking the corners off words. Up here, if you talked to anybody after 6:00 P.M., chances were they'd sound pretty blurry. "And in any case, he said"—up sprang another finger—"we'd never be able to see it because it was confined to the east side of the ridge. So what happens? I come home one day last summer and the cut has crept over the ridge, *and* it's a goddamn clear-cut! I mean, they spared a few specimen trees—"

"Specimen trees?"

"Yeah, you know, the big sequoias. The ones that presidents have their picture taken under."

"Wait a minute," Claire said. "You're talking about *sequoias?* They logged in a grove of giant *sequoias?*"

Sequoias were one of the secret treasures of this place. A relict species, Sam had told her, meaning they had once been widely distributed over North America, but when the climate changed they had retreated to a few mountaintops here in the southern Sierra. Before meeting Marcy and the other Friends of the Redwoods, Claire had naively assumed that such precious trees were protected.

"Oh, yeah, did I fail to mention that?" Marcy said. "But the point was, Pringle out-and-out lied to us!"

"Maybe he didn't know what was going to happen

once the loggers actually got in there," Claire said, thinking of her own often futile attempts to curb the 'nozzleheads.' "Maybe he doesn't have much control over them."

"Oh, he knew. I mean, he said it was a mistake; it wouldn't happen again. He says that every time. Like Gilbert. By about the third time I realized Pringle was just lying to us."

Claire was still unpersuaded. But it was time to go.

"Don't forget the meeting tomorrow night," Will said, following her to the door.

"Oh, 'n' listen," Marcy added, "we're all going to Casey's Friday night. Why don't you come with us?"

Marcy was now quite drunk, and Claire wasn't sure she'd even remember the invitation by Friday. Besides, Casey's held painful memories. "Um, I don't think so. . . ."

"Oh, c'mon!" Marcy said, and Will added, "It'll be a wonderful opportunity to network with the folks up here, explore our common ground—"

Even Marcy balked at this. "Jesus, Will," she said. "It'll be a hell of a lot of fun! They're getting a really good band up from Bakersfield, and everybody'll be dancing. Please come!"

Claire changed the subject. "You must have been hiking in a meadow, Marcy," she said. The earthenware vase by the door held deep blue cowled blossoms: monkshood, a flower of damp mountain meadows. She had to suppress an impulse to scold; Sam had not approved of picking wildflowers.

"I brought them, and yes," said Will, *"I've* been hiking in a meadow. A really beautiful spot."

"Someplace you feel really grounded?" Claire said, half hoping to provoke him into so exasperating her that she could dismiss him. It bothered her that she was fixating on this semi-vacuous hunk. Too much wine, she told herself. Too little sex.

Anyway, Will just smiled, disappointing her again. A nice smile, she couldn't help noticing; a nice man, when he spoke English instead of New Age. A nice man who was in love with Marcy.

He started to push open the door, then stopped, peered out a side window, and said, "Marce, you should replace this light. It's pitch-black out there."

"I know, I keep forgetting. Use the other door, Claire. The one you came in."

Claire left by the side door and followed the silvery paving stones of the lighted walk, which was itself only a few candlepowers up from total darkness. The brush whispered and rustled around her. A bird hooted like an oboe. She shuffled warily, feeling for the first step, but even so she missed it and nearly fell, clutching at nothing and saved only when her knee banged hard against a rasp-barked oak. When she straightened again, she was directly across from the official, never-used front entrance.

Something gleamed dimly from that front door.

For a moment she thought of a body floating in water. But the proportions were wrong, the arms caped, the body short and wide, like . . . like . . . *Moth!* She formed the word and writhed with revulsion, seeing a huge—an enormous—moth, splayed against the screen, pressing to get in.

But that was ridiculous. Of course it wasn't a giant moth. There was something else, she told herself as she inched toward the door, something that had that pale, big-bodied shape, something that should be sculling through the night, not just . . . hanging there.

Her mind flinched.

But when she was two feet away, the moon fell full on the eerie, inhuman face, and she had no choice but to see it for what it was.

"Marcy!" she half screamed. "Will!" Then she just stood, looking up at the barn owl someone had nailed by its soft white wings to Marcy's front door.

Chapter 3

Claire was dreaming too much. And Tuesday night the usual humiliating scenarios of her and Sam and Linda were invaded by the owl. Not the pathetic small body, torn by buckshot and nails, that had made Marcy curse and Will cry—though he'd had to work at it—but the face, that mask of a face, holy, implacable, alien.

About four she finally fell asleep. An hour later she was awakened by an eight-foot pair of castanets chattering right above her ear: a demented woodpecker was bent on drilling through the front of her cabin. If ever a bird asked to be nailed to a door . . . no. Not even in jest.

So once again she arrived at work late and exhausted. On rare occasions she could snatch a nap in the lab, but today she had scheduled a half-dozen field calls that would take her to every corner of the county. Ordinarily they were the part of her job she loved best, but now she planned her itinerary without enthusiasm, beginning at

Paul and Naomi Weissbergs', which made no geographic sense but would allow her to ease into her day.

As she passed through the lobby, the light glinted off the long freebie table where staff researchers distributed the fruits of their labor. A promisingly lumpy shopping bag slouched on one corner.

Too late for citrus, too early for tomatoes or peaches. She pulled the lip of the sack toward her and sniffed: a moldy, earthy smell. Onions. What kind of trials were they conducting on onions? she wondered. Self-peeling? Tearless? She shrugged and grabbed two papery globes.

She checked the station pickup for equipment and gas and headed north along J19, threading the foothills, passing the turnoff to Parkerville and the lake. A few miles later she turned west onto Avenue 164, realized her mistake, made a U-turn and traveled north to Avenue 194. The avenues were hardly mnemonic. A hundred years ago the Southern Pacific had laid out the plats for the San Joaquin, casting a vast taut net of roads and avenues across the Valley to contain its trackless marshes. And since the railroad was more notable for larceny than poetry, every town had the same street names—Oak, Maple, Walnut, Orange, Olive, Main—and Avenues One through Four Hundred and something divided the middle of nowhere into a neat grid.

Peach orchard, walnuts, apricots, peaches again—she whizzed along happily at seventy miles an hour. Suddenly an unfamiliar crop loomed on her right: low, strangely stiff, white. As she swept past, she saw it was a sprouting of small white crosses, homemade, draped with flowers. A Latino custom, marking yet another fatal car wreck on these lethal roads.

Whoa! She slammed on the brakes as she nearly ran up the tailpipe of a Mazda pickup carrying six men in baseball caps. Farmworkers, she thought; *oye, hombres,* let me by, and she pulled around to pass them.

But the Mazda wasn't the problem. The problem was a white Wal-Mart truck, tall as a town house so she couldn't see around it, but that didn't matter because all she'd have seen was another Wal-Mart truck. They always traveled in flotillas.

They had descended on the county suddenly, as if air-dropped onto the narrow two-lane roads of Kaweah County—ominous, hospital-white, like the trucks that carried the pods in *Invasion of the Body Snatchers.* Oh, Christ, here came another two, eastbound, spic-and-span and smug. Our Lights Are On for Safety! How Am I Driving? "Too slow," she snarled and pulled back into line.

In any case she had reached the Weissbergs' orchard, and she pulled into a dirt drive between rows of peach trees and stopped. By reflex she timed her breathing so that she exhaled as she slammed her door, avoiding a lungful of dust. But there wasn't much dust; the Weissbergs didn't use Roundup between their trees. Instead, nitrogen-fixing clovers and vetches ran down the rows, and a friendly insect-friendly hedge of clover, poppies, and yarrow rimmed the orchard. A stiff-eared jackrabbit bounced away from her, ricocheting between the berms like a pinball in play.

Paul and Naomi were waiting, Naomi unconsciously chic in broad-brimmed straw hat and overalls, Paul quite convincing in dirty jeans and a cap that said "Parkerville Lumber." They had moved down from the Bay Area a few years ago to buy this small orchard, knowing nothing about farming—they were lawyers—but really wanting this life for themselves and their young daughter.

"How's Hannah?" asked Claire.

"Fine. She's at playgroup. . . . Is that anything?" Paul

asked anxiously, as Claire reached up to finger a sickle-shaped leaf that was coated with gray. "Monilinia? I sprayed twice with sulfur during bloom."

"Road dust," she said, wiping her hands on her pants.

They walked the rows, pushing through the knee-high cover crop. Once Claire picked an almost-ripe fruit and Paul's forehead knotted again, but she began to eat it and he relaxed. Paul's face was constantly in motion. Even his scalp moved up and down like a freight elevator when he talked. Perhaps in compensation Naomi was as heavy-lidded and serene as a Madonna.

Finally she said, "Well, your zinc sulfate treatments seem to have worked. I don't see any sign of a deficiency. In fact, your crop looks pretty good."

Paul slumped with relief. "It ought to," he growled. "It ought to be the Cadillac of crops, after all the time I've put in lately."

"And not a billable hour in the lot," Naomi said crisply, and he grinned.

"That's true. I'm off the meter."

They headed toward the old-fashioned but air-conditioned farmhouse—ten o'clock, and it was already ninety-plus. Over a pitcher of iced tea in a kitchen large enough to feed family and hired hands, back in the days when hired hands were allowed in the kitchen, conversation turned from orchards to forests.

"So I hear you're coming to the meeting tonight," Naomi said. "Marcy's pulling you into our cabal."

"Yeah. I guess you heard about the owl, too."

"What owl?"

Claire told them.

Naomi was appalled, but Paul said he wasn't surprised, after the vandalism at Hazel's cabin and the recurring petition to have Cheryl fired from the library.

"And Marcy's brakes and Marcy's windshield," Claire said.

"And Marcy's provocation of the men in the restaurant," Paul finished. "She's gotta exercise a little judgment. She seems to think she's got diplomatic immunity, but this is a highly charged issue up here. Especially where you and Marcy are, Claire, up on the hill," he said seriously, making Claire feel suddenly uneasy. "Nayo and I"—he nodded at Naomi—"we're kind of insulated, being down in the Valley, but even we get murderous looks when we go into town."

"Which I don't understand," Naomi said. "Rationally, the farmers ought to be worried about what's happening uphill from them. They ought to want to prevent their water supply from silting up. They ought to be on *our* side," she said plaintively.

"Dream on," Paul said. "This has nothing to do with reason. This is like the Hutus and the Tutsis. People here have never forgiven us for having long hair in 1968."

"*They* wear long hair," Naomi pointed out.

"Doesn't matter, it's not rational. Though, to be fair, some of their friends and neighbors work in the mill."

"Some of their friends and neighbors belong to Friends of the Redwoods," Naomi said. "How come we don't count?"

" 'Cause they don't write country songs about reference librarians," Claire said, and they all laughed without enthusiasm. And then she asked, very diffidently, about Will Brecker.

Paul raised his eyebrows, and his hairline, in perplexity. "Well," he said, "he's either an organizer's dream or an agent provocateur."

"Really? What do you mean?"

"I mean he's this working-class kid from Parkerville—

he even worked for the Genes at the sawmill for a while—who's suddenly seen the light, environmentally speaking. I'm just paranoid enough to wonder about him. And Marcy was probably thinking with something besides her brain when she brought him into the group."

Claire, who had her own romantic ideas about handsome working-class boys with good politics, laughed a little nervously. But Naomi gave her husband a quick look, opened her mouth, closed it again, then said, "Oh, no, sweetie, Will's been in the group since the beginning. Marie told me. Only at first he was more of a gonzo Earth First type."

"I'm not reassured by that," Paul muttered.

"But then he started dating someone who was involved in some New Age recovery movement, and all of a sudden he's talking about 'tapes' and 'creating a space for anger.' But you're right about one thing," she said thoughtfully. "He *is* awfully good-looking."

Paul scowled and she laughed. "Sweetie, it's *you* who likes the sunny WASPs." Her husband looked away as she continued, "I'm the one who's partial to the dark intellectual type. And I'm afraid whatever Will may be, it's not the intellectual type."

"Unless he's playing a part," Paul said.

"Yeah," said Claire. "Isn't he almost a parody? Of New Age–speak, I mean."

"Oh, no!" Birdlike, Naomi cocked her head. "I think he's sincere enough. You've just never lived in Berkeley or Santa Cruz. You're sheltered out here."

"It's nice to think of this place as sheltered instead of deprived," Claire said.

"Parkerville *is* pretty much Old Age," said Paul.

"Dark Age," Naomi and Claire said simultaneously, and they all grinned.

When she left it was with a lightened heart. After two years in Kaweah County she was finally making some friends, and at the moment that seemed to compensate for exhaustion, heat, departed boyfriends, and dead owls.

Chapter 4

By seven-thirty that night the Friends had assembled at Marcy's. There was also, to Claire's surprise, an envoy from the enemy—a youngish man in a forest service uniform whose brass nameplate said A. Nilsson. Before the meeting they trooped out to look at Marcy's front door; she and Will had buried the owl under a cairn of smooth river stones, but you could still see a smear of blood between two nail holes, left as epitaph—and, on a more practical level, as evidence for Marie Martelli's husband, Tom.

After that everyone proceeded to nail A-for-Andy Nilsson to the wall.

"Who's monitoring those salvage cuts?" demanded Marcy. She was wearing a buttery silk sleeveless blouse over brown velvet leggings, and Claire began to wish that she herself had worn something besides her dreary one-step-up-from-T-shirt-and jeans. "I saw a load of ponderosa the other day that looked as healthy as you do, Andy."

Actually, at that moment Andy's good-natured ugly face looked a little pale. And before he could answer, Cheryl Preuss jumped in. "With all the drought-damaged timber up here, why has Pringle issued permits for new green sales on the forest?"

On the forest, thought Claire; she had noticed that this was the proper construction. Things were never *in* the forest, always *on*. She wondered whether prepositions were selected to put policymakers at one remove, looking down from a God's-eye position. In her own work, fields were planted *to* beans, cotton, wheat, not *with*— again, an idiom of domination, as if the land were entirely dedicated to its crop.

"And when is the district going to hire some scientists?" Naomi was asking. "Like a botanist? Under the terms of the memorandum of understanding, you were supposed to do that two years ago."

Finally, a question Nilsson could answer. "My degree is in botany," he said quickly.

"Yeah, but Andy, that's not what you *do,*" said Paul.

"There's no money—"

"C'mon, Andy. There's money to build logging roads for the Genes, but none to monitor the forest!"

"Paul, you know as well as I do that that money comes from different places."

"And *goes* to different places, too. The Genes' money goes right into the forest service's pockets."

"You don't have to tell me that," Andy said mildly. "That's why I'm here."

Paul flung up his hands, palms outward, in a gesture of exasperation or apology. "I know, I know, you're AFSEEE." AFSEEE was a reformist faction within the forest service. "But goddammit, Andy," he burst out, "why don't you people do your jobs?"

Andy flushed under his fair Scandinavian skin, and his round ears, which poked through his floppy hair, glowed like pickled beets. Against his green uniform they gave him a sort of festive Christmas air. "Look," he began loudly, but was interrupted by a sharp knock on the door.

Marcy jumped up. "That must be Dustin," she said, and in a moment she reappeared leading a Latino kid of about eighteen. "This is Dustin Gomez," she said. "He's from the res, and he knows the area where the two green sales are real well."

Claire looked harder at Dustin. The res—the Kaweah Reservation, was just south of Slate Mountain, and now she could see that he might indeed be American Indian instead of Mexican, despite his last name; most California Indians had Spanish surnames, one final and propagating insult from the conquistadors. He was of medium height, sturdy, with smooth acorn-colored skin and thick black hair pulled into a warrior's ponytail. A braided rawhide thong circled the strong column of his neck. Level brows met over his nose like the wings of a circling hawk.

He was, in fact, very beautiful.

At that moment Claire wondered if Dustin Gomez was in line to be Marcy's new squeeze. But he was just a kid, a baby, young enough to be her son.

Nevertheless, Claire shot a glance at Will. But when Dustin sank into the deep brown leather sofa next to Marcy, Will's clear blue gaze was perfectly amiable, if a little confused. Romantic notions from *Dances with Wolves* contended with the knee-jerk contempt of Parkerville for its own particular brand of American Indians.

Cheryl was hammering Andy Nilsson again. "You're

pretty new here, Andy," she said, her crisp reference-librarian voice issuing laserlike from under her mop of fluffy blond hair, "but you should know that this district has a history of not caring about anything except getting out the cut on the forest."

Andy looked pained and took a long swallow of beer. "Change the law," he said. "Getting out the cut is our congressional mandate."

"So is preserving the health of the forest," Naomi said.

He shrugged and loosened the collar of his uniform. "As you well know, we have to depend on congressional appropriations for that, and we don't always get 'em."

Marcy stretched out her velvet legs and draped an arm along the back of the sofa behind Dustin. Instead of leaning back against her, he bent forward, resting his arms on his knees, and there was a flash of silver against brown skin as his shirt fell open. "But you always get money for timber sales," Marcy said.

"That's direct revenue. Look, I don't like the situation any better than you do, Marcy—Ms. Hobbes. That's why I'm here tonight. But I got booted from my last position for subversive activities, and being a member of AFSEEE doesn't improve my standing with my boss, believe me. While I'm up here talking to you folks, Nelson Pringle is talking to some wise-use group down in Bakersfield." He made a sweeping gesture in the general direction of that city and overturned his glass of beer on the oak coffee table. "Oh, *merde*—I mean, shoot. I'm sorry."

He was given a brief respite as reward for jeopardizing his career, and to mop up the beer, and then Paul struck again.

"You think there's any chance of deliberate fire-setting this summer?"

Dustin looked up.

"For what?" Andy said, startled. "For the salvage?"

"Mm-hm," Hazel said. "Or for the fire-fighting jobs."

"Well, you folks know this area better than I do, but I'd be real surprised. I mean, I've heard about some of that in the Northwest, but I can't imagine anybody'd be stupid enough to try it down here. After four years of drought, this forest is a tinderbox."

Dustin resumed studying his hands.

Before they adjourned, Marcy passed out copies of the EA for the Bear Mountain green sale.

Claire received the phone book–sized document with dismay. "I don't know anything about Environmental Assessments, Marcy."

"Just check their botany," said Marcy. "Make sure they've considered the impact on any rare or endangered species in the area. Everybody, there's stuff to eat and drink in the kitchen. Will, would you bring me a glass of the fumé blanc that's on the top shelf of the fridge? Dustin, would you like a soda? Oh, by the way, folks, we might have to meet somewhere else next month. The kids from the reservation are having a powwow down in Riverdale on July Fourth, and they're going to be rehearsing up here in the living room. Right, Dustin?"

Dustin had wandered away and was leaning against the open doorway to the deck with his back to the crowd.

"Right, Dus?" she repeated.

Slowly he turned around, met her eye for a moment, then lowered his gaze and muttered something, exactly like a sulky adolescent.

Clutching her document to her breast, Claire left the house and headed down the walk.

Andy Nilsson was hoisting his wiry frame into a Chevy Suburban of that peculiar forest service algae green.

"Afraid you were Christian versus lions tonight," she said, startling him so that he bumped his head against the doorframe.

"Ouch! Oh. Hi. I'm used to it," he said, grimacing at the pain and at her comment. He had a droll mouth, with an upper lip like a trumpet player. "I really appreciate these grassroots groups; they keep us honest."

"Marcy would say you haven't been honest yet."

"That's probably true," he said, looking like a doleful camel. "It's changing; it really is. But you'll have to keep applying the thumbscrews, and tonight it was my thumbs in the vise." He grinned. "Or some more delicate part of my anatomy. Well, au revoir!"

She walked to her car in the dark. Reluctantly her eyes slid to where the owl had hung; then she brought them back and fumbled with her car door. Even on this side of Marcy's cabin the river was startlingly loud, like the rumble of trucks on the highway. Then she realized that the rumble was coming from behind her. A car was parked across the road, engine idling. Someone else from the meeting?

Evidently, because when she drove off the other car left, too, trailing her down the mountain to her road, then whizzing past as she turned off.

When she opened the cabin door the earthy coffee-ground aroma of skunk greeted her. Shit. Probably under the house. She'd have to deal with it sometime.

Inside, she flipped through the Environmental Assessment, her years in academia helping her over the unfamiliar lingo: MBF (million board feet), DBH (diameter at breast height), cap/suit (capable/suitable). From this first pass she gleaned two things. One was that the timber sale was smack in the middle of her viewshed: on the flank of Slate Mountain, directly below the clear-cut Marcy had pointed out the other night. The other was that there seemed to be no mention at all of sensitive plants. Misinformation she might have been able to correct, but with no information she was helpless. She was going to have to consult an expert, i.e., Sam.

Ah, well, she thought, maybe this was a sign. Sooner or later she was going to have to create a new kind of relationship with him or else leave her job, which was what she had done last time.

That was the *other* thing that had brought her to California.

Being left got easier; she was getting good at goodbye, as the country song—yet another she had absorbed through her skin and against her will, like a pesticide—would have it. Maybe youth was resilient, but age was resigned. When Phil left her, she'd had to move three thousand miles over; with Sam, it was only a few thousand feet up.

But still it was hard to be around him at work and not want something from him—something she couldn't even name and that Sam probably couldn't have supplied anyway. It wasn't simply sex; there were plenty of men around who would have provided that upon request.

Okay, maybe not. If there had been plenty, she wouldn't have been panting over Will Brecker. Men, touchingly, assumed that women never lacked for sexual opportunities, an attitude held over from the time of Emma Bovary, or at least from ninth grade.

All old news. She slapped a mosquito and retired to her nightly dreamscape.

It seemed like minutes later, though in fact it was four-thirty, that the woodpecker gave two or three sharp raps.

She gritted her teeth and waited for the unholy racket to commence. But that was it; he let her sleep. Maybe he had taken pity on her, or maybe, being male, he had simply left.

Chapter 5

In the morning her left front tire was flat.

And it wasn't until she had located the new jack, which looked like a lunar landing module, figured it out, located the cheap little balloon spare, strained her back loosening the goddamn lug nuts, wrestled off the tire and pushed the baby one on in its place, washed her hands—in short, till she had changed the tire—that she noticed that the *right* front tire was flat, too.

While she waited for Triple A she ran her fingertips over the nails driven deep between the treads on both tires. One she could easily accept as road hazard; two, no. She remembered those hammer blows before dawn, and last night's black car. Some asshole had crept down her driveway in the night.

It was the creeping rather than the tires that upset her. Also the injustice: why her? Why pick on *her?* She was no Marcy Hobbes, no Paul or Naomi, no linchpin of the environmental movement; she was just a relatively innocent bystander who happened to have attended a meeting.

As soon as she got to work she forgot the incident, lost in the minutiae of setting up her field trial: Did the literature really justify serious consideration of marigolds and neem as nematocides, or was that just old wives' tales/New Age gossip? Okay then, how many blocks? How many replications?

But night is altogether different, and that night as the sun set she began to think of secret, undetectable things they could do to her car. The brakes. A bomb.

She turned on all the outdoor floodlights and lay rigid in bed for hours, waiting, listening, wondering why she hadn't installed a car alarm. Why had she fallen for the Z-Lock 2000, an expensive antitheft device that protruded from the base of her steering column like a steel Tootsie Roll and was probably just about as effective?

Around midnight a dimly remembered sentence from Nancy Drew set her rummaging in her kitchen cabinets. She selected a box, carried it outside, and began to sprinkle a fine white line all around the car so that any disturbance would show. This should be salt or ground bone, she thought as she sifted, and I should be making a pentagram.

But even a ragged circle of Bisquick had a ritual quality that soothed her into sleep.

She dreamed of her parents that night, or at least of her father, or at least of a father she remembered before he got sick: glossy black hair and crisp good looks. He was talking to her mother, telling her how much he loved her. But Claire never saw her mother in the dream, had only a peripheral sense of her, sand-colored, sidling, transparent, like a ghost crab. In the dream her parents were younger than she but already parents, already *her* parents, and her father said reproachful and bewildered things to the grown-up Claire about her loveless, childless life. Things that he might indeed have said if he were alive, and that her mother *had* said.

She elbowed her way out of post-dream melancholy into resentment. It was unfair, she fumed, as if some agency other than her own brain—some Voice of America's Collective Unconscious—were broadcasting these things. It was unfair—she slammed her car door—to roll so much into one big softball and bean her with it. Sexual rivalry with her mother/sexual rivalry for Sam/grief for her father/grief for Sam/passive aggression toward her mother/panic over the solitary shape of her life . . .

She turned the key and went cold with horror. She had just remembered to be wary. Well, she thought as she scrambled out to examine the car, evidently not an ignition bomb. By now she herself had scuffed the line of Bisquick in two places, so it was unrevealing. But the tires looked okay, and when she pumped the brake pedal it seemed perfectly normal.

What else could she do? She started down the hill.

In a couple of miles she came upon a grand new Oldsmobile with a beam like the *Queen Mary* and a self-made man at the wheel. Figuring she was in for a slow ride down, she closed the gap between them to about a foot, just to let him know she was there. This was obnoxious enough that he pulled out at the first turnout, and she gave him a friendly beep and whizzed past.

It was when she braked for the next curve that the first alarm sounded, faintly: it seemed to her that the brake pedal dipped farther than was normal. But then the road leveled out for a quarter of a mile, and she told herself that she was just not quite used to her new car, that

Marcy's story had stoked her morbid imagination, that if someone cut your brake lines you noticed it right away. Marcy had said so.

But then the very hard granite walls on her right and the very empty air above the canyon on her left began to whip past awfully fast, and the alarms rang louder. She was having to shift down way too early to stay on the road. And by the time she hit the slalom course at three thousand feet, her foot was mashed against the floor and her tires screeched and a kind of sick dread throbbed in her gut.

She was in trouble.

Usually Claire's compulsion to rehearse disaster just made her morose—oh, sure, she was happy *now,* but what about tomorrow? Ever since Marcy's story she had been observing geographical features, weighing alternatives, fully imagining yet another Unlikely Bad Thing. And now a contingency plan for Brakes Fail on Mountain Highway had found its alphabetical niche in her brain between Airplane Door Flies Open and Caught in Front of Crumbling Dam.

Which was good, because at this moment she had no time to think about anything. Except making it around those deadly curves, taking them wide but not too wide, not too close to the sheer plunge off the side, laying on the horn, praying nobody was coming up the other lane. Shift down now! her subconscious told her, but she was already in second and still gaining momentum, the tachometer needle quivering, swinging toward the red, and when she tried, hopelessly, to force the gearshift into first, her transmission screamed at her. There was no arguing with syncromesh. Or gravity. *The emergency brake, stupid!* She grabbed the lever, which lifted easily in her hand, useless as a carrot.

Her subconscious already had considered and rejected as implausible or beyond her skill such television ploys as using friction against the steep roadcuts to slow herself. Her best, maybe only, option was racing toward her: the hairpin curve by the power station.

Just before the road bent sharply toward the river the vertical road cut on her right disappeared, and the uphill landscape opened out into a fairly gentle bank of oak and grass. There was even a short dirt road. If she could drive up onto that, it would slow her; if she missed it, she was sunk. Even if she happened to make the first curve, she wouldn't make the next one. She would go straight over the side.

Here it came . . .

Shit! She had forgotten the metal guardrail that lined the curve! Double shit, the fucking forest service had closed the iron gate across the dirt road!

There was a narrow opening between the gate and the rail, not really wide enough, not really the best place to turn off, but she had no time; she twisted the wheel violently, the car skidded out of control, clipped the railing *and* the gate, rocketed up the hill, bobbled over a couple of boulders, hit a good-sized blue oak, and crashed to a stop.

Chapter 6

I always wondered if that thing would work, was her first coherent thought, meaning: The air bag. It had inflated and deflated in such quick succession that she wouldn't have known except for the sour smell of whatever gas it used and the bag itself, dangling flaccid from the wheel, and the fact that she was alive. My new car! was her next thought, and she staggered out and moronically began examining fenders and bumpers before realizing she was way too shaky to stand. She dropped where she was, and for a long time lay flat in the brittle yellow grass.

Finally she sat up and took fearful inventory.

Her neck hurt, but not a lot. There was a quarter-sized bruise on her right leg where the Z-Lock 2000 had drilled into her thigh. Her left arm stung from a weird friction burn on the inside of her forearm. (Days later she realized she must have been pressing it against the steering wheel.)

And that was it, as far as she could tell. Incredibly, she appeared to be okay.

She waited for double vision or some other sinister symptom to manifest itself, but after five minutes she decided she really *was* okay and climbed unsteadily to her feet.

Now she examined her car. The car was not okay. Maybe, just maybe, not totaled, but not pretty: crushed front bumper, matching pleats on both sides from passing between Scylla and Charybdis, which had probably slowed her considerably, contusions and abrasions from branches and rocks, and who knew what she had done to the transmission?

She perched on a lichen-covered boulder and took a long swig from her water bottle. Now the ambulance would come, right?

After a while of the ambulance not coming, she understood that no one could see her and that the screech and smash, forever etched in her brain, had been heard by no one else. She walked up to the road to flag down a car, sat on the end of the guardrail, looked vaguely down the hill—and drew in her breath.

Six feet from where she had made her wild turn was another of those small white crosses: tacked-together paint stirrers draped with an ancient chain of ossified daisies, with a couple of initials written in the center. She had never seen it before.

No cross for her today; today she had been lucky. Not too long ago someone else hadn't been. She looked away from the cross and for the first time formulated the thought: Someone had tried to hurt her and hadn't much cared if he killed her.

Five minutes passed, but no traffic; even the regal Olds had long since coasted by. Finally she realized that if a car crashes in the woods and nobody hears it . . . you reach for your cellular phone.

The phone was such a recent extravagance, which the

University of California should have sprung for but hadn't, that she tended to forget about it. She tramped back to the car, started to dial 911—and hesitated.

This was not L.A. or Boston, with their anonymous bureaucracies. If she dialed 911, she knew exactly who would come: Search and Rescue from up the hill. They supported loggers; loggers supported them.

And she knew what they would do about her claims of sabotage: nothing. Or worse, call J. T. Cummings, who was the county sheriff, and hated her. And she would probably have to get a CAT scan and lose a whole day of work, and at the moment that seemed intolerable. She *had* to go to work; it was what she always did when bad things happened. The concentration, the routine, the normalcy, all steadied her. She had taken her SATs two days after her father died.

So she called B&T's Repair and Tow in Riverdale. Eldon Bonnet—he was *B*; the *T,* she suspected, was simply to balance the ampersand—arrived, told her that a lot of people didn't know how to drive down a grade, you had to watch your brakes, just last week the school bus had lost its brakes and crashed into the granite a quarter mile up, praise God no one was hurt. . . .

I didn't "lose" my brakes, she wanted to scream; someone took them! But all she said was "Check out the brakes."

"Oh, they'll be fine after they cool down."

"Just take a look at them. But don't fix anything until I tell you to."

When they got to the garage, she walked down the street to the office of the chief of police, Tom Martelli. But his Blazer wasn't parked on the street, and nobody responded to her knock. She'd call him later.

Claire caught a ride to work with another peripatetic

farm adviser. At ten Eldon called to say that her brake lines had been loose, so that they lost fluid gradually as she came down the hill.

"Loose, not cut," Claire repeated.

"Yup. Both lines, too! I never seed that before. That's why they started makin' 'em with two independent lines, so if one system goes, you still got you two good br—"

"And the emergency brake?"

"Cable snapped. You had yourself a run o' real bad luck."

"Yeah."

The weasels had learned from Marcy: a slow drip was better than a cut because it would take miles for all of the fluid to leak out. Suddenly Claire was violently disgusted with these cowards who oozed under cars, performed their trivial technical tasks—a twist here, a snip there, no big deal, easier than hooking up a washing machine—and oozed out again, absenting themselves from the consequences. It was like carpet bombing from thirty thousand feet. Or building the bomb in the first place.

Now she really had to call Tom.

She hadn't communicated with Tom since her breakup with Sam. He had been Sam's best friend, insofar as old-fashioned, private men like them had best friends. But he and Claire had a mutual, if strange, history, too, as sporadic collaborators in Tom's police work.

Still, they had always had an edgy, ambivalent relationship, and that at least didn't seem to have changed. "You know," he said after she told her story, "you got to go easy on the brakes when you're comin' down a road like that. You ride 'em, they'll go out on you. Just last week a school bus—"

"Jesus, Tom, didn't you listen? My brakes were tampered with!"

"Loose, I thought you said."

"Loos*ened,* both of them, and the emergency brake was cut."

"Snapped, I thought you said."

"Tom, it's a new car! This is the same thing that happened to Marcy last—"

"Marcy Hobbes?" he said quickly.

"Marcy Hobbes. You know, smashed windshield, owl nailed to door. That Marcy Hobbes."

"What's this about her brakes? Marie told me about the windshield and the owl, but I never heard about no brakes."

"Maybe Marie didn't know. Marcy noticed the problem right away, so nothing happened. But they're getting smarter."

"They?" he repeated vaguely.

"The loggers!" Her voice rose with exasperation. Tom could infuriate her faster than anyone except her mother and certain ex-boyfriends, people who otherwise seemed to have nothing in common. "I mean, they've been harassing the Friends of the Redwoods for months."

"Who's been bothered besides Marcy Hobbes?"

"A lot of people, most of it petty stuff. And now me. And they're escalating; next time they're going to kill somebody!" She paused, then added the obvious. "That could include Marie."

There was a long silence. "Look," he said eventually, "the only reason I know anything about this is because of Marie. None of it is my jurisdiction. Your accident ain't in my jurisdiction. You got to call the county sheriff for your insurance report."

"J.T.?" she said in dismay.

"Not the great man himself—he ain't gonna come over— but some deputy."

"Yes, okay. But Tom, what about the other stuff?"

"Other stuff? Yeah, yeah," he said when Claire started to sputter. "Even if there is some pattern of harassment here, I can't do nothin'. So far you got incidents up on the hill, that's J.T., and maybe some in Parkerville, that's Parkerville Police. Somethin' happens in Riverdale, I'll get right on it."

"Oh." Like last year, she thought; two men had drowned, and when the third victim was courteous enough to die in Greater Riverdale, Tom had said excitedly, "This one's *mine!*"

"But I got to tell you," he was saying, "this petty vandalism's pretty hard to solve, unless you catch somebody in the act."

"I don't call tampering with my brakes petty. I could have died!"

"Yeah, but you didn't."

"Sorry."

"Listen," he said, relenting a little, "call Ricky Santiago. You know, my former deputy. He's with the sheriff's department now; he'll be sympathetic."

Ricky, whom Claire had introduced to the most beautiful woman in Kaweah County, was downright friendly, but he wasn't very helpful. When it came to the harassment of the Friends, the sheriff figured the Friends were asking for it. "I'm just reporting what J.T. says," Ricky told her hastily. And as for Claire's car, he would stop by B&T and talk with Eldon. But while he, Ricky, might personally believe that someone had tampered with her brakes, it was going to be impossible to prove—or to convince J.T.

"What's it going to take for J.T. to investigate this stuff?" Claire asked.

"Um . . . somebody gettin' killed, I guess."

*   *   *

As a last placating comment, Ricky had suggested she call the other people who were at the meeting to find out if anything else had happened last night.

She did, and it hadn't. Except that Paul and Naomi, who had left before her, had noticed the car. Black, Naomi thought. "I know," she said when Claire was silent; "there're a lot of black cars."

"Yeah." Claire said, "I wonder why they didn't follow you?"

"Maybe they knew we lived way down here in Flatland. If they'd cut *our* brakes we would have rolled fifty feet." Naomi paused. "Or maybe because of Paul."

"You mean, they picked me because I was a woman alone?" Claire bristled at the sexism of the criminal classes. And for the next six hours of returning phone calls and rescheduling field calls, whenever she thought about the accident it was with this same half-amused indignation. Her neck reminded her not to move too fast, and when she checked her thigh, the mark of the Z-Lock 2000 had ripened to the color of a Thompson seedless grape, but she congratulated herself on her recuperative powers. She seemed to have recovered from the trauma of the incident.

In fact, she had not yet begun to deal with it.

Chapter 7

At six Claire was headed for the lot to commandeer a vehicle for the next few days when Sam pushed open his office door.

"Hi," she said cheerfully.

He regarded her warily, wondering at her cordiality. She wondered at it herself. But there was some reason she needed to talk to him, something the day's excitement and maybe the impact of the crash had knocked right out of her head. She really was going to have to go to the doctor at some point, for the insurance if for nothing else. . . . Botany, that was it! Rare plants in the Bear Mountain sale!

"What do you know about rare plants in the area east of Forest Service Road S23J54?" she demanded.

"Sorry, I don't know the logging roads by number. Is that near Slate Mountain?"

"Yes. There's a proposed green sale in the area, and someone asked me to review the EA." She could hear herself rattling off "green sale" and "EA," trying to impress him.

But he didn't miss a beat. "There's nothing about sensitive plants in the EA?" he asked, and she shook her head. "Can you show me on a map exactly where it is?"

"More or less."

He spread a topo map across his desk and leaned over her while she examined it. Ostentiously she bent her elbows so she wasn't touching him, a gesture that probably escaped him. His mouth was just above her right ear, and for a moment she heard a catch in his breathing, a small, helpless sound.

But he must have been clearing his throat. Because when she said, "There's S23J54, that's the southern boundary of the sale," he answered in a perfectly normal voice.

"Believe it or not," he said, "I think I read that Jim West from Fish and Game found a rare species of *Calochortus . . .*"

He paused as if for a student's reply, and she heard herself say obediently, "Mariposa tulip."

"Right, and it was in this area somewhere. Some subspecies of *Calochortus invenustus.* Hold on, I think it's in the new Jepson." He pulled the new *Flora of California,* which was nearly the size of the *OED,* down from the shelf and leafed through it while Claire recalled what she knew of mariposa tulips. In a state full of spectacular wildflowers, they were one of the most gorgeous, but that was hardly scientific. They were in the . . . the lily family, she thought, despite the name, which came from their tuliplike blooms—three petals, pearl or yellow or rose or tangerine, overlapping one another in precise, tender curves.

"Here it is," Sam said. "*Calochortus invenustus* subspecies *westii*. Slate Mountain mariposa tulip. Jim West and Bob Bartlett found it on the west slope of Slate Mountain at about forty-five hundred feet. That sounds like where your green cut is, all right, but let me call Jim and find out more specifics."

This is why you consulted experts, she thought, half pleased and half resentful. Not only did Sam know about the rare flower, he was a personal friend of the guy who had found it and had his phone number in his Rolodex *and* got hold of him on the first try.

"Uh-huh," he was saying, looking at the map. "Uh-huh. A meadow . . . yeah, yeah, I got it. And that's as far as you went? Okay. Thanks a lot, Jim. Hey, listen, you'll have to come up for some trout fishing before the season's over. Yeah, give me a call. Well," he said, hanging up, "Jim thinks this *Calochortus* will be on the Native Plant Society's next inventory of rare and endangered species, which means it doesn't yet have official protected status, but the forest service usually respects the Inventory."

"And where exactly was it?"

"On the margin of a meadow, right here"—he stabbed the map—"on the perimeter of your sale. But there might very well be more within the sale area. He didn't have time to search farther north; he hopes we'll check out the other wet areas and find all the populations."

"So if we did find it in the sale area . . ." she said, thinking she'd found a way to stop the chain saws.

"They would modify the sale," he finished.

"Modify? Not cancel?"

"Hell, no. Plants don't get respect like fuzzy animals with big eyes. They'll just 'flag and avoid'—work around 'em. Theoretically. But it would delay the process some, too, while they documented it. . . . District got a botanist down there yet?"

"Not officially," she said, thinking of Andy.

"Well, then, they'd have to call in somebody else to locate it. And in any case, it's worth doing for purely scientific reasons. Let's go out tomorrow—"

"Wait a minute," she interrupted. This was *her* project, part of *her* new life. "You don't have to—to interrupt your weekend." She was going to say "tear yourself away from Linda," but just managed to restrain herself. "There's no reason why I can't do this myself, I know what a marip—"

She ended in a little hiccup. There was a reason she couldn't do this herself.

She was afraid.

All day she had managed to distract herself, but now when she thought of hiking through the mountains alone, she felt it: the will-numbing, gut-churning fear of the prey for the predator. Her left hand crept to her neck.

God *damn* those bozos! What right did they have to ruin one of her primary pleasures, a solitary walk through the forest? Might as well kill her as make her afraid to live her life!

"What?" said Sam, who had actually noticed that she was in some distress.

Bluff it out, she thought, though who she was bluffing she couldn't have said. "Nothing. I had a little accident today; I guess it shook me up. I was just saying," she continued before he could sympathize or in any other way encourage weakness, "that I can do this myself. I know what a mariposa tulip looks like and I've got the illustration . . . oh," she said as Sam pushed the *Flora* toward her. "Okay, there is no illustration. But I have the description."

She read it to herself, translating from Botanese to English: the Slate Mountain mariposa tulip seemed to have one or more flowers per stem. The flowers were white or lilac-tinged and sometimes had a purple spot below the nectary—she'd have to look up "nectary" later.

"Doesn't sound too tricky," she said confidently, though in fact she was thinking how difficult it was to identify something from a purely verbal description. Two very different faces that you would never mistake would sound identical: eyes dark brown, she thought, looking at Sam; ovate, 2.5 centimeters apart, surrounded by fringed membranes; nose, sort of . . . clavate, puberulent. . . .

Without comment, Sam pulled the book toward him and recited a passage.

"That's what I just read," she said.

"No, that's the description for plain old *invenustus.* Not the Slate Mountain subspecies."

"Oh." Then, humbly: "What's the difference?"

"Well, range, for one. *Calochortus invenustus* is found farther south, even down in the Tehachapis. So if you find something that looks like it near Slate Mountain, it's probably the rare subspecies. But if you're unsure, the fringed membrane around the nectary in *invenustus* is densely short-branched hairy, and it's long-hairy in the subspecies."

"Oh. Great." A pause. "You think I'm not going to be able to find it by myself."

"I think it's not going to be easy. You don't know the area, and you don't know plain old *invenustus,* much less this subspecies. Look, let me go with you. I know you don't like my company, but if you're serious about helping delay this timber sale, you'll be a lot more effective if I'm with you. And I'd love . . . I'd love to go with you."

On the one hand she was relieved, but on the other she hated to pass up an opportunity to deny Sam something he'd love to do. But she realized he was right. And she *had* told herself she wanted to resume some sort of professional relationship with him.

Or, she was fooling herself and simply looking for an excuse to spend time with him.

Or, she was fooling herself and simply afraid to be alone in the woods.

"Okay," she said finally. "Tomorrow, you said?"

"Yeah. About nine?"

"Fine," she said. "By the way, what does 'invenustus' mean?"

Sam had no idea; it wasn't the kind of thing he was curious about. He picked up his *Field Guide to Pacific Wildflowers,* which called it "shy mariposa tulip."

"So 'invenustus' must mean 'shy,' " he said, but that didn't seem right. There was another Latin word for "shy," wasn't there?

"Oh, and while I've got you here," he was saying, "Terry and Shannon will be up in two weeks. I know they'd like to see you, but I don't know how you'd feel about that. . . ."

He trailed off. Sam's boys, who lived with their mother in L.A., were part of the reason he had left the distinctly unmaternal Claire for Linda, who had two boys of her own. Or at least the boys had precipitated the schism. But Claire bore *them* no ill will; had, in fact, liked them quite a bit by the end of last summer's visit. And right now she certainly liked them better, or less ambivalently, than she did their father. She even missed them, sort of.

"Sure. Bring them by the lab—they enjoyed that last year."

"Great!" he said. "And maybe we can all have dinner together."

"Maybe," she said sourly.

He walked with her to the parking lot, where she unlocked one of the station pickups. "Hey, where's your gorgeous new car?"

"Garage," she said briefly.

"Tune-up?"

"No, somebody cut my brake lines," she said airily, stepping up into the cab, and had the great satisfaction of watching his face. *That* had impressed him.

Chapter 8

But in fact she was not nearly as nonchalant as she wanted to be, and it was more fear of returning to her empty house than a craving for music that made her stop at Casey's. Marcy's party was happening: in the lot a malachite-green Jaguar and a black Mercedes gleamed opulently between the pickups and panel trucks and all-terrain vehicles and horse trailers. The Jaguar was Marcy—the windshield must have arrived—but who was the Mercedes?

On her way in she stopped, as always, to read the bulletin board, an indispensable resource if you needed your chimney swept or your septic tank cleaned. You might discover you needed something that you hadn't even known existed.

As she scanned, a smudged photograph caught her eye. It was a state prison escape bulletin from down in Corcoran, and the scowling face belonged to Ramirez, Geraldo. Alias: Pelon. Crime and term: murder with use of firearm, controlled substance; twenty-one to life. Five-foot ten, two-fifty. Oddities: two fingertips missing, right hand.

Case in point on the inadequacy of verbal descriptions. No one would recognize Geraldo Ramirez from this handbill. Even the missing fingers were not much help; so many men around here had lost fingers—or an eye or a couple of inches of leg—to a combine or sawmill or meat-packing plant. And the nth-generation Xerox of a bad photograph simplified its subject to anonymity: he might have been one out of five Latino males in the county of Kaweah.

She jotted down a few people who were advertising firewood, and noted that Will Brecker had posted his name as someone who did odd jobs. After entertaining a brief X-rated handyman fantasy, she pushed open the door to Casey's—then hastily stepped backwards and took a great gulp of fresh air. There were no smokeless zones in the bistros of Riverdale. Fortified, she plunged inside.

What with the dim lights, thick smoke, and loud, loud music, she took a moment to make sense of the scene. Evidently the "great band from Bakersfield" had canceled; it was just two guys and a Rhythm Master, as usual. But with a couple or six drinks inside them, people seemed just as happy and in fact good music would have been wasted on them. She saw Marcy near the bar, flanked by a pretty blond girl and a man Claire didn't know.

"Claire!" Marcy called. Her hair was tucked up so that soft tendrils framed her face, which was pink with excitement or tequila. "Meet my daughter! Laurie, this is Claire Sharples, a scientist down at the UC experimental station."

"Neat!" said Laurie. "Are you a biologist?"

"Microbiologist, by training."

" 'Cause I'm a bio major, too. At UC Santa Barbara."

"Oh, and, Claire," Marcy said, "this is Stewart Connor." Pause. "My husband."

Claire nearly dropped her drink. She didn't know which astonished her more—that Marcy had a husband, or that *this* was him, this odd, spindly man whose elaborate cowboy regalia—fancy stitched shirt, stiff jeans, turquoise bolo—just made him look ridiculous. After a moment she remembered to smile, and he nodded to her, not meeting her eyes, as if he knew exactly what she was thinking, as if this mixture of disbelief and pity was how Marcy's friends always reacted to him. She felt a sudden sympathy for old Stewart. Consort to Marcy was no easy role.

But with the din of the band and the crowd he and Marcy were one foot too far away for conversation, so she half listened to the tedious details of Laurie's freshman-year curriculum and watched the room. Paul and Naomi and Will were sitting at a table in another corner. Don, Claire's contractor, a big beefy guy with disco sideburns that were graying from the bottom like cigar ash, was drinking alone in the corner. Aha!

She made excuses to Laurie and was headed toward him to talk about her stove when a terrific female singer suddenly joined the band. The guitar player got better, too. She looked back at the empty stage and realized that it was Wynonna Judd on the jukebox; the band was taking a beer break.

Halfway to Don, Marie and Tom Martelli intercepted her.

Marie she greeted warmly and reassured her as to her own health; Tom she regarded with a certain coolness.

But he gave her his usual mild smile and barbed banter.
"Hey, there. Brakes work?"

"On the truck? So far."

"Steering?"

"So far."

"Fall over any corpses lately?" This in reference to *last*
summer's troubles.

"Nope. No contact of any sort with any bodies in a
long, long time."

Marie giggled. "Maybe you'll get lucky tonight," she
said, her black eyebrows rising like wings. Like Paul and
Naomi, Marie and Tom were perfect complements: Marie
all delicate angles—long sharp nose, pointed chin, articu-
late collarbone—and Tom rounder by the year, especially
the belly that was beginning to pooch out over his belt.

"Maybe I should take lessons from Marcy," Claire said.
"Did you know that guy over there is—"

"Her husband," said Marie. "I know. He lives in L.A.
and comes up here almost every weekend."

"I would never have guessed she was married. That
must be number two."

"Two?"

"Mr. Hobbes," said Claire.

"I thought Hobbes was her maiden name."

"Nope. She said number one gave her a decent last
name, and Laurie." Claire was proud to bring new information to the table: Marie was a serious gossip. Also, surprisingly, a serious Christian; evidently the two were not
mutually exclusive. "But what about Will?" she said.

"And Dustin," added Marie.

"Dustin? That kid from the reservation? Are they . . . ?"

"All I know is she sure paid him a lot of attention last
night."

Last night. Was the meeting only last night? "But he's just a kid!" Claire said again.

"He's twenty-five."

"He can't be!" exclaimed Claire. Still twenty years younger than Marcy, but not quite so grotesque as a teenage squeeze.

"He is. And he's mighty pretty."

At this point Tom rolled his eyes, observed that all women ever thought about was sex, and headed for the bar, leaving Marie and Claire to speculate freely about Marcy's rococo love life and whether Dustin was a player and what Will thought about Dustin and what Stewart thought about Will.

This last question was answered when the band resumed. The Rhythm Master began to burp out a rumba, but the guitar player gave it a kick and it settled down into a slow waltz, and Marcy asked Will to dance. Stewart glowered impotently as they swayed in the middle of the floor.

Claire watched until the tune ended, then looked around for a place to settle . . . and everyone she knew had dissolved into the murk. She was alone, conspicuously alone, and the band began to play an old Merle Haggard tune, and suddenly the last few years dropped away like a dream. It was as if she had just arrived in Kaweah County and didn't know a soul and was drinking at Casey's, haughty, scared; as if she didn't yet know that she would be loved and not loved, that she would know three men who died violent deaths, and narrowly avoid some violent, messy end herself—and that she would still be living here two years later. Two fucking years!

The disorientation was like nausea. She wondered whether she had hit her head after all. She sat down hard on the nearest chair and pressed the heels of her hands against her eyes, and when someone tapped her on the shoulder she half expected it to be Tony Rodriguez, dead these two summers.

But instead she looked up into the blue eyes of Will Brecker.

"Wanna dance?" he said, and she was back in the present.

"Um . . . I really don't know how to dance to this beat, Will," she said, flustered. "What is this, a two-step?" While she had developed a grudging appreciation, or at least affection, for country music, she still found it rhythmically quite resistible.

"Texas two-step. Couldn't be easier. C'mon." He held out his hand to her.

Reluctantly she stood. "I'm not a very good follower," she warned him.

"I don't think of it as following and leading," he said. "It's more of a flow."

"Well," she said, "at least show me the basics, so I won't be embarrassed." He demonstrated the one . . . two . . . one-two pattern, put his arm lightly around her back, and they were off.

Will wasn't a bad dancer; he was poised and graceful, an athlete, and after so many months of celibacy Claire received a definite erotic charge from the pressure of his hand on the small of her back and the nearness of his mouth. But he was tentative. If she stumbled, which she did often, he stopped helplessly until she tugged on him. If this was a flow, she controlled the tap. She personally found this somewhat intriguing, but she couldn't help wondering if he was as passive in bed as he was on the dance floor—and if that was why Marcy was at this moment leaning against the bar elbow to elbow with Dustin Gomez, laughing with her head thrown back.

From the far end of the bar poor Stewart was shoulder-
ing his way toward his wife. Shamelessly Claire maneu-
vered Will toward the action, only to be defeated by the
decibel level of the band. She saw the pantomime—
Stewart's mouth opens, Dustin scowls and leaves, Marcy's
mouth opens—but heard not a word. For all she knew
they were talking about soybean futures.

Then abruptly the song ended. "—throw it in my face,"
Stewart happened to be yelling at that moment, and half
of Casey's stopped whatever it was doing to look at him.
Will dropped Claire's hand. The new Will believed in
trust and open dialogue, but the essential Will was genetically coded to fight over women in bars. So his feet took
a half step toward the happy couple and the rest of him
stayed put, until he was leaning backwards like a man
caught in a gale.

Marcy hardly needed a champion. "Stewart," she said
in the calm, sweet voice she had used with the loggers
the other morning, "it's nothing."

"It's always nothing!"

"You agreed to this arrangement. You can move up
here if you don't like it."

"You know I can't leave my work."

"Then accept the fact that I'm going to have a life up
here!"

"A life! What you have is a—"

And at that moment the band launched into a deafening and approximate rendition of "I've Got Friends in
Low Places." Stewart was seen to slam his drink down on
the bar and leave.

Claire turned back to Will. "Thanks for the dan—"

"I better go see Marcy," he probably said, and walked
away.

"Well, that certainly let the bat out of the cage," said a

voice near Claire's left shoulder. It could only be Marie, who was both Mrs. Malaprop and a great folk poet. Her small, knowing grin made her look just like her husband.

"Somebody should—" Claire began, and Marie cupped her ear. "Somebody should shoot those guys," she shouted, gesturing toward the band.

"For bad music? Or bad timing?"

"Both."

"They're all we got," Mariè said. "How was dancing with Will?"

"A little disappointing. But he's so cute."

"He's so what?"

"Cute!" she screamed.

Marie nodded. "Will's everybody's *first* boyfriend," she yelled cryptically, but Claire was too hoarse to pursue it, or anything else. She jerked her thumb toward the door and mouthed "good-bye."

But Casey's performance art showcase wasn't over for the night. Claire took a last glance in the direction of the bar on her way out and saw that Marcy was embroiled with yet another man: this one scrawny, elderly, and pugnacious, wearing a cap that said Sierra Wood Products.

Gene Doughty Sr.

Gene Senior seemed perfectly comfortable conversing at the top of his lungs. He emphasized points by jabbing his finger about two inches in front of Marcy, who looked composed but slightly irritated.

Poor Marcy, thought Claire, moving closer. All she had wanted to do tonight was get sloshed and dance.

Will, having summoned his nerve for Stewart and not exercised it, decided to intervene.

"Gene," he said, leaning around Marcy, "I sense that you need to know that your feelings are being respected here."

But over the years old Gene had chosen to create plenty of space for anger in himself. "Butt out, Brecker," he snarled.

Will blinked and took a step forward, right arm cocked, face flushed. Then he caught himself, and the mellow waters rose and covered the id's messy debris.

Bad graft, thought Claire. Exotic varietal frequently reverts to its robust native rootstock.

The entire population-at-the-moment of Casey's was gathered in an attentive semicircle, and suddenly Claire didn't want to play audience to Marcy for one more second. To witness the romantic drama of Marcy's life was to acknowledge the emotional void in her own.

She cleaved a path through the crowd and made for the door, pausing at Don Henson's table to remind him about her stove. "Tomorrow, for sure. Eight-thirty," he promised in his halting country drawl, and she nodded abstractedly and stepped outside.

The heavy door slammed, shutting off the clutter and riot of the bar, leaving Claire in the pooled silence of the night. She took a few steps toward the highway, faced the mountains, and tilted her head back—very carefully—to look at the black sky. The longer she looked, the more stars she saw; the rim of the galaxy, a whole smudge of stars, arched overhead. A meteor flared briefly like a synapse firing.

At the moment it was hard to take seriously the schemes that played out on this fingernail of turf on this insignificant little planet. Nobody, she declared with two-beer bravado, *nobody's* scaring me off this mountain—

Someone coughed right beside her, and she flinched and ducked.

No blow landed. Presently she straightened and turned to the right. But there was nothing, only blackness; then a small star glowed red, grew, dimmed. Someone was pulling on a cigarette, maybe ten yards away. It was only darkness and fear that had put him at her shoulder.

She peered, but still saw nothing.

A sudden thump, as if someone had pounded the roof of a car, and then a rough male voice said "Fuck it!" The red cigarette-star fell to earth, the car door swung open, and by the interior light she saw a cowboy hat sail onto the front seat like a wedding cake. Then the speaker slid behind the wheel and drove away.

The driver was Stewart Connor. The car was the black Mercedes.

So that was the secret of Stewart's charm, and the secret of Marcy's money—no secret at all, the oldest trick in the book. Marry a rich man.

A rich man with a black car. Like the car that had sat across from Marcy's cabin last night, engine idling.

Claire could certainly imagine Stewart stalking his wife, taking horrified, prurient notes on Marcy's extracurricular activities. She could even imagine him tampering with his wife's brakes.

But not *her* brakes. And as Naomi had said, there were lots of black cars out there.

Chapter 9

When she pushed open her cabin door she was greeted by a familiar skunky smell, a smell that would ripen nightly in her living room unless she did something about it. But she was still in a slightly intoxicated state of interstellar exaltation and decided there was room in her home for all manner of beasts—a generous thought that was tested not long afterward when she pulled back her bedcovers and discovered a fluffy mouse nest made of stuffing from her pillow and peppered with little mouse turds.

Exaltation has a short half-life. By the time she changed her bed, her radiant mood had disintegrated into something inert and heavy. Fear. Claire tried to reason it away: she really was an unlikely target, a bit player in the Friends of the Redwoods; the vandals, whoever they were, had settled on her at random last night; it was just bad luck. Only now, of course, they did know her. Knew where she lived.

The lock on her front door was a joke; there was nothing she could do about it. But she latched the windows and wedged her sliding glass doors shut with dowels, sprinkled her Bisquick, and slept.

No woodpecker drilled in the dawn on Saturday morning. She poked her head outside and peered up at the section of siding he had been excavating. Maybe he was truly gone. But if that was the case, then why—looking straight down—why was there this line of pelletlike bird shit on the threshold, which she had swept only yester-'day afternoon? She swept again and this time remembered to examine her flour membrane, which was intact. Also, in the sane light of morning, ridiculous.

At eight-thirty on the button Don the contractor appeared.

He ambled through the hallway toward the kitchen and glanced down the opening to the cabin's lower level, where the steep makeshift steps were more like a ladder than a staircase. "These stairs ain't to code," he said unnecessarily. "You ought to get 'em fixed." Then he looked at the stove and the fusebox.

"I'll git it working, but I'm gonna have to trace these wires. That means I prob'ly won't have time to fix your bedroom *and* your hall lights today. Which you need most?"

"Bedroom," she said immediately, remembering her shinbone.

"You sure? You ain't afraid of falling down them so-called steps in the dark?"

"No." It was a relief to find something she was unequivocally not afraid of.

"Okay, bedroom it is. How do I git under the house?"

They opened the door to the crawl space and rocked

back as the concentrated odor rolled out. "Whew. You got a skunk," said Don, master of the obvious.

"I know. How do I get rid of it?"

He shook his head dolefully. "It's near impossible. You might ask the county trapper. He's with County Ag. That's in Parkerville, at Maple and Main—"

"I know where it is," she interrupted, huffy at being mistaken for an outsider—a flatlander, a weekender. "I work with Ag, you know."

But Don couldn't hear her; he was squeezing his bulk past the water heater and the furnace.

Sam was past due, so she hurriedly packed a day pack and her camera, and waited. Nine-thirty: she unwrapped the bread and cheese and made herself a real sandwich. Nine forty-five: she forsook her camera and macro lens and tripod for a pad and pencil. Ten of ten: she unbraided, brushed, and rebraided her hair, considered and rejected a different pair of earrings. Ugly women always wear big earrings, a fellow graduate student had once remarked to her, to deflect attention from their faces. Argentine, he had been, the jerk; must have thought of himself as refreshingly frank, since Claire at that moment had been wearing candelabra-sized assemblages of beads and silver filigree. She regarded herself in the mirror. Was she ugly?

No. She was plain. Individually, there was nothing wrong with her features—her eyes were even remarkable, light green under her level brows—but collectively they didn't add up to prettiness. Too androgynous, perhaps, like her body. Where Linda, Sam's Linda, was round and womanly, Claire was tall and angular, with long wrists and ankles, broad shoulders, small breasts, narrow hips. Some men like it, some didn't, but Sam, she had thought, belonged to the former category, and she changed to a tighter pair of jeans so he could consider the question for himself.

Five after ten: where the hell was Sam? This was so typical! She was trying to read the Environmental Assessment through a haze of exasperation and anxiety when she heard a vehicle roll down her driveway.

"Sorry," Sam called breathlessly, sliding down from his new Toyota 4x4 sports utility vehicle. "Had to take Kevin and Douggie to Little League practice."

This was the simple truth, no doubt, and not intended to show her how busy and fulfilled he was with his new life and new family, which was how she received it. Even his new car, which she had of course seen in the lot, seemed to signify the erasure of all traces of their life together.

But Sam wouldn't have bought a car or . . . or a house in the mountains, say, for symbolic reasons. In any case, he didn't need to protect himself from her with gestures; he was perfectly happy.

"You sell the Valiant?" she asked.

"No," he admitted, somewhat sheepishly. "It's in the driveway. I'm sort of a pack rat. Hate to part with old things."

Like me? she wondered. Do I fall in the category of yellow stacks of *National Geographics* in the garage?

"Hey, this is a great place!" he was saying enthusiastically, with no indication of mixed feelings about Claire's new life.

She caught herself. This was going to be a very long and excruciating day if she dissected Sam's every word and action. If she was going to make a transition in this relationship, she just had to take him at face value. That's how he took himself.

"Needs a little work," she said.

*   *   *

They drove east up the highway about a mile, then turned south on a road that snaked toward the base of Slate Mountain. After one mistake they found the old logging road that marked the southern boundary of the green sale and headed east again. The sports utility vehicle was in its true element, not in a parking lot in Hollywood or in a suburban driveway but negotiating the badly eroded, deeply rutted roads of Kaweah County.

The mountain loomed before them, green and gray and white-crowned. Around them the landscape was brushy and open. Once she would have taken this for a natural phenomenon, but she had learned that in country that generally supported dense forest, a clearing that was too dry to be a meadow was probably an old clear-cut. Once you knew this the evidence was conspicuous, and as they jounced along, she saw the old stumps everywhere, overgrown by whitethorn and Sierra currant. Not a good-sized tree left standing . . . until they got to the sequoias.

They came upon them suddenly—one massive cinnamon-colored column standing alone twenty feet from the road and then, off to the right, three grouped together on the flank of the slope and another two beyond them. All huge, all ancient. Specimen trees, Marcy had called them.

"Could we stop for a minute?" asked Claire impulsively, and Sam braked in the middle of the road.

"We've still got another mile to go before we're close to the meadow," he said, consulting the map.

"I know. I just want to look at the trees. I can't get used to them; it's like seeing elephants in the wild."

"We'll be seeing plenty more where we're going," he

complained—Sam had hiked through these trees all his life and was blasé about them—but he pulled off.

She climbed the road cut and laid her hand flat against the trunk of the nearest sequoia. She thumped it like a drum; thick, fibrous cocoa-matting bark guarded the quick, the cambium, buried within. When she looked straight up it was two hundred feet to the lowest branches, and the clumps of needles seemed so sparse. Hardly enough biomass to keep that pillar of fire alive.

It was a mid-sized tree, only about fifteen feet across, not a thirty-five-foot colossus. Giant sequoias were bigger than their cousins the coast redwoods, and older. And of course not in such lush habitat; the southern Sierras were surrounded by desert and would be desert themselves but for six thousand feet of elevation. In arid lands, she thought, it's not anatomy but altitude that's destiny.

"Let's walk from here," she said.

"Okay, but we may not have time to do anything but find Jim's original population. And that won't do you any good; it's outside the sale area."

"That's all right. Once I've seen them I can look for other populations on my own. I brought my sketchbook to help me recognize them."

They climbed under a sky as blue as a pilot light, Sam effortlessly as usual, Claire, who was in good shape at sea level, breathing hard in the thin air.

"Look!" she said suddenly, passing a perfectly conical four-foot tree with a soft fringe of blue-green needles. "A baby sequoia! That's the first one I've seen!"

"Uh-huh. And let me point out that it's in the middle of an old clear-cut. You know, sequoias need sunlight to regenerate. Logging is the closest thing to natural fire succession, and now that we're suppressing fires—"

She stopped dead. "C'mon, Sam, you're not trying to argue that a clear-cut is the equivalent of a fire!"

Sam had kept walking. "Well," he said over his shoulder, "it creates an opening in the canopy."

"Yeah, and scrapes or erodes away all the topsoil, and exposes shallow root systems."

He finally turned to face her. "Since when are you a forester?" he said with some heat. "You'd never even *seen* a sequoia when I met you."

"I hardly knew what a peach tree looked like, either!"

He resumed walking. "You are a fast learner, I'll give you that."

"Some things I never learn," she muttered, but he was upslope and probably hadn't heard. Anyway, she was right. Nobody really knew how to "manage" sequoias. They were on a whole different timeline from humans; they had always managed themselves.

She and Sam passed through a plantation, a tree farm of ponderosa pine planted by the forest service to mitigate the clear-cut—and to provide a new crop for the mills in forty years. It was not flourishing; looked, in fact, like a pathetic Christmas tree farm. Those seedlings that had survived the tangle of buck lotus and whitethorn were water-stressed and beetle-damaged. Claire remarked magisterially that the monoculture single-age approach to reforestation encouraged disease.

Sam, who had halted to wait for her, looked amused and superior. "You're suddenly pretty interested in this issue."

"I've gotten involved with some people—"

"Paul and Naomi's group?"

"Yes," she said. "And Marie Martelli and Hazel Batts and Cheryl Preuss, and Marcy Hobbes, of course. . . . What?" His mouth had turned down.

"Oh, Marcy, Hazel, Cheryl—that group strikes me as a bunch of lonely middle-aged women with too much time on their hands."

"What?" His politics had deteriorated since he left, or else he no longer bothered to watch his mouth. "If that's what they are, then it's exactly what I am, too!"

"Claire, you're not middle-aged."

I'm old enough, she thought, to regret my past just exactly as much as I anticipate my future. "I'm thirty-six! Jane Austen died at forty-two!" she said as if this proved some point.

"Look, forget I said it. Anyway, I'm really talking about Marcy. She's kind of a fanatic."

"That's how men always dismiss women who are passionate about politics!"

A jay squawked angrily; Sam, on the other hand, shrugged his thin shoulders and resumed walking. She climbed, to the sound of her own harsh breathing and the raucous colloquy of the jays. Gradually the low thrum of an engine rumbled into her consciousness and she squinted up at the sky. A big-bellied transport plane was making its way steadily northward.

"That's a C130!" Sam said, closer than she'd thought. "There must be a fire!"

"Does that thing carry water?" she said, interested in spite of herself.

"Retardants. PhosCheck. Borate Bombers, they call 'em—and look, here come the choppers! Must be a good-sized blaze, maybe up in the Little Kern canyon. Hey, if we head back to the car right now we can drive up to the lookout and find out what's going on!"

"What about the *Calochortus?"*

"We'll still have plenty of time! C'mon!" Without waiting for an answer—naturally—he tore down the mountain while Claire scrambled after him.

The 4x4 rattled along through open pine and fir, Claire half lost. Not disoriented; she could always see the mountain, but she couldn't keep track of the particular strand of logging road that Sam confidently picked out of the skein. Suddenly they came around a curve and saw, briefly, the fire lookout station, perched on a needle of rock like a hat the wind had dropped. Then it was lost behind the trees. Another half mile and they pulled up behind a blue pickup at the bottom of a steep, zigzagging trail.

"It's steep but short," Sam said. "See you at the top."

Jesus, Claire thought, watching him sprint up the path, didn't he know they were at eight thousand feet? Cursing him for a thoughtless son of a bitch and herself for a weenie, and vowing to take conditioning hikes every weekend from now until snowfall, she pushed herself along the switchbacks.

It was dense fir forest here, shady and quiet except for the crunch of her own feet. Now and again she slipped on the litter of dead branches, elegantly curved and bleached like tusks. Once she stooped to retrieve a small egg-shaped cone, then scanned the canopy in vain for the distinctive ragged profile of the sequoia that had produced it. Must have rolled pretty far, she thought, turning the cone between her fingers. It was segmented and chewy-looking like dried figs on a string, and when she tapped it, dozens of seeds poured into her palm— minute, flaky, each with a black spot in the center, like frogs' eggs rolled flat. That black speck—that sequoia on the head of a pin—reminded Claire of why she had become a biologist.

The trees thinned, and she began to see the sharp gray

peaks of the High Sierra far to the north. Ten minutes of trudging and she was ready for a water break. After the next switchback, she decided, rounded it—and stopped abruptly.

Before her was the face of the huge dome of exfoliated granite that supported the lookout station, still invisible; to her right, a sheer drop of a thousand feet; to her left, a flight of metal stairs leading, apparently, up to heaven.

She ascended the Beanstalk. The stairs rang with every step, fifteen of them, ending in a landing in the middle of the air, from which another flight proceeded at an angle to the first, like switchbacks in the sky. Twenty stairs, another landing; the wind gusted violently from her left, the north, and she had a brief fierce vision of herself lifted up and over the railing, maybe snagging it with one hand as she went by so that for a moment she blew stiff and horizontal like a flag in a hurricane, then peeling off and cartwheeling slowly through space, down and down. . . . She moved to the exact center of the stairs. Another flight—now she could see the bottom of the lookout; a landing, and then the final steep climb. Ten steps . . . eleven . . . twelve . . . gasping, she pulled herself onto the enclosed catwalk that circled the structure and leaned on the railing to catch her breath.

Directly to the north was the valley of the Little Kern River, then a range of decent-sized mountains, and then the 14,000-foot peaks: Olancha, Langley, Whitney. Directly across from her was the rest of the dome, split off into the needlelike plinth that drew photographers and rock climbers. Directly below her was . . . nothing, and she sat down hard on the catwalk with her back to the view.

When she had stopped panting, she entered the twelve-by-twelve room where Sam and a competent-looking woman in green uniform and braids were poring over a map.

"Where—" she began, but Sam put a finger to his lips as a voice crackled over the radio. A mellow California kid who sounded like he was giving a surf report—sounded, in fact, like Will Brecker.

"Uh, that's a roger, one helicopter—no, make that two, two choppers on the way from California Hot Springs."

"There," said Sam, pointing north. He handed Claire the binoculars, being careful, it seemed, not to touch her. "Like I thought—up along the Little Kern."

She scanned, saw the brown plume of smoke on the far side of the valley. "Is it bad?"

"Naw," said the woman. "They'll have it knocked down in a few hours—whoa, I hear the choppers!"

Sam grabbed the binocs and ran to the window.

"Was it a lightning strike?" Claire asked.

"Nope," the ranger said.

"Arson?" Claire asked, remembering the discussion at the meeting.

"Who knows? Probably just some idiot with a cigarette. Maybe on a pack trip, 'cause it's wa-a-y back in there."

This seemed to Claire to comprise everything important about this fire: it had been started by a human, it was far away, it was going to be put out. Some other time she might have had more curiosity—the lookout station itself was fascinating, for example, tiny but complete, like a lighthouse or a yacht, and the woman who staffed it was probably an interesting character—but there wasn't much time left to find the Slate Mountain mariposa tulip. She pointed this out to Sam, who continued to stare out at the horizon, monitor the radio, and look at the map.

Fuck you, she thought, and "I'll start down," she said.

In a moment she heard his steps ring on the stairs behind her.

"Does she stay there twenty-four hours a day?" she asked, forcing amiability to distract herself from the blue void.

"Lainie? No, she's got a boyfriend down the road. She leaves after five, spends the night with him, then comes back in the morning."

"She hikes up this trail *every day?*"

"Naw."

"Oh."

"Mountain bike."

"Oh." *Conditioning hikes. Every weekend.*

If you knew how to pick out S23J54 from S21J54 and S23J55—and Sam did—Bob Bartlett's meadow was just to the south of it. Claire and Sam began walking, ascending gradually, and soon found themselves in a quiet grove of smooth sequoias and beveled ferns. Here the trail was broad and they walked side by side, their feet stirring the soft duff to rise and sparkle in the slats of filtered light. Neither spoke. After ten minutes they cleared a low ridge and looked down on a patch of broad pleated leaves— corn lilies, a sure sign of moist mountain areas.

"That's the meadow," said Sam, whispering for some reason. In a moment he began to pick his way down to the western edge of the opening, followed by Claire. They circled clockwise, past wild geraniums and sneeze-weed and rein orchids and something white that was shaped like an atomizer bulb and had the wonderful name of "bistort." Three-quarters of the way around, Claire saw an orange lily with recurved petals in the center of the meadow and made for it.

"This won't dry out till August," Sam called as she sank up to her ankles in muck.

"Thanks," she said, squelching back to "shore"—and then stopped.

An inch away from her right foot was a small tulip-shaped white flower. Now she saw four or five others gleaming like stars through the tall grass at the edge of the meadow. *Shy,* she thought, bending down.

Sam hurried over.

"Is that it?" she asked as he dropped to his knees in the damp earth and examined the flower with a hand lens.

"I think so," he said after a moment. "Here, look at the hairs around the nectary."

She knelt beside him, accepted the lens, and crouched over the blossom.

"See 'em?" he asked. "Way down in the throat," and she leaned forward. The sun laid a warm strip across her back where her shirt lifted away from her jeans. Their legs brushed and she moved away—or maybe she only thought about it, because she could still feel the pressure from hip to knee.

"Right here," he said softly, spreading the petals apart with two long fingers.

The gesture struck Claire as explicitly sexual, and she jerked upright. Sam seemed to be looking at his own hands with a kind of horror, as if he'd never seen them before. "Here," he said, shoving the lens at her, "you hold it."

After a moment she bent over the bloom again, separating the petals herself and trying to concentrate on fringed membranes around nectaries and not on Sam's ragged breathing beside her, or the unsteadiness of her hands.

"Thanks," she said in a near-normal voice. "I think I've got it," and handed him the lens.

"Good," he muttered, pocketing it.

Though there were a few hours of light left, they headed straight to the car. Sam didn't sprint ahead; he walked behind her, silent.

"Now that we know the lay of the land, and the flower," he said with effort once they were rattling toward the highway, "we can go back this week and look for more populations."

"*I* can go."

"Alone?" he said after a moment, hands tight on the wheel.

"Sure, alone. Why not?" she said, as much for herself as for him. "I live alone, I'm out in the field alone every day. Some of the places I visit for work are almost as isolated as this."

"Well, that's not such a great idea either." Pause. "You ought to think about getting a gun."

"A *gun?*"

"Yeah. A handgun. Or a twenty-two, for your car."

She actually considered this for a quarter-second, something she would not have done two days ago. But, "Look, Sam," she said, "I know everyone in Kaweah County thinks of a gun as a personal accessory as indispensable as a toothbrush, but I'm not that assimilated. Just forget it!" and they finished the ride with no further conversation. At her cabin they slid down from the jeep and faced each other across its high blue hood.

"About the gun . . ." he said.

"Sam, for Christ's sake, forget the gun! You're just—" She stopped.

"Just what?"

"I was going to say that you're just bringing up the gun to avoid talking about what happened."

"I'm bringing it up because I think you need a gun. What happened where?"

"In the meadow! Don't tell me you . . . I mean, didn't you feel . . ." She faltered. What *had* happened? It suddenly seemed possible—likely, even; horribly likely—that *nothing* had occurred, that her fevered, sex-starved imagination had transmuted a little mundane botanizing into Molly Bloom at Gibralter. Foreplay by flower! Jesus! She was hallucinating!

Sam could have maintained plausible deniability, but he did the decent thing. "Yes," he said after a moment, "okay. I won't pretend I didn't feel . . . something. But I really don't want to have this discussion," he added, backing away.

"Oh, well, of course, that's your right," Claire said. "I mean, that's the point of leaving someone. You don't have to argue with them anymore. Only eventually, you run out of women."

By now her voice was thin and lethal, a verbal garrote. But it was her only weapon; all Sam had to do was to catapult himself and the jeep out of earshot, which was certainly what she would have done.

But he didn't; he stood there and took it.

"Look," he said after a moment, "what do you want me to say? That I still find you desirable? That Linda's jealous of you? That I wanted to fuck right there in the mud? Is that what you want to hear?"

"Well, it doesn't hurt," she said, "especially the part about Linda."

He didn't smile. "Claire," he said, and came around as far as the front bumper. "Claire. Sure, I have feelings for you—"

"Feelings?" she interrupted. "What does that mean?"

"Didn't I just tell you?"

"Not really," she said, merciless, and his face twisted.

"I've never not loved you," he said eventually, and as she was working out the double negative, he threw up his hands as if measuring the one that got away. "What do you want from me? We've been over this! Love was never the issue! I love you, and I love Linda, too, in a different way. But it doesn't make any diff—"

"Are you happy?" she said, and immediately wished she hadn't. Why ask a question when you didn't want to hear the answer?

"Happiness . . . isn't the point," he said, looking away from her. "I wasn't raised to be happy; I was raised to do the right thing. I want to be a good father to my kids, and I want to have a home where they can live with me, and you don't want to be a stepmother!"

This was a gross oversimplification of a painful struggle Claire had waged with herself over the past year—a weighing of her feelings for Sam, her doubts about their relationship; her fear of dissolving under the steady drip of family demands, like her mother; her discomfort with his boys, their hostility toward her—but in sum it was accurate.

"We've been through this!" he was saying. "So even if I do have these . . . feelings for you, I'm not going to act on them. I mean, if I didn't jump you today, my God . . ."

Oh, she thought dismally, so that's what this afternoon came down to: a test of their self-control; a test passed impeccably, except for some heavy breathing.

"Good luck with the *Calochortus*," he said woodenly, lifting himself into the car. "Call me if you need help."

Paralyzed with unhappiness, she watched him back away. What did it mean when a man, a man—well, let's face it, a man you probably still loved—said "I love you," the most significant phrase in Western civilization, and it wasn't a solution or a prelude to a catharsis of pity and terror or a prelude, in fact, to anything at all, but had no implications whatsoever? What kind of a world was that?

An adult world, she supposed, feeling the pull of the receding car like a wave tugging sand from under her feet.

Chapter 10

Brushes with death are good for a sense of proportion.

Claire was no longer dreaming of Sam and Linda but of falling from great heights—in dream poker the ace of spades generally beats the jack of hearts. Though each house has its own rules; after Saturday's encounter with Sam she dreamed that he and Linda were backing her over a cliff, but by Sunday night she was back to simple life-threatening scenarios.

On Monday morning she swept bird shit from the deck; in fact, she swept for fifteen minutes—anything to put off driving down the mountain. The woodpecker seemed to have left, but if he was drilling elsewhere he was returning to her front porch to metabolize. This struck her as strange—anything to put off driving down the mountain—and she looked up into the deeply shadowed peak of the A-frame for signs of him.

There *was* something. A sort of decorative frieze in the peak of the roof, two rows of little newellike structures. I didn't notice gingerbread up there, she thought, when suddenly the woodwork . . . writhed. She shivered with instinctive repugnance for something that's not supposed to move but does—a stick that's a snake—ran inside to get her binoculars, and peered up into the eaves. A little face looked back at her—a line, in fact, of little feline faces.

Bats.

There must have been two dozen bats, packed together like chocolates in a box. She lowered the binocs and watched, half fascinated, half revolted. A bony knuckle of wing poked up and stretched—a sudden angle, like a sail, among all those round heads—then another wing, then another, rippling down the line. There was a high-pitched chittering like the squeak of a Styrofoam cooler, which she realized she'd been hearing for days. Abruptly revolted again, she stepped back—she liked the little round nugget heads but not the skeletal wings—and just in time, as a pellet of guano hurtled to the deck. Then they all resettled and it was quiet again.

"Order Chiroptera," said Storer and Unger's *Natural History of the Sierras,* which she grabbed from her shelf—anything to put off driving down the mountain. "Small mammal, delicate of form, mouth wide, ears large, paper-thin; pelage dense"—zoologists had their own Teutonic ideas about syntax—"wings formed of thin webs of skin between bones of arm and 2nd to 5th fingers on each 'hand.' . . . During the day bats, singly or in groups, hang by their hind claws in dark crevices in trees or rocks, some in caves and some in buildings."

And some in mountain cabins.

Finally she did drive down the mountain—at fifteen miles an hour, hands in a rictus grip around the truck's steering wheel, testing the brakes before every curve. She arrived at work sweaty and shaking.

But there was bounce in the old gal yet, or at least a capacity for massive denial. By Tuesday she was up to twenty miles an hour, and with every hour that passed without further incident, her fear faded. Tuesday after work she took a walk on a nearby trail, willing herself to relax at what she knew were harmless sounds. Wednesday she walked a little farther, and by Wednesday night she was dreaming about Sam and Linda again. It was a relief.

But she still drew a line of Bisquick around her truck every night.

Don the contractor showed up very early one morning to finish the hall wiring, but overnight the water heater had broken and bumped it from the queue. As he headed back down to the crawl space, he took a look at her unswept deck and said helpfully, "Bats."

"No kidding. How do I get rid of them?" and knew an instant before he answered what he was going to say.

"Git you a shotgun. You could pot quite a few while they're hangin' there."

She was ready.

On Thursday after work she prepared herself to go in search of the savage Slate Mountain shy mariposa tulip.

Still in the UC pickup—the body shop claimed it would reconstruct her car by the following week—she drove toward Bartlett's meadow, where she and Sam had found the first population of *Calochortus*. Then she began to walk north. In about a half hour she came to an old overgrown logging road—SN23J1, by the topo map, and smack in the center of the proposed sale.

The road ended at a steep flatiron ridge, which she

climbed, slowly. Once a loud rustle in a dry chinquapin brought her to a panicky halt, but she saw a flash of blue through the dull green leaves and began trudging again. Bluejays. Lead-footed, brass-voiced, jays were the heavy metal of the bird world.

A line of sequoias had strung themselves out along the top of the ridge. One giant had been half hollowed by fire, and she stepped clear into its tarry heart, feeling a simultaneous sense of transgression and safety. How could anyone with an eye or an imagination have logged these trees? Nineteenth- and early twentieth-century photos showed two or three sweating men working from all sides with crosscut saws, a slow and agonizing process, like amputating a limb. And unprofitable: the huge trees shattered of their own weight as they crashed to the ground.

It was this fact more than moral revulsion that had changed forestry practices. Loggers began to leave the giants alone, taking only the small sequoias and the whitewood—i.e., everything but the redwood—from the groves. And then Cheryl Preuss and Hazel Batts, Sam's "lonely middle-aged women," had raised holy hell so widely and effectively that the forest service had promised to revise its policy. No more logging in the groves, they said, though the problem of what constituted a grove remained, and the larger question of whether there should be any logging at all on this dry, fragile forest. (*On* this forest. She caught herself and grinned at her own mimetic nature. *You all. On the forest.*)

And the forest service had agreed to periodic public meetings like the one scheduled for . . . tonight, she suddenly remembered. She'd better not stay too late in the woods.

Below the ridge to the north was a clear green area

that might be a meadow and therefore habitat for a shy mariposa tulip. She left the shelter of her hollow and cautiously worked her way down to the meadow, slipping once and straining the ankle that had not quite recovered from last year's fall. Corn lilies: yup, a meadow, and she walked slowly along the western edge, watching her feet, glancing across the opening. There was another orange lily, but this time she didn't slosh after it; she could see that there was a little stream running right through the middle of the meadow. Here, closer to the edge, was a deep purple shadow of a bloom, cowled and complicated. Monkshood. She remembered Marcy's bouquet.

And there—just there where the land rose and the conifers began again—what was that? A patch of white rock? She strode toward it, heart accelerating as she began to pick out individual tulip-shaped blooms. *Calochortus,* yes! Fishing in her pocket for a hand lens, she knelt and examined a large violet-tinged flower. *Invenustus,* she thought, but was it the subspecies? She bent to examine it, and for a moment had an acute sensory memory of the other afternoon and Sam's body next to hers. Nevertheless she peered deep into the throat of the flowers. Around the nectary were the long hairs she and Sam had found in the *Invenustus* subspecies *westii.*

"Ha!" she said out loud. Jim Bartlett's rare subspecies, and right in the middle of the green sale. This ought to derail the locomotive of the rapacious Genes! (She thought "locomotive," but what she imagined was a coffin gliding along its mortuary rails, toppling into the furnace.)

Her discovery so elated her that she forgot to be nervous on the hike back to the truck.

The public hearing was held in the Riverdale VFW, which was itself an appendage of the Sierra View Convalescent

Home, which in turn was affixed to the lending library—the whole concatenation of fake Mission-style modules strung along the highway like postmodern pop-it beads. Claire pulled in next to a utility pickup with a bumper sticker that said "Wise Use—Don't Lock Up the Forest."

"Don't lock it up" was, in Claire's opinion, simply the sound bite of anyone opposed to protection of public lands.

On her way in, she checked the Sierra View bulletin board, because you never knew. "4 Sale," someone had written in a spidery script, "Cressent wrench. 2 wood shoe trees. Flashlite with battrys. See Clyde, Room 233."

Jesus. Some elderly Arkie—Sierra View was almost exclusively a warehouse for the remnants of the Dust Bowl—some elderly Arkie was reduced to selling a used *flashlight?* She was tempted to march into room 233 and write Clyde a check, but she didn't. Instead she walked into the VFW hall, to cold folding chairs, cheap buckled paneling, and black-and-white photos of men in uniform, some of whom now sat in their bathrobes next door in Sierra View. In front of the mostly empty chairs three green-shirted forest service people and two flip charts stood at attention, ready to inform such members of the public as had bothered to appear.

There were really only two groups with enough of a vested interest to haul themselves out to the VFW meeting hall for this—the antagonists: the Friends of the Redwoods and the sawmill faction.

There were the Friends in the third row, so far minus Marcy, but including her escorts, Will and Dustin. Like bookends. Will looked up and gave Claire a smile that warmed the whole cold room; Dustin didn't acknowledge her. He looked almost like a grown-up beside the three Indian teenagers in the same row. The kids all had warrior haircuts—shaved up to the ears and drawn back in a ninja-style ponytail, or stiff and bristly in front with a little finger of braid down the back. Two of them looked every bit as tough as they had hoped but the third, baby-faced and bespectacled, was merely sweet.

An empty row as buffer, and then came the sawmill people, mostly young families. There was the blond logger from the restaurant, holding a very fair, elfin little girl on his lap; to his right sat a haggard-looking young woman with a blond baby in *her* lap. A slightly older boy leaned up against her. None of the kids could have been over five.

Could this young father have crept under her car, clipped a cable here, loosened a coupling there, and sent her hurtling down the mountain to her doom? She couldn't believe it. She looked around for his toothless buddy, but didn't see him.

The Genes appeared—Gene Junior, open-faced and pleasant-looking in khakis and sport shirt; Gene Senior scowling in terry-cloth golf shirt and white linen shorts embroidered with little red lobsters. Andy Nilsson wandered in and stood indecisively near the back. Claire started to speak to him, but just then Marcy swept by.

"Marcy," Claire called, catching up to her, "I found something really exciting today! A rare flower, a mariposa tulip. Just north of SN—um, SN23J1, so it's right in the middle of the sa—"

"Sshh!" Marcy frowned fiercely, and her eyes darted around the room. "Not now!" she said in a melodramatic whisper. "I'll talk to you later!" Marcy's paranoia, thought Claire, stung. True, a few heads had turned around to look at them, but what of it?

"Hi, everybody," Marcy was saying to her friends in a normal voice. "Dustin, you came! Great! And you brought my kids! These are some of my kids who are going to be rehearsing for the powwow up at my cabin," she added to the group at large.

At that phrase, "my kids," Claire winced and she saw Dustin's mouth tighten for a moment. She studied him. Next to the fine angles and planes of Will Brecker's face there was something unformed about him. His considerable beauty was of surface rather than feature: of symmetry and vivid coloring and smooth skin and thick hair and shining eyes. Of youth, in other words. What would it be like, she wondered, sliding against that sleekly muscled body? Like sex with a dolphin?

He saw her watching him and she flushed, but he held her gaze and coolly shrugged out of his denim shirt as if to say, go ahead, lady, get an eyeful. Underneath he was wearing a black tank top, and again there was the glint of silver. Only this time she could see that it was a spectacular squash blossom necklace—and no Kmart knock-off, either. The subtle veined stones glowed like a Santa Fe morning, and the silver hung heavy from his brown neck. He twitched under the weight like a dog in a new collar. A little trinket from Marcy, perhaps?

"Sit with us, Claire," Marcy said. "Dustin can scoot over."

"Oh no, no thanks. I've got a seat closer to the back," she said, and found a chair with a group of indeterminate loyalty that included Don Henson and her neighbors Dora and Leroy, and Andy Nilsson.

"You're not sitting with your team," she whispered to him.

He grimaced. "I'm not sitting with either team. I'm trying to play it very, very cool here. If I lose *this* job, it better be for a darned good reason! Like shutting down

logging on the whole forest; *that* would be worth getting
bounced again."

"Dreams of glory," Claire said, then shut up, because
they were starting.

The meeting was called to order, conducted, and carefully orchestrated by Marcy's nemesis Nelson Pringle, the
head of the local forest service district. A weathered man
in his fifties, Pringle had the air of aggrieved innocence of
someone who had worked for thirty years under one un-
ambiguous mandate—"get out the cut"—and had been
winding down toward placid retirement when overnight
the rules were changed. Suddenly everyone hated him.
The environmentalists had always hated him for rape and
pillage, but now even his erstwhile pals at the mill had decided he was a jackbooted government thug for attempting to regulate, however feebly, public lands. Nelson's
eyebrows rode halfway up his forehead in perpetual disbelief; his high voice quavered with suppressed outrage.

Nevertheless he carried authority. And Claire, having
presented a few seminars in her time, admired his technique: (1) bore everyone into a coma with complicated
flip charts illustrating some dense but irrelevant subject,
in this case the forest service budget; (2) after your audience is too demoralized and restless to stick around,
open the discussion; (3) define the terms of the debate
so that those people who do hang in there don't even
think of the important questions.

There's always someone, however, who outwaits and
outwits you, and as a former attorney Paul Weissman had
an enormous tolerance for bullshit. A few people posed
timid and bewildered questions about the budget; then
Paul stood and asked about salvage. The loggers were
taking healthy trees out, he said, and immediately chip-
ping the leftover branches to destroy the evidence.

The logging contingent had already left to put their fidgety offspring to bed, or there might have been a fight. As it was, Pringle promised solemnly to look into the matter.

"Why are you offering green sales at all when there's so much beetle-and smog-damaged timber?" Hazel demanded.

"Now, Hazel, that's a whole other topic, and it's late. We'll go into it next time," Pringle said. "Meeting adjourned."

"Why do we have to resort to Freedom of Information to even find out about the sales?" Cheryl said loudly. "We're entitled to that information!" But Pringle and his minions were already packing up.

"What a waste of time," Andy grumbled to Claire. "Nice to see you, though. Actually, would you be interested . . . Oh, hi, Marcy, uh, Ms. Hobbes."

"What a fucking waste of time," said Marcy, taking Claire's elbow and drawing her a few steps away. "Paul's telling Pringle so, right now. What were you saying about a rare plant in the sale area?"

Claire told her.

"Fabulous!" Marcy exclaimed. "Can you show me where it is?"

"Sure. Saturday?"

"Great. I'll call you!" She gathered up her entourage and left.

"I'm sorry," Claire said to Andy, who was examining the photos of the fortieth reunion of the veterans of D day. "You were about to ask me something when Marcy interrupted."

"Was I? I don't remember."

When she walked out to her car, the Friends of the Redwoods were gathered around the green Jag in attitudes of concern, as if at a sickbed. Claire assumed the unreasonable car was on strike again, refusing to crank under these barbaric conditions. Then she noticed that it seemed even longer and lower than usual. Her eyes wandered to the front tire, which was sort of . . . *flowing* onto the asphalt like a Dali soft watch. The rear tire was also no longer round.

She approached the group. "Let the air out, huh?" she said moronically.

"Worse," said Will, who was squatting beside the left front tire. His index finger traced the black rubber lips of a long wound. "All of 'em, just like this. And—" he rose, looking at Marcy—"if you want the same kind we'll have to send to L.A. again. These are *special.*" He gave the word a nasty turn.

Marcy shrugged. "That's the least of my worries," she said, rattling a ragged sheet of white paper between thumb and forefinger, then folding it into a neat square.

Claire's phone rang at eleven-thirty.

"It's Marcy. Listen, don't . . ." The rest of the sentence was lost in a jet-engine roar.

"What? I can hardly hear you, Marcy," said Claire.

"Sorry. A Wal-Mart truck just went by. I'm at a pay phone right by the highway; I think my phone is tapped. Anyway, I just called to tell you not to say anything about these plants to anyone. I don't think anybody heard us tonight, and I'd like to keep it that way." Pause. "Especially after what happened tonight."

"You mean the tires."

"That, and the note on my windshield. It was sort of a threat," she said diffidently.

" 'Sort of a threat'?" echoed Claire.

Marcy cleared her throat. " 'Bitch,' " she recited primly,

" 'keep your fancy car and your fancy twat'—I hate that word—'out of our business or we'll ram them both.' " Claire sucked in a quick breath. "And there was a little drawing," Marcy was saying. "It looked kind of like a fetus with measles. I thought the right-to-lifers were getting on my case, too, but we finally figured out it was supposed to be a spotted owl." She laughed.

"Marcy! You should get some protection!"

"Naw, it's just some moron blowing off steam. I was gonna chuck the note, but Paul made me take it down to Marie's and give it to Tom Martelli. I'll call you Saturday morning about looking for that flower."

"So you did give the note to Tom?"

"Yep. Talk to you Saturday."

Finally, thought Claire as she hung up, finally someone had been threatened right in downtown Riverdale, two hundred feet from Martelli's office. He couldn't claim that wasn't his jurisdiction.

Now he would do something.

Chapter 11

Tom did do something: on Friday morning he stopped by and talked to Randy Unsel, the toothless logger.

And left again.

"He had an alibi," he explained to Claire on the phone. "Three people corroborated he was drinking at the Antlers during the meeting."

"Sure," she said, "three employees of Sierra Wood Products!"

"Well, not employees, exactly. But prob'ly friends of employees," he conceded, and caught her in mid-windup. "Look, Claire, I'll tell you the same thing I tell Marie. You all have set yourselves up to be pretty unpopular with a lot of folks. The penalty for that is gonna be petty shit like this, and there's not a hell of a lot anybody can do about it."

At lunchtime Claire stopped by the county agricultural office, in the new complex that had replaced the storefront between the 3-7-11 Tavern and Mindy's Book Fair. Better lighting, same decor: wall-sized maps of all the labor camps in the area, for the benefit of understaffed growers and labor contractors.

The county trapper was summoned from the back room. He sauntered out, an ordinary big-bellied man in polyester and Dacron; Claire had been hoping for buckskin and raccoon cap.

"I have a skunk, I think," Claire said. "Under the house, I think. So I thought maybe a Havahart trap," she concluded firmly.

"Sure," he said, surprising her; she'd figured an assault rifle, or plastique or nerve gas, would be more his style. "Got just the thing, right here." He set the trap on the counter—an aluminum cage about the size of an accordian sewing box, with solid plates at either end.

He showed her how to bait and set it. "See, them plates at either end prevent the little varmint from seeing you, and as long as he don't see you he don't spray."

Was this experimentally verified? she wondered. "Should I call you when I catch him?" she asked.

"Oh, no!" He thought a moment. "You got a pond on your land?"

"A pond?" she said, puzzled. "No, I mean there's a river, but it's a good quarter-mile away."

"How 'bout a waterin' trough or a big basin?"

"Just the bathtub . . . Wait a minute—" she said, as she caught his drift.

"See, the thing to do, once you catch the sucker, you just drop the whole trap in water somewhere."

"*Drown* it? Then what's the point of the Havahart trap? I thought you'd just . . . take it somewhere and let it go!"

"Hell, no! I been skunked once or twice, and I don't

plan to let it happen again. And them critters come out of there pissed off!" He considered her. "You want the trap?"

"Yes." She would figure something out later. "Now let me ask you about bats."

Powerful spotlights, he suggested. "Though sometimes they like that. Warms 'em up." Steel wool in the cracks of the eaves. She thought of the stairway to the lookout and imagined herself on a twenty-foot ladder. What about leaving them there? she said. Maybe putting something up to catch the guano? Use it in the garden?

The trapper handed her a Xerox entitled "The California Fruit Bat," and she scanned it. Rabies . . . encephalitis . . . histoplasmosis . . . toxoplasmosis . . . Okay, she'd try the steel wool. Maybe she could get someone else up on the ladder. As she was leaving, she heard the trapper call wistfully, "You could take out a lot of them with a shotgun."

A few blocks south on Main, and she noticed an intense odor of zoo wafting forward from the trap in the back seat. She pulled into what had always been the Joy Jug Gas and Convenience Store but last week had become merely another Exxon station—her quality of life was constantly eroding—and rinsed out the trap. Then she continued south for a block and parked.

To her amazement the Parkerville Library had a Latin dictionary; she hadn't imagined anyone in Parkerville needing Latin—Future Priests of America, maybe. *Invenustus, invenustus* . . . There it was. The opposite of *venustus,* which came from "Venus" and denoted all things lovely and charming. *Invenustus* was therefore unlovely, uncharming. "Homely," the dictionary suggested. "Shy" had been a euphemistic stretch on the part of the Pacific field book. Though if that delicate crocuslike flower was homely, she'd have to see *venustus* sometime. . . .

"Unhappy in love."

What?

Thinking her subconscious had kneecapped her, she blinked and read the passage again. Nope, there it was: "*invenustus*. In Catullus and Cicero, 'unhappy in love.' "

Well, no wonder, she muttered darkly, and returned to the station.

"Where are we going?"

It was Saturday, and Claire and Marcy were supposed to be driving to the rare and homely *Calochortus* that would spike the wheels of the Genes. But even Claire could tell that Marcy was not following either the logging road that led to Bartlett's meadow or SN23J1, which would take them straight to Claire's population. Instead she had turned south, keeping the mountain on her left and wrestling the car along this washboard road. Not the Jag, of course, which was temporarily retired, but an old silver Isuzu Trooper with a creased door. On the dashboard were a couple of opened envelopes addressed to William Brecker.

Marcy flipped up the short brim of her white painter's cap. She had done her curly hair in two schoolgirl braids which, in combination with the cap and the oversized white T-shirt, somehow managed to make her look not ridiculous but winsome, like a model from a catalog so hip that you weren't even on its mailing list.

But right now Marcy was about as winsome as a backhoe. "I want to check out this salvage sale first, look for violations," she said. "You'll have to take some pictures."

"Oh," Claire said shortly. Maybe Marcy's boyfriends found her imperiousness charming—she could certainly imagine Will longing to follow orders, or to be punished for failing to follow orders—but she, Claire, didn't respond well to imperial fiat. In fact she felt disappointed; she felt . . .

Jilted, she realized suddenly. What had happened to the friendliness, the confidences? Corked back up like the Chardonnay, and Claire felt like a spurned lover. Marcy made uncertain, eager suitors of everyone.

"What's wrong with salvage cuts?" Claire asked, rebelling. "Cutting a few dead trees would open up the canopy, let in sunlight for seedlings."

What's wrong with eating babies, it makes more room for other babies, she might have said from the sudden silence in the front seat.

But Marcy replied patiently, as if to a small child. "First of all, they don't want a few dead trees; they want them all. There wouldn't be a snag left for nesting or to replenish the soil if it were up to the Genes! And they don't stop with the dead trees. They love salvage sales because they don't have to go through an Environmental Assessment, and then once they're in, they take whatever they think they can get away with. Dead, dying; it's all definition, right? I mean, all trees will die someday. But," she said, as the Trooper labored up a rise, "if we *catch* them taking healthy trees, we can shut down the cut with an injunction. Maybe."

"Oh," said Claire, humbled. "So what are we looking for now?"

"Any signs of recent logging activity . . . shit!" The truck stalled and rolled backwards. Marcy cranked it and coaxed it up and over the hump, her tanned, lightly freckled arms working the gearshift with confident expertise.

"Is this Will's car?" Claire asked.

"Yeah. Worthless!" she said, venomously and ambiguously. They rocked on through mixed country, brushy and cut over, then dark with blue-needled fir and yellow pine. Some of the trees had blue asterisks sprayed on their trunks. "Whoa!" said Marcy abruptly, killed the engine, and in a moment was scrambling up the steep road cut with remarkable agility.

Claire followed, finding handholds in the exposed roots that poked through the raw red clay. When she hauled herself to the top of the bank, Marcy was squatting about twenty yards upslope from her, examining a downed tree, freshly cut. The chain saw had neatly split the asterisk into two blue setting suns. So the mark must mean "Kill me," thought Claire; the arboreal equivalent of a yellow Star of David.

"This one's still got the choke line on it," Marcy said, pointing to the steel cable wrapped tight around the trunk. "They jerk 'em out by helicopter when it's this steep."

Claire looked around her. What with drought, beetles, blister rust, and smog, right now there were so many dying conifers in this forest that their orange needles gave the mountains a spurious look of autumn. At her cabin she had watched three magnificent sugar pines die one by one, bim-bam-boom, down by the river. But here was a tall, healthy ponderosa—a few dead needles in the crown, but basically fine—with a blue star on its fissured trunk. And a white fir, same thing. And another. Why were all these robust trees marked for death?

"These look like really healthy trees," Claire said.

"Oh, sure. They're high-grading."

"What?"

"High-grading," Marcy repeated. "They cut all the biggest and best, so the forest's gene pool is gradually impoverished."

"Huh," said Claire after a minute. Kind of like Parkerville, she was thinking; the best and the brightest left before they could reproduce. But . . . "How can they mark these trees for *salvage?*"

"That's something I'd like to know myself," Marcy said.

"Who marks the trees? The loggers?"

"Oh, no. The fucking forest service. Do you have your camera?"

They documented the site, and then Claire was ready to return to *Calochortus invenustus*. But instead Marcy continued along the same road, following a trail of homemade paper-plate signs tacked to trees, as if for a company picnic. Only these led to something called Landing 7.

"One more stop," Marcy said, detecting Claire's restlessness.

Landing 7 proved to be a sort of elephants' graveyard, a lumberyard in the forest: a bulldozed clearing surrounded by neat piles of raw logs, which Marcy immediately began to inspect, clambering up the nearest stack.

"I'm checking to see that they were all dead when they were cut," she called. "Look for this blue ring of fungus around the outside; that means it had started to decay when they brought it down."

Claire watched her balance on top of a stack, her crisp khaki safari pants red with sawdust. Out here this afternoon Marcy was a woman transformed; even the rhythms of her speech had slowed. "Grounded," as Will had said, but in the literal, the electrical, sense, as if her prodigious energy could finally complete some circuit instead of fizzing and sparking her into hyperactivity and semihysteria. Evidently she had to be bushwhacking up a forty-five-degree slope, or slightly drunk, to be at peace.

So Claire began at the other end of the lot, checking every stump-end for a gray-blue ring of fungus. Sometimes she would forget what she was looking for, lost in the intricate pattern of rings, cross grains, and "galleries"—the secret journeys of beetles through the heart of the tree, sinuous as Sanskrit. Suddenly she noticed a different, cruder alphabet, written in yellow spray paint along the whole length of the bottom log of the last stack: GOMEZ*FRANCISCO*HERRERA*CONTRERAs. The letters were square and well formed, all but the last two, which the author had had to shrink and deform to fit in.

"Marcy," she called, "are some of the loggers Mexican?"

"Not usually," Marcy said. "Mostly white redneck types, like those guys at the restaurant and at the hearing. Why? Oh," she said, reading the names. "Well, there might be some Hispanics in the crew, doing the dirty work, flagging, stuff like that. Or guys from the res. I could ask Dustin." Her voice changed as she uttered the name, and for the first time that day she seemed silly. Well, if she was, thought Claire, she wasn't the first otherwise bright, energetic human to be silly over attractive young humans of the opposite sex—look at JFK.

Or at Claire Sharples, salivating over Will Brecker.

"I ever tell you my strategy for having fun and not getting hurt?" Marcy said out of the blue, and then, without waiting, "Never date a man who's smart *and* good-looking. One or the other. See, that way none of 'em have power over you. Except," she added, turning back to the stack, "sometimes the pretty ones turn out to be smarter than you thought. Or the ugly ones grow on you. Then you're in trouble—Oh, God," she said abruptly, lifting a hand to her mouth. "Listen to me. Ugly ones, pretty ones—I sound just like my first husband!" She paused and added in a low voice, "Sometimes I think Gilbert won after all."

Claire was not paying attention; she was staring at those yellow names.

If someone had sprayed "Riley" or "Johnson" on a log, she would have wrinkled her nose and dismissed it as childish vandalism, the conjunction of a can of spray paint and an idle hour. But as it was, she saw before her a profound existential gesture, the desperate need of the powerless to be known, like lifers scratching their names into the hard stone of their cells. And all because the names were Spanish.

Like undulant fever Claire's romantic attitude toward the Mexican farmworkers of Kaweah County was serious and recurring. Even a few weeks spent last summer in a squalid motel for migrant laborers hadn't cured her. She had *liked* the place; her neighbors and the language that teased at the edges of her hearing like a secret once known but forgotten and the music of tubas pumping from pickups, Dopplering down the road. She had even made friends, insofar as that was possible, and had witnessed the precariousness and rigor of their lives. And therefore the notion that some loggers might be *Mexican* came as a revelation: for the first time she saw them as human beings and saw what was at stake for them. She could even manage sympathy for a run-of-the-mill Anglo logger if she imagined him as a blond, wan Latino.

"Problem?" called Marcy from the other side of the yard, when she saw Claire standing motionless. Claire tried to explain.

"Oh," Marcy said, puzzled. "I've got nothing against the loggers, really. They're shortsighted, maybe, but I understand it's hard to take the long view when you're worried about your next meal. No, I reserve all my contempt for Gene, that greedy bastard. And the forest service. They've got no excuse."

As far as they could tell, all the logs in the yard but one had been properly salvaged—"They must be taking the others out right away," said Marcy—and they set off for the mariposa tulips. In Will's Trooper they were able to push up the old logging road almost to the meadow, and from there recapitulated Claire's hike: up the ridge, a moment for each to stand in the hollow sequoia and commune with Gaia, then down the steep slope to the meadow.

"Oh, look, there's some monkshood," Marcy said, and then, when they came to the *Calochortus,* "These? But I've seen these before." She cupped a white bloom in her small hand. "Mariposa tulips, right?"

"Yes, but these are a rare subspecies."

"Really? They look just like the others."

"Really. Trust me."

"Well, we need to document them. Maybe we should show them to Andy Nilsson. . . . No, maybe not; I'm not sure we can trust—"

A branch snapped up by the hollow sequoia. They both froze.

"Deer?" said Claire, fighting the urge to whisper.

"Or somebody watching us," Marcy said, as Claire had known she would, and abruptly took off toward the ridge, scrambling up the loose talus. In the moment before she decided to follow her, Claire thought she heard movement through the brush at the top, eastward toward the mountain, but she didn't see a thing.

"I'm sure someone was spying on us," Marcy said when Claire joined her.

"Not . . . a . . . deer?" gasped Claire, leaning on her knees to catch her breath.

"No, I think it was a person," Marcy said firmly. Clearly the idea, the drama of it, appealed to her.

Claire, who really, really didn't want it to have been a person, because she had just gotten over feeling nervous

about traipsing around alone, said, "How would someone have gotten up here without us hearing a car or seeing him?"

"Easy. From the other logging road."

"The reservation's just south of here, isn't it?" Claire
said suddenly. "Not far overland?"

"Oh, a couple of miles, I think," Marcy said vaguely.

"But why would anyone watch us?" Claire continued.

Which was a question with too many answers, and
Marcy just shrugged.

That evening on her deck Claire sipped smoky Glen-
fiddich and watched the colors leach from the world, as
her rods shut down and her cones kicked in. Having no
such light-dependence, a bat skittered above her and
snatched breakfast from the air. Oh, yes. The bats. She vi-
sualized Don reaching high above his head to stuff the
eaves with steel wool, his bulk teetering on a ladder like
a baked potato on a straw. No. Someone slimmer, more
agile, more . . . *more like Will Brecker,* suggested her cun-
ning subconscious, and she realized she had been thinking about him ever since that smile at the public hearing.

And really, why not Will? He was perfect: a handyman,
probably a rock climber . . . and he had some free time
coming up, since Marcy seemed to be stalking other game.
Claire drained her glass, sat for a moment, then ducked inside and left a message on his answering machine.

Back on the deck the evening had deepened, and she
took in lungfuls of night-saturated air. The skunk, she
thought, sniffing; she still had to deal with the skunk.
She hadn't been able to bring herself to set the trap. Tomorrow, for sure. Possibly. Maybe. She forgot about it.

Where had she and Marcy been today? she wondered,
staring at the base of the mountain. Toward the south,

she reckoned, at, say, six thousand feet, which put them right about—there.

Right where that light was shining.

Was it? She blinked; she wasn't sure. Was that a light, faint and unsteady? She ran inside for her binoculars, returned, scanned blackness. Nothing. She wasn't even sure if she was aiming at the right place.

But on Sunday, of course, infected as she was by Marcy's paranoia, she had to check on the population of *Calochortus.* The pickup bottomed out in the first quarter-mile of SN23J1, and she had to hike a good three miles before she saw the ridge ahead of her. Wearily she trudged up and over it, not even pausing for the traditional pilgrimage to the hollow sequoia, and stumbled, grumbling, down the north side. Past the blue monkshood, the orange lily, straight upslope to the white mariposa tulips . . . the white . . .

Oh, my God, they were gone.

At first, she couldn't believe it, even though this was what had led her up here. She whirled, she looked, she dropped to her knees and parted the grass with her hands—but the flowers, the delicate sculptured flowers, had disappeared entirely. She couldn't even find a long-bladed *Calochortus* leaf, only pockmarks where the bulbs had been pried out. Someone *had* been watching her and Marcy yesterday, and he had been thorough.

She looked up at the ridge, thoroughly spooked, and started for the car.

Like poor little Snow White she stumbled through the forest, hallucinating in the white knots of oaks the faces of killers she had known—Manny Aragon, Jay Cardenas, and then, halfway to the car, that blurred face from the handbill at Casey's, the escapee from Corcoran. She was very sorry she had remembered him. Maybe Sam was right about a gun.

But she reached the car unmolested. And then she somehow took a wrong turn, and lost a half hour traveling east toward the mountain instead of north toward the highway, and when she tried to reverse course, her right rear wheel sank into a ditch and she had to dig herself out. So she was not in good humor to receive Marcy's triumphant exclamation over the phone.

"I told you!" she said. "I told you someone—"

"Yes, all right," Claire snapped, "but *who,* Marcy? It has to have been someone who heard us talking at the meeting on Thursday."

"That's almost everybody! The Genes, the sawmill people—"

"No, they were already gone." She had been thinking about this for the last two hours. "Your group was still there, and those kids from the reservation—"

"My *kids?*" said Marcy, scandalized. "Oh, no, Claire. I know they look tough, but that's just attitude. They would never do something like this. Nature is sacred to them. But all the forest service people were there . . . Andy Nilsson!" she exclaimed, and Claire flinched. "He was standing right next to us!"

"Oh, I don't think Andy—"

"I've never trusted that guy!" Marcy said. "I bet he's a, what do you call it, double agent"—she stopped, and giggled—"pretending to pass on information to us, but actually reporting back to Nelson Pringle!"

Will had left a message, returning last night's call. Because it was business he was at his best, husky voice straightforward, free of jargon and mannerism; she could hear his local Okie accent. "Sure, I'd like the work. But you know bats are pretty sweet little animals. And they eat mosquitoes."

She left another message, explaining about guano and histoplasmosis and rabies, and around ten-thirty he called back.

"Okay," he said, "you convinced me. As long as you don't want me to hurt them, or poison them—"

"No, no!" she said, touched. "Just deter them. With the steel wool."

"Sure. How about if I look at it tomorrow evening after you get off work? Say around seven?"

"Perfect. The bats will be gone by then."

"Good." A pause. "I've been hoping for a chance to get to know you better anyway," he said. "I felt like we sort of resonated the other night, and you seem like a good person."

Whoa, she thought, hormones sluicing through her veins. Not *that* good.

Chapter 12

As she drove down to work on Monday morning the temperature rose by the mile. It was going to be a scorcher, and foul. When the canyon opened up, she could see what she was about to breathe: air like pond muck, squashed flat under the cooler mountain air that had rolled down on top of it, and by the time she passed the lake her mouth tasted like galvanized aluminum—a vivid childhood sense memory, like the chalky taste of Play-Doh. Could she have once licked a garbage can? People worried about Alar on their apples but never seemed to think about the other crap Valley crops took in on a routine basis through their little stoma.

Just beyond the fork in the river at the east end of Riverdale someone had stretched a blue banner between two telephone poles. "This weekend," it said, "Mountain Days! Crafts, food, music," and then a demoralized "Much More," as if the publicity committee had almost immediately run out of imagination and vocabulary. Claire groaned at the thought of the weekend traffic on Riverdale's main street, which happened to be the only route to her house. Then she remembered this morning's staff meeting and would have groaned again, except that the threat of the day's heat made her actually look forward to two hours in a controlled climate.

And Ramón Covarrubias from County Extension was going to talk to them about his work with the Small Farm Project.

She was curious about his work. Somehow, in the heart of this land of industrial-strength agriculture, a few Mexican and Southeast Asian families had managed to buy plots no bigger than suburban backyards, which they cultivated by teaspoon and watered with sweat. The good ones, the lucky ones, coaxed enough food from their land to sell at farmers' markets or roadside stands. As she drove through the county she would see their plots—colorful, richly textured, ad hoc—squeezed in among the monotonous, orderly orchards. Some had ingenious cat's cradles of string supporting strange Asian vegetables: pale squash, pendent eggplants.

And somehow UC Extension had decided that these small farmers—Claire always thought of Hobbits—were a good thing, and had graciously undertaken to offer them the largesse of its technology and expertise.

So it was a good-intentioned, underfunded program. Kaweah County had only recently hired a Small Farm Adviser, and Ramón was it. Fiftyish, with black hair streaked with gray and a big square face like a tractor driver in a Soviet Socialist Realist mural, he was, Claire assumed, a local boy, son of farmers or even farm laborers. He delivered his presentation in a deep, easy voice that reminded her of Jay Silverheels.

"A woman called from the reservation down here,"

Ramón said finally, absently hitching his belt to a more comfortable latitude. He was not fat, but solid, and Claire idly observed the brown fingers of his left hand. The inevitable line of gold winked back at her. "She's an interesting case; I've never worked with anyone on the reservation before. Mostly they run cattle—"

"Which they find at the end of a long rope," said Mac Healy, meaning the Indians had rustled them, and everyone snickered.

"But she has a little orchard," Ramón continued, ignoring him. "Apples. Granny Smiths. And I've helped her put in some specialty vegetables until the trees start producing again. But I'd like a plant pathologist from here at Citrus Cove to take a look at her trees. They've been neglected for years."

"Aw, Ramón, what's the point?" Mac said. He seemed to have picked up the baton of racist curmudgeon from Jim LaSalle upon the occasion of Jim's recent incarceration. "You know she won't stick with it. They should keep to horses and cattle out there. Because of the water," he added hastily, seeing Claire glaring at him—he lacked Jim LaSalle's shamelessness in these matters. "They don't have access to water."

"They do have water problems," Ramón conceded.

Claire raised her hand. "R-ramón," she began, stumbling over the name because she always wanted to give that initial *r* an authentic Latin rub (she couldn't pull off the *rr* in the middle of Covarrubias without a sort of glottal windup) even though Ramón himself never did, and most people at the station called him Raymond. "I don't know if I'm the person to help your client, but I'm really interested in the small farm program. I'd like to talk to you about enrolling a friend." Luz, the beautiful Luz, inamorata of Deputy Enrique "Ricky" Santiago. Luz Perez had passed briefly through the ramshackle migrants' motel last summer, dragging two kids and four pots of chlorotic tomatoes behind her.

"Sure. I'll stop by." A smile split Ramón's somewhat wooden face.

Sam was at the meeting, head bent over notebook so that all she could see was an oval of thick dark hair. *Pelage dense,* she thought. She felt detached from him this morning because she was thinking about Will—not seriously, but enough to make her feel protected.

The whiff of indifference is a powerful aphrodisiac, and after the meeting, which concluded with Ramón telling what he had learned about the Laotians this week, Sam approached her obliquely, tacking around the furniture as if fighting some powerful opposing force. Eventually he stood before her.

"Lunch?" he asked.

"No, thanks," she said triumphantly. "I have some errands to run. But I brought you this." She handed him a folded wad of newspaper clippings.

She had been collecting stories of gun fuckups. Modesto, a father accidentally shoots his two-year-old while cleaning his pistol. Bakersfield, a fifty-four-year-old woman is shot with her own gun while trying to protect herself from an intruder. Fresno, a six-year-old finds his father's gun under the mattress and accidentally shoots his little brother. And her personal favorite: Orange County, a guy shoots his sister-in-law for no apparent reason and takes off in a '74 Plymouth Duster. He runs out of gas and ideas in Chrysolite, Colorado, and wanders over to a bus bench to think. In the next two hours the county sheriff, a highway patrolman, *and* the police chief each come by and question him because they all know he's not from around there, and there isn't but one bus a day through Chrysolite and that not for a while yet. As he is talking to the police chief his gun slips out of his waistband, slides down through his pant leg, and dumps out onto the gravel. He's arrested and extradited to California.

"What's this?" Sam asked.

"Just some light reading."

Parkerville Hardware had exactly two packets of steel wool. "How much you need?" the clerk asked belligerently, as if it were Claire's unnatural lust that was the problem here. Customers, with their constant and insatiable desires!

"Lots." But Parkerville Hardware didn't have lots of anything, except—she looked around—leather work gloves. There were two boxes, made in China, size Humongous. And shovels; they seemed to have plenty of shovels. It was like shopping in the former Soviet Union. GUM had stocked four zillion potato peelers, when what the people wanted was toilet paper.

"We'll be getting some in next week," he said.

"I need it today. Sorry."

"You might try Wal-Mart."

The noon sun was not kind to Parkerville. It backlit the dusty signs for Chuck's Hobbies and Karla's Klassy Wrap; it glinted off the smeared windows of Gil's Kamera Korner—what was it about *k*'s? Some nostalgia for the Klan?—Mindy's Book Fair, Betty's House of Balloons, and Pat's House of Beauty; it probed the tawdry mysteries of the Brau Haus and the 3-7-11 Tavern (Booze Cards Come On In). Claire shrugged impatiently. She needed steel wool, pantyhose, Advil, and a cordless screwdriver—none of these exotic items in late twentieth-century America, and none to be found at Betty's or Gil's or Pat's or Chuck's.

Giving Parkerville up to its fate, she drove north, following a line of tall white trucks.

Along the strip between Parkerville and Alma a few narrow olive plots lingered, ghosts at the feast of Pizza Huts and Carpeterias and JiffyLubes. And when Claire arrived at the asphalt vastness of Wal-Mart Plaza itself she couldn't remember what it had replaced. Orange groves, maybe? That was almost the worst of this land conversion—the 'dozers seemed to scrape away collective memory.

Well, let it go, she thought grumpily. Let it all go. Once it was tulare and shallow lakes; now ninety percent of the native wetlands were gone to farmland; soon ninety percent of the farmland would be gone to strip malls and housing tracts. If this was highest and best use of America, then let every growing thing go to Mexico, and she'd go with it.

But for the moment all of Mexico was right here at Wal-Mart. The Word in the parking lot was definitely in Spanish. Or sometimes Laotian or Tagalog. The brown faces were a comforting antidote to Wal-Mart White, to the antiseptic trucks, the hospital-like sign, and, when she stepped inside, the lunar fluorescent lighting.

She stopped and blinked like a hick while the Third World flowed confidently around her. My God, it was overwhelming, it was a continent of a store. She had entered in, say, Mobile, Alabama; up in the Rust Belt she found shelves crammed with steel wool, all grades, and finally settled on some the consistency of pubic hair; she wheeled along the fifty-fourth parallel, stopping out of outrage and fascination in Idaho to look at the gun counter; then a leisurely trip down the Coast for pharma-

ceuticals, with a quick detour to Reno for ladies' underwear; and finally checked out in Tijuana.

She looked down at her cart. Steel wool. Pantyhose.
Battery-operated cordless screwdriver. Detergent. Ramen
soup. Condoms. That should cover it.

After work she sat on the back deck to wait for Will.
Then she ducked inside, grabbed a stack of what looked
like magazines from her desk, and resettled herself, and
while the sun sank on another sweltering Valley day, she
drank cold Dr Pepper and studied her catalogs.

Woodstoves, cable-knit sweaters, mohair mufflers,
plaid flannel pajamas, down comforters . . . just as her
mother spent the long Massachusetts winter nights poring
over seed catalogs and planning summer gardens, so
Claire endured Kaweah County's endless summer by fan-
tasizing about winter.

But this year she would have it. Not a clammy Valley
winter—dreary weeks of toxic tule fog so thick you had
to drive with your door open to see the yellow line—but
the real thing. Snow . . .

No, she thought, setting down the can of soda, no
snow yet. This was a ritual fantasy and she had to follow
the rules. First, autumn: oaks turn, yellow leaves do hang
upon those boughs or are plastered onto wet black
roads, morning frost burns off like smoke. Okay. Late autumn: astringent air cauterizes the lungs, cedar logs in
woodstoves smell like new pencils. At night the stars are
hard, glittering. Then . . .

Then one morning you wake to white light and know
that while you slept it snowed.

Snow! It squeaks under your feet. It transfigures. It
raises the stakes and changes what's important: not color
and detail but shape and slope. Not that pothole in your

driveway, but the thirty-degree climb at the end.

And in California, when winter becomes tedious you just put your sneakers back on and drive down the hill.

Will showed up just before sunset, and she described the bats' schedule: gone by afternoon; hunt at twilight; settle in sometime during night; hang around till sun gets too warm.

No problem, he said, but he'd have to borrow a ladder—or maybe top-rope himself from the roof.

"Ladder," she said firmly. "Want a soda?"

"Just water, thanks. Nice pictures," he said, following her through the hall where she had hung her photos and pausing in front of her Folded Hills series. "I like this one. Seems like the light is coming up through the grass. Like the ground is shining."

This was exactly what she liked about that photo, and she looked at him in surprise. Maybe Will had hidden aesthetic depths. Maybe he was a diamond in the rough after all.

"Kirsten taught me about pictures," he said. "She was a photographer too."

"Kirsten?" she asked, pouring two glasses of good mountain water.

"A woman I lived with up here. She was from the Bay Area, and she went back a few years ago."

Before she was forced to ask rude follow-up questions he added, "We were in Recovering Adult Children and ODA together."

"ODA?"

"Overdependents Anonymous," he said. "I didn't know anything about the recovery movement until I met Kirsten."

It *would* be Kirsten, she thought. Or Traci or Staci or

Lori with an *i*. She pulled the table out from the ceiling—neither the table nor the laws of gravity were suspended, but in an A-frame the walls and the ceiling are the same—and asked, "What happened to you two?"

"Well, we were both working the Program, and we both agreed that Kirsten's work was going faster than mine and that she had evolved to a higher spiritual plane and that it was time for her to move on," he said rapidly.

She dumped you, translated Claire, watching a drop of sweat slide from Will's hairline across the two fine lines that trailed away from his eye like the wake of a speedboat. It slid over the ridge of cheekbone, down the long concavity of cheek, past the gold earring to the sharp jaw. Her own head was a good five degrees warmer than her feet: the thin roof-ceiling-wall slanting six inches above them still held the day's heat.

"So she went back to Berkeley," he was saying. "I've had a couple of relationships since then, but it was never really magical, nobody had worked through their stuff, till Marcy."

Claire didn't know what "stuff" was, but she suspected Marcy still had plenty of it. She was tempted to bait him again. But Will had stopped speaking suddenly and looked confused, so she laid her hand on his arm. He covered it with his own callused, useful hand.

Once upon a time she'd had a boyfriend, a perfectly nice kid with a perfectly legitimate South Boston accent, who one day out of the blue had begun to talk like Kwai Chang Caine of the TV series *Kung-Fu*—gently, serenely, haltingly, as if surrounding perfectly ordinary words with moats of silence would lift them into wisdom and significance. Bad poets felt this way about expanses of white paper.

And now Will. Okay, maybe he wasn't a mental giant,

but he had once had an authentic self, a personality and vocabulary. And now they lay like orange trees under concrete, buried under the rip-rap of somebody else's words. *Resonate. Magical. Stuff.* Maybe science, where one word equaled one and only one thing, was too precise; maybe language, like steering, should have a little play in it. But the jargon Will used was sloppy. It obscured the truth; it offended her delicate sensibilities . . .

Which were those of a narrow-minded snob. She could use a little play in her, too. After all, he at least was trying to talk about his feelings, unlike some men she had known quite recently. And maybe he had been desperately unhappy and violent and alcoholic, and now he was merely unhappy.

Or, maybe she was desperate to make excuses for him because he was so good-looking.

Or—

Will interrupted what could have been an infinite regress. "I'll come by around five tomorrow," he said. "The bats should be gone by then." He gave her a parting hug—comradely, she supposed, but goddammit, it set her buzzing.

Chapter 13

The knowledge that Will would be waiting for her made Claire run through Tuesday's field calls with mounting impatience, checking her watch with remarkable precision every seventeen minutes. Wherever she was, she wanted to be at the next place: almonds, navel orange worm in, let's get on to peaches; peaches, brown rot in, let's get on to walnuts, to olives, to oranges. . . . Christ, can't you people solve your own problems? Finally, at seven, with the sun setting in her rearview mirror and a pulse thrumming in her solar plexus, or lower, she tore up the hill.

There was no sign of Will—that is, there were *signs* of him, the Trooper with its "Stop Irradiating Food!" bumper sticker was parked in the drive and the ladder was propped up against the house and the eaves now sprouted a dull metallic moss, but there was no actual Will. Then he appeared from around the side of the house, a pornographic vision of sweaty torso and faded jeans.

"Just finished," he said, and rubbed his hair, which was loose. "I feel like a guano-head."

"Would you like to take a shower here?" she heard herself say.

"Yeah, that would be really good!"

While the shower ran, she pulled a Dr Pepper from the refrigerator, sank into the couch, and held the cold can against her temple. Jesus, it was hot, even up here; that south-facing glass wall, ever so scenic, turned the place into a greenhouse. As soon as Will left, she would strip to her underwear. . . .

Why wait? was a question that occurred to her, especially when Will appeared, aromatic and freshly laundered and wearing nothing but a blue towel draped from his waist. There was a flash of color from his right bicep.

"That was magical," he declared, then, looking down at his nearly naked self, "Sorry," which she didn't believe— he must have known how he looked. "I just couldn't face these again." He held up a tangle of dirty jeans and T-shirt. "I'll get some clean clothes from my truck."

Why bother? was another stumper.

What she dredged up, while she watched him walk out of the house and wondered why men had stopped wearing kilts, was the fundamental axiom that one shouldn't have sex with someone one didn't know and couldn't talk to.

But what did *knowing* someone really mean, when ninety percent of what you thought you knew was projection? And talking was overvalued anyway: many words had passed between her and Sam during the course of their relationship, but still they had failed to communicate.

There was AIDS, of course; that was a real argument. But it wasn't a *moral* one. It was based purely on fear, a fatal variant of high school's injunction to not go all the way because you might get pregnant. And besides, she had condoms, and besides, Will was screened, in a sense: he was Marcy's boyfriend.

Yes. He was Marcy's boyfriend, sort of, and Claire was her friend, sort of.

But Marcy seemed to be in the process of ascending to a higher spiritual plane, Will-wise. And maybe Marcy was part of Will's attraction: Marcy was a certified desirable woman, so if Claire slept with Will, maybe that made her a desirable woman too.

And if Sam had managed to detach love from happiness, why shouldn't she detach sex from love? Why shouldn't she?

Her R-brain, the ancient lizard-brain that lay under her cerebellum and controlled the basics, stirred and snarled. Cut the crap, it said. You're horny. You want to get laid. It feels good. Whoops, heads up, here he comes.

Here he came, all right. Fully dressed, in creased jeans and T-shirt. He draped her towel over the back of the rocking chair and handed her something.

It was an invoice for twenty-four dollars.

He must have seen something in her face, because he said anxiously, "Is it too much? I figured three hours at eight dollars an hour. I gave you a reduced rate, but if it's too much—"

"No, no, it seems very reasonable."

" 'Cause I can make it less. I hate having to charge my friends money at all. I'd rather live under the barter system, you know, like the Indians, uh, Native Americans. They weren't into possessions at all, they had this thing called potlatch. . . ."

He trailed off. Possibly Dustin Gomez was testing Will's belief in the spiritual superiority of Native Americans, and Claire certainly didn't have the heart to tell him that potlatch could be a very brutal business, sometimes culminating in the murder of slaves as a final flashy sacrifice of one's material goods.

"Twenty-four?" she repeated, foraging in her purse for her checkbook. Thank God she hadn't made any overtures. Once more she had misread a situation. It was like the other afternoon in the meadow with Sam; she was investing every available male with her own sexual longings.

"Could you use help in your bedroom?" Will asked abruptly.

She cleared her throat. "What?"

"There's a pile of paneling—"

"The *paneling!* Yes, uh, yes, I was hoping to do it myself, but I'm not getting around to it."

"Just give me a call. Anytime. I could install solar for you, too." He slipped her check into his wallet. "I've gotta go right now; I'm supposed to have dinner with Marcy. I think," he added, grimacing. "But some other day"—and here he drew her into what was either a comradely hug or a lover's embrace, his damp hair pressing against her face—"some other day I'd really like to share some heart space with you."

"I'd like that, too, Will." God help her, she meant it. Even the part about heart space.

He left. She picked up the damp towel, shapeless now and smelling of nothing but her own soap and her own shampoo—as if she had indeed conjured Will out of her own desire, like an incubus. An incubus who had to rush off to have dinner with his girlfriend.

*   *   *

The body shop had reassembled her Toyota—minus, at her request, the Z-Lock 2000—and relinquished it on Thursday. It looked all right, but to Claire it would never be the same. From now on she would always see, or imagine, slight irregularities, color mismatches, pulls to the left or the right. One of them had lost its, or her, innocence.

And one of them had gained six inches of clearance, too, because on Saturday she drove SN23J1 toward the missing *Calochortus* and found it pretty smooth going. But when, after forty minutes, there was still no sign of the sequoia ridge or the *Calochortus* meadow, she realized the easy road was of course the wrong road. Back down toward the base of the mountain; then there was a turnoff, a hard right to the east, and this time she banged her muffler almost immediately and bumped to a halt two hundred yards later. *This* was the road.

She pulled on her pack and started hiking. At the Thursday night meeting everyone had urged her to continue her search for other populations of the Slate Mountain mariposa tulip, and she figured the logical place to start was the site of the missing population. From there she would work north, as she had before.

But she had started late, and the wrong turn had cost her an hour, so by the time she began to walk it was high noon, and hot—a hot blue noon, in which the sky itself seemed to radiate heat, like her ceiling. As she trudged through the brushy landscape the sky pressed down on her. She felt its weight, its menace, like a diver at the bottom of the Pacific Rift; her eardrums trembled with it until her pulse and the cicadas' shrill merged into one dizzying roar.

The dry detritus of the old logging road crunched under her feet. Finally the prow of the ridge showed ahead. Once she reached the top and sat in the shelter of the hollow tree, she knew she would be okay. Up the switchbacks; she cupped her hands around her eyes to shut out that vertiginous blue so that all she could see was gray—boot toes, packed dust of the trail, roots snaking across it, granite pushing through it. The throbbing in her ears grew louder. Wondering if she was really ill, she lifted her canteen to her mouth, and as her head tipped back she saw the helicopter. It was directly overhead, moving east.

Then she smelled the pleasant, resinous tang of woodsmoke. Treesmoke.

And if she could smell it, that meant the wind was blowing toward her, driving fire before it.

Heat and head forgotten, she scrambled up to the edge of the ridge and looked anxiously toward Slate Mountain, where the helicopter was just disappearing. No smoke— no, wait, there *was* something, on the far side of the peak. A faint stain against the sky. Even through her binoculars that's all it amounted to, a subtle yellow smudge. She closed her eyes and felt the wind against her eyelids, not strong, but steady, and blowing from the mountain.

Maybe she had better turn back, she thought uncertainly, but now that she was finally up here she hated to leave. She looked down at the meadow and squinted at the far side, as if the *Calochortus* might have magically regenerated. Then, since she was holding her binocs, she scanned slowly across the lush green, picking out the leaves of the corn lilies and the orange leopard lily and some rose-colored geraniums and, in the tall grass directly below her, where the trail ran out onto level ground, a fallen log. Funny, she didn't remember it. It lay perpendicular to the trail, a short pier jutting into the meadow. . . . She looked again.

Then she started down, slowly at first, picking her way, then faster, cutting off switchbacks, sliding wildly down the loose talus like a skiier. Her weak ankle twisted under her and she grunted with pain, but hobbled doggedly downward, thinking, Fallen log. It must be a fallen log.

It was a small log, weathered to the color of chino. A helicopter shuddered overhead again, and Claire's heart thudded in time; later she remembered horror, or fear, but in fact what she felt at this moment was pure excitement. The horror came later.

The log wore chino pants. And a khaki shirt. And a blue bandanna. It was lying face down, head to one side, toes in, arms straight out like wings. Well before Claire knelt and brushed away the soft brown hair she knew it was Marcy.

Chapter 14

She looked like a child napping, but Marcy wasn't
asleep. Claire lifted a small wrist, and a few long stalks
fell from the limp hand. Monkshood, she noted automatically, frowning in concentration as she felt for a pulse.
Nothing, but then her hands were shaking, and she
didn't even know if she was looking in the right place,
and sure enough she felt for her own pulse and couldn't
find it, either, even though the blood was roaring
through her ears like the Red Line thundering into Central Square.

Try the carotid artery. Her own was jumping under her
skin, and she pressed her hand just below Marcy's jaw-
bone. Nothing. C'mon, Marcy, she thought, getting angry,
because look at her, she was fine, there wasn't a mark on
her. She slipped her fingers underneath the neck and
squeezed from both sides, gently throttling. Yes. Yes, it
was there, Marcy was alive, she was okay—

Her hand came away black with meadow muck and streaked with red.

With an involuntary cry of disgust she scraped it against her overalls and then on the grass, scrubbing violently.

What had happened here?

She looked up at the ridge. Had Marcy slipped on the trail as she had, smashing her head against the rough granite as she bounced down? Neat-footed Marcy? It was hard to believe, but here she was. Hesitantly Claire reached for the left shoulder to roll her over—then stopped.

"Heads is delicate," Tom Martelli had once, memorably, said, in another situation, and so was necks. And backs. If Marcy had taken a header down that cliff, Claire knew she should think twice about moving her. But it was hard to restrain herself, not just because she wanted to help but also because she needed to *see;* she was inflamed by curiosity. Examining the wound was as essential to the doctor's well-being as to the patient's.

But for the moment all she did was tug at the hair trapped underneath Marcy's face, digging in the soft dirt until it pulled free, matted with mud and blood.

She rocked back on her heels, winced at the twinge in her ankle. What next? Should she really leave Marcy bleeding into the mud while she went for help? A deep thrumming that she felt rather than heard made her look up, expecting another chopper. But this time it was a "Borate Bomber," cruising toward the mountain.

The fire! She had completely forgotten it! She narrowed her eyes and saw that the smudge was now a distinct plume of dirty yellow trailing straight up behind the peak of Slate Mountain.

"Hey!" she screamed at the C130, semaphoring her

arms, dancing around. "Hey! SOS! Down here!" The plane parted the sky like water, far too high and regal to take note of her. A helicopter was a better bet.

But if that fire was coming closer, she *was* going to have to move Marcy.

She could do it—Marcy was small, and Claire was a tall, strapping woman—but she couldn't move her easily or gently, and she couldn't move her very far. Not for the first time in her life she cursed her gender's lack of muscle mass. Who cared that you could live off your own fat in an open boat for three weeks, when what was more commonly required was the ability to bench-press your own weight?

She looked around. The meadow was a natural firebreak, clear and moist. It seemed to her that someone in the center, right where the stream cut through, might survive even a major inferno. Out of the bottom of her pack she pulled the silver thermal blanket that Sam had insisted she always carry, even on day hikes in midsummer, because you never knew. She unfolded it and began to wriggle it under Marcy. It was the old tablecloth trick in reverse: get it *on* the table without disturbing the cutlery. Or single-handedly make a bed with the patient in it, as nurses did every day—but Claire was no nurse, or she would have started pulling from the side instead of the bottom.

Up to the knees, no problem; under the hips, not bad; but then she progressed slowly, and by inches. Each time she had to start at the feet, gathering the material, then easing it up the whole length of the body, like threading elastic through a waistband.

And every time she looked up, that plume was higher. But it seemed also to be shifting slightly to the right.

Good. Maybe it was moving south instead of west. Up to
the shoulders—

She was on her feet, waving, before she even saw the
chopper. "Down here," she yelled at the sky—there,
heading back to the west. "Here! Help!" She knew he
couldn't hear her, but somehow she couldn't wave and
hop if she didn't also scream. "Help! Mayday! Shit!" as he
cruised over, cruelly indifferent.

It took almost five minutes to work a good foot of
bunched fabric up as far as Marcy's neck; then she more
or less tunneled under Marcy's head, cradled it an inch
off the ground with her right hand while she pulled the
blanket under with her left—a messy, awkward business,
and rougher than she had hoped. When she finished, her
forearm was smeared with blood and she started to feel
for a pulse again, but decided there wasn't time. And
maybe she didn't want to know. Instead she grabbed the
bottom edge of the blanket, curling her fingers into the
stiff selvage, and began to pull.

Nothing happened.

Abruptly cold with disappointment, she realized it
wasn't going to work; this whole twenty minutes that
could have been spent hiking for help had been wasted
on a misbegotten scheme . . . and then the blanket broke
loose. Its slick metallic fabric began to slide across the
rough grass. Like an exceedingly slow, stately royal barge
pulled by one cursing slave, Marcy inched toward the
center of the meadow.

But after thirty feet Claire was trembling with exhaustion. Every step sank her to her shins, and soon she
would be up to her knees; the muck sucked at her legs
like wet snow or quicksand. She had stumbled so often
she was black with mud; she couldn't even find a clean
patch of skin to wipe her stinging eyes.

Her stinging eyes . . . She looked up at the mountain and caught her breath. The smudge was now an angry yellow-gray thunderhead boiling up behind the mountain, and as she watched, little white motes floated gently through the air and came to rest on her arm. Ash.

Hopelessly she looked at Marcy. It had been a half hour since she'd found her; she could have been almost at her car by now, goddammit—

"Hel-lohhh!"

The voice came from the ridge. She whirled, at least from the waist up; her feet stayed glued in the muck, and she fell. When she struggled upright again, she could see a figure skittering down the steep trail, stumbling exactly where she had stumbled but recovering neatly. "Hallo!" he called again.

Beware! hissed her mind, but she had nothing to beware with, not a cubic centimeter of fight or flight left, and her muscles relaxed. As long as she could stop dragging this damn blanket, she didn't care who the caller was. And surely anyone with evil intentions wouldn't be hailing her. Or have tripped; somehow his clumsiness was proof of virtue.

"Hello!" she called weakly. He was coming into the meadow now, a small man jogging at a steady pace. As he neared she could see brown hair flopping with every step, and then the blunt features. . . .

Andy Nilsson, in black shorts and T-shirt; she hadn't recognized him without his green uniform. She forgot her suspicions, almost sobbed with relief.

"Claire!" he said, "I saw your car back down the road, and I thought I better warn you about the fire. . . . My God!" he exclaimed as he looked carefully at the blanket. "Is that . . . that's Marcy!"

"Yes. She's hurt and —"

"My God," he said again, "how could she—I mean, she was just—Is she unconscious?"

"Yes, I was trying to move her to the meadow where she might be safe."

Andy had sunk to his knees by Marcy's figure. "I have a first aid kit in the truck, but I'm afraid all I'm carrying is moleskin and a snakebite kit." He halted when he saw the smear of blood across the blanket's silver surface. "Jesus Christ," he whispered, "what happened to her?"

His voice shook, and suddenly she missed Sam's macho stoicism. Irritating in love, reliable in crisis. "I don't know. I've been afraid to look—no, don't!" she warned as he reached for Marcy. "Don't! It's not . . . not squeamishness. I was afraid I'd hurt her more."

"Oh, no! No, I don't want to hurt her! But maybe the two of us could turn her over pretty gently—"

It came roaring over the ridge. Andy dropped flat, and Claire slapped her hands over her ears.The noise was intolerable—*whap-whap-whap,* like being punched in the belly—and then the chopper swayed to the ground at the east end of the meadow.

It was rescue, but it felt like assault.

A guy in windbreaker and cap climbed down and started toward them, straight across the muck, backed up, and trotted around the southern edge of the clearing.

"You got a problem here?" he shouted over the *whap-whap-whap.*

"Yes!" screamed Claire. "Can you turn that thing off?"

He turned away, whipped his hand across his throat, and the pilot killed the engine. Andy was up again, trying to clean himself off.

"You got a problem?" the guy repeated. Under his blue

cap his skin had the shiny, scraped look of a redhead scorched by years of Valley sun. "I'm Bill Murphy, Cal Department of Fire. We were working this blaze and we saw the solar blanket."

So it had been worth something. "Yes, there's an injured woman—"

But he was already pulling at Marcy's shoulder. "Give me a hand here, buddy," he said to Andy. "She fall?" he asked, looking up at the steep face of the ridge.

"Yes," said Andy.

"I think so," Claire said. She was prepared to scream imprecations if Marcy's head lolled or her neck twisted, but the two men flipped her as handily as a burger on the grill. Claire bent forward, bracing herself against Andy's shoulder, against shock; she had once seen a man with half his face smashed in. But Marcy's face just looked dirty, really, especially her left temple, which was a tarry mess of black and red.

"Oh, brother!" Bill said, shaking his head and feeling for a pulse. "I ain't gonna touch this." He waved his partner over. "Bring the stretcher," he yelled, then turned back to Andy.

"This lady—" he began.

"Marcy Hobbes," said Claire.

"This lady," he repeated, ignoring her, "is just hangin' in there. We'll fly her down to Parkerville. Now, I ain't got room for you two in the chopper, but I can radio for somethin' to pick you up. Fire might be headin' this way; it's hard to tell."

"My truck's just over the ridge," Andy said.

"We'll be okay," said Claire. "Where are you taking her?"

"Mercy Hospital."

"We'll meet you there."

"Yeah." He hesitated. "Yeah. In fact, let me get your names," he said, pulling a scrap of paper from his jacket pocket. "Because if she don't pull through, the sheriff will want to talk to you."

Chapter 15

Claire and Andy trudged back up the ridge, or rather Claire trudged and Andy trotted. At the turning of every switchback he would pause and wait for her, and when they came to that last steep stretch he offered a hand, and she was too exhausted to turn it down. As he hauled her up a knot of muscle slid under the skin of his thin upper arm like a mouse through a python. Her own arm was still streaked with mud.

"Ah, God," she groaned, sinking to the ground under a sequoia. "I'm sorry, I have to rest for a minute, Andy. I wore myself out trying to move Marcy."

He hesitated, looked down the trail. "But what if she . . ." He shrugged. "I guess there's nothing we can do for her," he said and squatted beside Claire. "What were you trying to do down there, with the blanket?" He opened his pack as she explained. "Huh," he said when she finished. "That was pretty smart."

Too tired even to preen, she said, "Was it? I'm not so

sure. Maybe I just should have gone for help. Because the fire *didn't* come this way, and maybe she'd be in better shape if I hadn't moved her."

"No, it was a good call," he said, unscrewing his canteen and offering it to her. "A half hour one way or the other wouldn't have made much difference anyway. She'd probably already been laying there for a while."

"I don't think she was. No, I don't think she'd been lying there very long." The water tasted slightly of mud, which she realized after a moment had come from her own lips. Jesus, she thought, she must look like she'd been dipped in pig shit!

"Why not?" asked Andy while she pulled her own water bottle from her pack and made a rudimentary attempt to wash her face.

Why not? She had to think about it for a moment. "Because she had picked a bouquet," she said finally, "and it was still fresh."

"Hmm." He shifted so that he was also sitting with his back against the sequoia. "You're right; this feels good," he said. "I'm a little shaky myself."

She looked at him. Uniforms tended to make people, well, uniform, but in his shorts and T-shirt Andy was like a daddy longlegs: short body and long, loosely jointed, bamboolike limbs. How incongruous that he had the face of a prizefighter—that flat nose that took a dip as if it'd been broken, and that permanent embouchure, like a mouth guard tucked under his upper lip. An undercoat of sickly green seemed to show through his biscuit-colored skin, but maybe that was just the tree-filtered light.

When he saw her observing him, he said quickly, "It's not like I'm new to these situations or anything. In my job you have to fish people out of the river from time to time, or scrape them up when they fall off rock faces.

But it's different when it's somebody you know." His elastic mouth stretched, turned down. "My girlfriend was killed by an avalanche four winters ago—No," he interrupted himself, as if answering an accusation, "not girlfriend. Just someone I liked. A lot. It happened right in front of my face; one second she's there, and the next . . . I looked for her eighteen hours a day for a week."

"Wow," she said, and didn't know what to say next. For one thing, this discussion of "my girlfriend," even oddly qualified, was a jolt; she had, she realized, assumed that Andy was gay. Lots of botanists were, and he didn't seem to be generating a sexual field, in *her* presence, anyway. "Did this happen up here?" she said lamely.

"Idaho. I worked out of Coeur d'Alene"—(pronouncing it carefully, in the French way)—"for ten years; they posted me out here just last year." Pause. "As punishment for insubordination, like I said, but I was just as glad to leave after Jan died." He took a swallow of water. "Anyway, you can't work up in the mountains without seeing some bad accidents. And most people who fall off cliffs look a lot worse than . . . than Marcy."

Claire's damp bandanna halted midway between water bottle and muddy neck. It was true. Marcy had looked fine. No bruises, scrapes, abrasions, the kind of thing you would naturally accumulate in bouncing down a cliff. Plus—

"The monkshood!" she exclaimed. "Marcy couldn't have fallen down the cliff . . ." She trailed off and looked at him uncertainly.

It was a big forest. Why had Andy appeared at just that moment, in just that place? What had he said, kneeling by Marcy? "She was just . . ."

"Were you and Marcy up here together?" she asked abruptly.

"Together? Oh, no!" he said, reddening, as if the question were somehow suggestive. "I did see someone on the far side of the meadow, but I didn't realize who it was. No, I came up to see this famous tree, the hollow one, because somebody at work told me about it. And then I wandered off to do a little botanizing, maybe find that *Calochortus*. And then I heard you calling." For a moment the sun shone through his round ears. She'd once taken a photo in western Massachusetts of a particularly intelligent-looking sheep, backlit so that its ears were that same luminous pink. Andy was the most innocuous being in the world.

"You were saying . . . ?" he prompted.

"Oh. Well, I don't see how she could have fallen," she said, "because she must have picked the monkshood down below, in the meadow. And she was still holding it."

"You're sure?"

"About what? I mean, I'm sure it was monkshood! Maybe I should go back down and find it—"

"I'll go," he said, and scrambled to his feet. She watched him career pell-mell down the trail, skidding and sliding, losing and instantly regaining balance, so that she was simultaneously alarmed by his clumsiness and amazed at his powers of recovery. From the rim of the cliff she directed his search.

"They'd be right at the end of the trail—about ten feet to your left, I think," she yelled down to him.

"I don't see anything."

"There were about five stems. They'll have dark blue flowers and ranunculusy leaves—you know, deeply lobed—"

"I *know* what monkshood looks like, for Christ's sake," he called testily, and she smiled at the inversion of her relationship with Sam. "I just can't find 'em! But I can see the smoke pretty good from here, and it's probably moving to the south of us." Silence. Then, "Nope. I just don't see 'em. Is it important? Because I think we should go down and see how Marcy is."

She thought about looking herself, glanced at the smoke, changed her mind. "No, it's not important. Let's get out of here."

Andy jogged back up, breathing hard, a forelock of light brown hair pasted to his forehead. "So," he said, as he twisted to put on his daypack, "you're saying that if she picked these flowers . . . you're saying . . . you're not saying somebody attacked her?" His voice squeaked suddenly, and she realized how jaded she'd become.

"It happens," she said flatly, indulging in a little macho posturing as reparation for two years of rank-pulling by those battle-hardened veterans Tom and Sam.

"Well," he said after a minute, "after the owl and all, I guess I wouldn't be that surprised. And something happened to your brakes, too. Right?"

She nodded.

"They ever find out who did that?"

She shook her head. "Let's get down to Parkerville and hope Marcy's all right."

"Yeah. For one thing, if somebody hit her he could still be hanging around."

Andy drove the rutted road the way he hiked—a little too fast for his ability, so that he was continually misjudging and continually compensating. Every now and then they glimpsed the smoky sky to the east and south of the mountain. The enormous plume had billowed out at its crown, like a tree flowering. The wraith of a thousand trees.

"Lucky you came along when you did," she remarked, probing a little out of habit, no longer really suspicious. "Could she have surprised somebody setting the fire?" She was remembering the discussion at the meeting, but even as she answered her own question he shook his head.

"That fire started miles away."

They came to her car and he asked if she felt okay to drive. "Of course," she said.

"Well, hang on a minute, just the same." He twisted around in his seat and reached behind him, cursed, slid out of the van, climbed into the back and dropped to his knees and elbows. For a minute he was a waving rump and a continuo of grunts.

"Son of a bitch," he gapsed, finally dragging what appeared to be a length of pipe from under the back seat.

It was a shotgun.

"Take this, just in case. Here's a couple of shells. You know how to use it?"

Irritated and touched, she took its cold barrel into her hand and shoved the shells in her pocket. "Yes."

"Good. I'll meet you at Mercy Hospital."

"Fine."

"Oh. Claire. Where *is* Mercy Hospital?"

Chapter 16

Mercy Hospital was, in fact, in Parkerville, and Parkerville was on the other side of Riverdale, and Riverdale was experiencing Mountain Days: Claire had forgotten about Mountain Days. By the time she squeezed through the town she was feverish with frustration. Andy had found the hospital; his green van was in the lot, right next to a Gatorade-colored Kaweah County Sheriff's Department Cherokee, which was next to Tom Martelli's black-and-white Blazer. The presence of so many authorities filled her with nonspecific dread, which was not allayed by the sight of the big boots and soft belly of Sheriff J.T. Cummings himself, blocking the corridor. He was talking with Marie and Tom and Andy and a slight, very dark young man who looked sixteen but nevertheless seemed to be a doctor.

"How is she?" Claire called, hurrying up to the crowd.

Andy turned a stricken face to her. "She's still unconscious," he told her in a voice that wobbled. "Dr. Mukherjee was just filling us in."

"As I've been telling your friends, she's seriously injured," the doctor said. He had a musical East Indian accent and soft plum lips. "There's major trauma to the left frontal lobe—"

Claire interrupted. "But she's going to be okay, right?" she said, almost indignantly.

But Dr. Mukherjee didn't jump right in. Instead he pulled a pencil from his breast pocket and revolved it slowly between thumb and forefinger. A strand of black hair fell across his glasses, reducing his apparent age to twelve.

"It's too soon to tell," this child told them. "She's in surgery right now. If . . . when she recovers consciousness, we can evaluate her more fully. She may not be . . . she may require some rehabilitation."

Claire missed entirely the second half of his sentence. She was thinking about surgery and that they would have shaved Marcy's head. The image of those brown curls tangled around used syringes at the bottom of a Dumpster made her realize for the first time that something irrevocable had happened here. "Did I hurt her by moving her?"

"No, I wouldn't think so. There's no injury to neck or spine. In fact, there are no—"

"Do I understand that you found her, Miss Sharp?" Sheriff Cummings interjected.

Claire's eyes flicked quickly across his pink visage. "Sharples," she said wearily. This was an old game; J.T. had known her name for two years. "Yes. At the foot of a ridge near the base of Slate Mountain."

"Right at the foot of the ridge. So you reckon she fell."

She looked at the sheriff again. His lipless mouth, which seemed to recede by the year, as if his whole face were caving into it, was set in a horizontal line. J.T. had made up his mind. "Well . . ." she began hopelessly.

"Pardon me, Sheriff," said Dr. Mukherjee, "but I'm not sure this lady fell."

Oh, miracle!

"No?" J.T. said loudly. It was unfair that such a stupid man could carry such authority.

"No," Mukherjee said uncertainly. "As I started to say a moment ago, there are really no injuries other than the blunt-force trauma to the left temple. Nothing that would indicate a fall in rough terrain: no abrasions, no broken bones—"

"How about her forearms?" Tom interrupted. "Her hands?"

"No."

J.T. was staring at Mukherjee so hard that Claire actually thought he was considering the implications of this revelation. But no: "How long you been practicin' medicine, *Doctor?*" was what he said.

"A year," the young man said with dignity.

"And how long you been here?"

"At Mercy Hospital? About six—"

"No, I mean *here,* in America."

"Five years. I don't see that this is relev—"

"I been sheriff of Kaweah County for twenty-one years come September, and I seen a lot of people come off cliffs. Some of 'em are hamburger, but some don't have hardly a mark on 'em. This victim was wearing long sleeves and long pants, ain't that right?" He swung his head ponderously in Claire's direction.

"Sure, but—"

"Well, that would've protected her."

"From a fall like that?" she said incredulously, but Cummings shrugged, as she had known he would, and turned away from the group.

Mukherjee made his escape. "Excuse me. I will check on Mrs. Hobbes's surgery," he said, and walked briskly down the hall. His rubber soles squeaked loudly on the linoleum and out of nerves and near hysteria, Marie and Claire began to giggle, adding to the consternation of Paul and Naomi, who had appeared at that moment.

"How is she?" asked Naomi, and Marie, sobering immediately, told her what they knew.

"What does he mean, rehabilitation?" Paul said in a strangled voice. "Does he mean Marcy will be . . . be brain-damaged?"

"No!" said Andy loudly.

"Of course not!" said Claire. "He meant . . . All he meant was . . ." Then they all looked at one another, taking in this possibility for the first time. Thinking about Marcy as other, less than she was.

"Let's just wait to see if she pulls through before we worry about that," Tom, ever tough-minded, said.

"Did anyone tell Will?" Claire asked suddenly.

"I left a message," said Marie. "But I don't know when he'll get it. He's probably working the fire. He always does. Laurie's driving over from Santa Barbara. And I talked to Stewart in L.A."

Oh, yes, Stewart. Claire had quite forgotten Stewart.

Meanwhile Tom was heading toward the door, mumbling that he had to get back to the office. After an instant his wife followed and caught up to him by the entrance. Against the white window of light they were two black cut-paper figures, as comic as Punch and Judy: Marie bent forward from the waist, chin out, nose out, sharp elbows out; Tom one gentle swell from collar to belt, where the curve was cruelly cinched and lifted.

Eventually Tom left and Marie returned, her eloquent eyebrows pinched into a scowl.

It was impossible to predict how long Marcy would be in surgery, the doctor had said. Still, none of them wanted to leave. They drifted outside, where the temperature was about a hundred and five, and settled under a big sycamore at the edge of the parking lot. Andy swung his leg across one piebald branch that ran parallel to the ground and straddled it.

"I just hope they catch the bastard who hurt her," Claire said—before he hurts another one of us, she added silently.

"Hurt her? I thought it was an accident," Paul said sharply.

"J.T. thinks so. I don't."

"Well, how about Tom, Marie?" Paul pressed. "Can't he handle the investigation?"

Marie picked up a broad, palmate sycamore leaf. "No," she said, tearing it carefully along the central rib. "Tom can't touch it"—tearing down the right-hand rib. "The national forest is the county sheriff's jurisdiction"—the left-hand rib—"and that means J.T."—clenching her right hand and crackling what was left of the leaf. "Ol' thanks-for-the-check-Gene-just-tell-me-what-you-need J.T." She brushed her hands briskly, and pulverized leaf exploded like seed from a burst pod.

"The Genes!" Andy said. "You don't think they did this?"

"Who else?"

"Nelson Pringle," offered Paul. "Sorry, Andy, just kidding."

"A disgruntled boyfriend," said Claire, then wished she hadn't.

Naomi sighed and leaned back against her husband, tucking her corolla of flame-colored curls under his chin.

"I can certainly believe somebody attacked her. She wasn't—*isn't,* one of those people who haven't got an enemy in the world."

"That's the way to live," said Paul. "When I go, I intend to leave the police a mind-boggling list of suspects." He tightened his grip around Naomi. "Including my long-suffering wife."

"Yeah," Andy said, kicking his legs back and forth along the branch like a kid. "She was—*is,* something. I don't know. Formidable, I guess. *Formidable,*" he repeated, this time pronouncing it in French.

"Unpredictable," Claire said. "I didn't know she could be funny, but she was," losing the battle with the past tense. "Especially when she was drunk."

Naomi said that Marcy was a complex woman, that she respected her, but that she could be . . . "difficult," she finally said. "She had to have what she wanted."

"What is this, a eulogy?" Paul interrupted, and his wife pulled away and looked back at him. "How do we know she's not going to be okay?" he said. But his forehead collapsed, and Marie picked up a leaf and began another fastidious dissection, and Claire stared at the hospital door.

"I wonder if she's out of surg—"

Cra-a-ack!

A shockingly loud report like a rifle shot made Claire for some reason throw her arm across her eyes, as if the violence were visual not aural. When she looked again all she saw was Andy, flat on his back on the ground.

There was a stunned silence. "Andy?" she said hoarsely . . . and he opened his tea-colored eyes and began to laugh. Then she saw the white sycamore shrapnel and litter of dull green leaves: the branch had snapped at its base and now twisted along the grass like a huge serpent.

"Good-bye, Old Paint," he said, sitting up and brushing himself off. He caught sight of the deep, ragged wound torn along the trunk. "Oh, God, look what I did! I feel terrible!" And in fact he sounded as if he might cry.

"You won't believe what I thought," Naomi said shakily, her serenity shattered like Andy's tree. "I thought it was a gunshot. I thought someone was picking us off—you know, our group. First Marcy, then the rest of us, one by one . . ."

"Nayo!" said Paul, surprised and tender, and pulled her toward him. Claire, who had thought the same thing, wondered why no one ever gathered *her* up in his big arms and told her everything would be all right. Even when she had men in her life, they seemed to assume she didn't need, or wouldn't accept, such simple comfort. Maybe they were right.

In any case, that last surge of adrenaline had just about depleted her. Horizontal seemed like a good idea, and she leaned back on her elbows, then eased herself onto the grass. For a moment she looked straight up at the glutinous late-afternoon sky, then closed her eyes.

"Are you all right?" Marie's voice, soft and southern.

"Tired," she said. "Hungry. Hot."

"Lord, I should think so!" Andy's voice, high and reedy. "After dragging Marcy halfway across the mountain!"

"Go home," Marie said. "I'll call you if there's any news."

Claire sat up abruptly. "Call me anyway," she said with a meaningful look, and tottered away on legs shaky with fatigue.

But Paul stopped her in the lot as she was sliding into her car.

"You know, Marcy and I clashed sometimes in the group," he said, his adenoidal voice rougher than usual, "but I . . . she was . . . she was really a special person," he ended. "Seems like you two were good friends."

"I don't know about that. I don't know if Marcy had friends, exactly, and my feelings about her were more complicated than that. Like Naomi's."

"Naomi," he repeated. "Naomi's scared."

"I don't blame her."

"Yeah," he said abstractedly. "You really think this was an attack?"

"I don't want to think so, but yes, I do."

His forehead folded with worry. "Because of all the harassment?"

"That, and the way she looked when I found her. I don't see how she could have fallen off that cliff."

"Me neither," he said. "Isn't Tom going to do anything about it?"

"I'm not sure, Paul. It's not his jurisdiction, but it's not like him to be so meek about technicalities."

"I guess you know Tom pretty well. Marie said you worked on some cases with him."

Claire thought she could see where this was leading. "Sort of."

His eyes shifted to the grassy area where Naomi and the others sat, then back to her. "Well, I'll let you go," he said, and relinquished the car door. "But I hope this gets resolved soon. Because otherwise we can kiss the Friends of the Redwoods, and the redwoods, good-bye. People are gonna be too freaked to go on. Oh, and Claire," he added casually as she started the engine, "do you have a gun?"

Chapter 17

She drove one-handed, rooting in her pack for her sandwich and shoving everything that had happened in the last four hours, including her conversation with Paul, to the bottom of her mental in-pile. Instead she planned the perfect nap. What if her bedroom was too hot? How could she triangulate the fans in a one-windowed room for optimal effect? What—*whoops!*

The cars in front of her had come to an abrupt stop. Mountain Days.

Far be it from her, thought Claire, stopped dead in traffic, to begrudge pathetic little Riverdale any influx into its civic coffers, which were probably pilfered by its inbred officials anyway . . . Far be it from her, but wasn't this illegal? Closing off a state highway? The thought of a class action suit was consoling, but after fifteen minutes she hadn't progressed past Milt's Donuts 'N' Videotapes, and the aroma of tri-tip barbecue was driving her wild.

So she pulled into Milt's parking lot and wove on foot

between the harried drivers, lobbing amused glances through their windshields now that she was a pedestrian. Main Street was constricted to one and a half lanes by a line of booths on the south side, selling traditional mountain crafts like tie-dyed T-shirts. Remembering her conversation with the Weissbergs, she wondered why tie-dye and long hair had been taken up by a slice of American society that still nursed a grudge against the sixties. But then, it was all very confusing, she thought. The paranoia about the federal government, that used to be *us*, and now it was *them*. The only thing that was constant was the rift down the middle of the country.

Holographic pendants, airbrushed plaques of the Sermon on the Mount . . . beyond the Karaoke for Rent booth—a blue plastic tarp strung from poles, empty except for the proprietor who sat smack in the middle of the weird blue light, his head in his hands—was "Genuine Indian Jewelry Handcrafted by Native American Artists from the Kaweah Reservation." Claire suspected that the Kaweah tribe's silverwork tradition dated back to about the first time tie-dye came around; nevertheless she couldn't resist the shiny things.

The motifs were all Navajo or Zuni, but there were some nice pieces. The craftsman behind the counter had silver hair in a thick braid and a brown, familiar-looking face, folded around the eyes. "Billy Gomez, certified Indian silversmith," his card said.

She considered a pair of silver saguaro earrings, a long way from their native habitat. "Are you related to Dustin Gomez?"

"Yeah," he said. "You want to see those?"

"No, thanks. Not yet."

The beat of rap pulsed from somewhere: a boom box behind the tent. Billy Gomez's support group—a young woman with black hair that fell like a shawl around her shoulders, and three teenage boys—were eating fry bread and barbecue from paper plates. Claire looked closer. The kids were Dustin's friends, the three ninjas from the forestry meeting. She saw now that the boy with the wire-rimmed glasses was much fairer than the others; his long ponytail was not crow-black like his friends' but medium brown, not much darker than her own.

At that moment he glanced up. An indescribable but intense emotion contracted his baby face and he stood abruptly, dumping his tri-tip in the dust, stumbling over his chair, and finally disappearing behind the tent. Claire whirled to see what it was that had startled him and saw nothing, except the wise-use booth across the street.

"Multiple Use!" said the banner. "Don't Lock It Up!" and below that, "The Issue Is Control!" Nelson Pringle and another uniformed forest service person were leaning against the table, talking with Gene Senior. Claire sidled over just in time to hear Gene declaim, "Now these endangered species. I say if they can't survive on all the public land there is in California, maybe it's time for the Lord to call them home!"

She laughed, she couldn't help herself, and turned back to Billy Gomez's booth. The boys had disappeared, and someone was sitting next to the girl with his arm around her shoulders and his face buried in her hair. He looked a lot like Dustin Gomez.

At the tri-tip stand so many slavering carnivores stood between her and burnt animal that she decided she was sleepier than she was hungry. So she was making her way back to her car when she heard two vaguely familiar voices coming from behind the blue karaoke tent. One was high and aggrieved, the other old and cranky but still with plenty of volume: Nelson and Gene.

"Totally unfair!" Gene was roaring, and "We agreed!" Nelson said.

At that moment the blue karaoke gent cranked up "Feelings," overwhelming the end of this highly provocative discussion.

Claire drove up Main, scowling at the heedless pedestrians who crossed in front of her. On the way up the mountain she ate trail mix out of a Ziploc bag.

She had just curled into fetal position on her bed when the phone rang.

"No news," said Naomi's slightly nasal voice. "I mean, Marcy's out of surgery, but she's not conscious. Mukherjee said there was severe trauma and a lot of swelling. But they can't really tell anything yet."

"Oh." Sleep, she thought. I am supposed to be asleep.

"Oh, and Marie had to get back to the kids," Naomi was saying. "She said to call her if you wanted to."

Wearily Claire dialed the Martellis' number.

"You've got to convince Tom to work on this," she said without preamble, a telephone technique she had in fact learned from Tom. "Cummings will just drop the ball, I mean he won't even pick it up, if it begins to look like any of the timber people are involved. Which they obviously are." She desperately wanted the sugar and caffeine of a Dr Pepper and began to pull the phone toward the refrigerator, paying out the cord through thumb and forefinger to straighten its kinks. She knew it was too short.

"Claire, you know what he said. This is J.T.'s case; Tom has no—"

"Jurisdiction," Claire finished, easing the cord past the table, untangling as she went. "But I don't think that's true. The note on Marcy's windshield and her slashed tires—that's his jurisdiction, right?"

"Right."

"So can't he make the argument that the attack is re-lated to that? I don't understand why Tom isn't more ag-gressive about this; it's not like him." She moved around the kitchen counter. The telephone plus her left arm were now stretched to their limit, which was one foot from the refrigerator handle. "Besides, I would think he'd be—" Worried about you, she started to say, but stopped. If Marie wasn't scared, why provoke her? "I think you should talk to him," she said.

"Claire, why don't we just wait till Marcy recovers con-sciousness and *tells* us what happened?"

Claire tugged gently, yearningly, at the cord.

"Then there won't—"

Click. Buzz. Claire cursed, snapped the jack back into the handset, stalked back to the desk and redialed Marie, realizing as she punched the last digit that she'd forgotten the Dr Pepper after all. "Sorry. What?"

"I said, if we wait till Marcy can tell us what happened, maybe we won't have to have an investigation."

A flowchart unreeled in Claire's mind, a line of binary boxcars bumping each other down the track: (1) Marcy regains consciousness, yes/no; (2) if yes, she can speak, yes/no; (3) if yes, she makes sense, yes/no; (4) if yes, she remembers what happened, yes/no. It was a rickety ride over a shaky trestle.

Marie, interpreting the ominous silence, said. "Okay. I know. But why me? You'd be a lot more persuasive."

"Me! You're his wife!"

"Sure, but we're not exactly Bill and Hillary, you know, I mean basically Tom believes I'm a slithering idiot. But you're a scientist," she said, dropping her voice comically on the last word, making a joke of resentment.

"An honorary male."

"Right."

Claire really didn't want to butt heads with Tom Martelli right now. "How about if we both approach him?" she suggested after a moment. "Good cop–bad cop?"

"You mean smart cop–dumb cop," said Marie, and interrupted Claire's objection. "I'm not serious. But I have the kids, I don't see how I can come today. I can promise to work on him at home, though."

"You could withhold sex," Claire suggested.

"Naw, he wouldn't notice. Not lately. I'll nag him when he gets home. But you should talk to him now."

Claire reminded Marie about Mountain Days; Marie pointed out that Tom's office was at the east end of town, before festival traffic. Claire proposed to drive down in forty minutes, after a nap; Marie pointed out that Tom might have left by then. So Claire washed down an Advil or three with a Dr Pepper and took a shower. For a long time she stood under the lukewarm spray, half asleep, half-mesmerized by the threads of black muck that swirled through the clear water like Janet Leigh's blood in *Psycho*. Or Marcy's blood, smeared across the silver blanket. Threads. Thready. What was a "thready" pulse? Had Marcy's pulse been thready in the meadow? Did Marcy still have a pulse? Would Marcy ever be the same?

She gave a vicious twist to the hot water spigot and gasped at the shock of pure cold water. When it began to be tolerable she ended the shower, dressed, and drove down the hill.

Chapter 18

"Well, well," Tom drawled when Claire walked into his cinder-block office behind the firehouse, "why am I not surprised?" He laid down a ballpoint pen and swept a manila envelope over the lined yellow pad on which he'd been writing. "I suppose Marie's been bending your ear."

"Marie and I are of one mind about this, Tom," she said, dropping into a plastic chair the color and texture of used chewing gum. A corner of yellow paper showed, and she scooted her chair right up to the desk, but could see nothing. "You know Cummings is not going to pursue this assault."

"Accident."

"Assault," she repeated.

"What's your evidence?"

She ticked off points on her finger. "One. The condition of the . . . of Marcy. Even the doctor thought she wasn't banged up enough for someone who'd fallen. Two. The monkshood."

"Monkshood?" getting it right this time. "What is that?"

"It's a flower, and it grows down in the meadow, not up on the trail. Three, the number of people in town who might have wanted to harm—"

"Wait a minute," Tom said. "Granted, Marcy had a lot of enemies; she was a dangerous woman—"

Dangerous? "Dangerous to the local logging industry, maybe."

"Whatever. You're mixing two things here: whether she was attacked, and who attacked her."

"But surely," she said, "if an accident is ambiguous"— she didn't think it was all that ambiguous, but she was making a point—"and the victim has a lot of enemies *and* there've been previous incidents, you want to look harder at that accident."

Tom stared at her with vacant blue eyes. Not the blue of fourteen thousand feet, like Will's; more of a Club Med blue, a snorkeler's wet dream blue.

"And by the same token," she continued pedantically, "if you have a close personal relationship with some of those enemies, then you might be reluctant to admit that the accident was ambiguous—J.T.!" she said hastily, as Tom's face suddenly changed. "I'm talking about the Genes and J.T.!"

"Good. Because if you think I—"

"No, no. I just don't understand why you aren't more concerned about this."

"I can't afford to be concerned. It's not my jurisdiction."

In a paroxysm of exasperation she slapped his desk. "The note and the slashed tires are your jurisdiction!"

"Yeah, they are. And my suspects for those particular

misdemeanors are half the adult population of Kaweah County—no, scratch the 'adult.' Anyway, I turned the note over to J.T. He's investigating the other—"

"J.T.!" she screeched. "J.T. would be just as happy if the Friends of the Redwoods vanished in a little puff of smoke!"

Tom muttered something that sounded like "—not the only one."

"I don't understand this jurisdiction business," she said.

"Well," he said in a singsong voice like a kindergarten teacher, "it's like this. Let's pretend Kaweah County is the ocean, and in it are some islands." He touched his fingertips together to make the sun in "Eensy-teensy-spider."

"The big island in the middle"—fingertips in a circle again—"belongs to the Parkerville Police; the medium-sized island"—fingertips—"belongs to the Alma Police; and this itsy-witsy little circle way down here—"

"Yeah, yeah," Claire said, irritated.

"Is Riverdale," he continued blithely. "All the rest of the big, big ocean"—arms flung wide—"is the county sher—"

"What I *mean* is," she interrupted, "that last year when one of those drownings happened in your—on your witsy-bitsy little island you were elated because it meant that you could investigate *all* the drownings! Now this is exactly the same sit—"

"No," he said, "it's not the same at all. That was a bona fide murder, in my jurisdiction, that happened to be re-lated to the previous deaths. Now we're looking at a probable accident"—she noted that "probable"—"and some minor nonviolent vandalism, with no particular rea-son to think they're connected." He paused. "I. Have. No. Authority. You understand?"

Claire looked sullen; Tom looked vaguely troubled and added, "Tell me again about the flowers."

Now, this was better. "The monkshood? Or the *Calochortus?*"

"Calo-what?"

"*Calochortus.* Slate Mountain mariposa tulip. Someone stole it." She pushed her chair back an inch or two from the old-fashioned mahogany desk. "It's a flower."

A long pause, then Tom said politely, "Someone stole a *flower?*"

"A *rare* flower." She leaned into the word and then explained the situation.

"So this rare tulip thingy would have stopped the timber sale," he said finally. "Like the spotted owl."

"Well, no, not actually *stopped.* Just delayed." Now her chair was three feet back from his desk, and she tensed for the slap of scorn to follow.

He stared at her for a moment, allowing one eyebrow to lift a few centimeters. "This may come as a shock," he said gently, "but flower-napping is not generally a motive for attempted murder."

"Yeah, but if she stumbled on the guy who was stealing them, or on somebody who was doing illegal salvage—we were trying to shut down that whole salvage operation, you know."

"Never mind that, I understand that. It was the other flowers I was talking about. The monk—the monkey stuff."

"Monkshood. What do you want to know? *Aconitum columbianum,* a member of the ranunculus family—"

"Where were they? Lying next to her?"

"Nope. In her hand," she said pointedly.

He nodded, and his eyes lost focus again. "I'll tell you, Claire," he said eventually. "In my experience, the simplest explanation is usually the best one. And the simplest explanation is that Marcy fell down a real steep cliff.

People fall down cliffs in the mountains, and she was a city girl."

She was a mountain goat, Claire started to say, but Tom stopped her.

"That's what *I* think happened, and it's not because the Genes contribute to *my* campaign, I can tell you."

And how did she manage to hang on to that bouquet falling down that cliff? she started to say, but again Tom stopped her.

"And even if somebody did attack her," he said, "which I'm not saying they did, there's no reason to connect it to this other trivial stuff; there's been no previous violence. And anyway, it's not my case."

It was a dismissal. Claire stood and walked toward the door. But at the last minute she pivoted and saw him bend over and begin scribbling on his yellow pad. He lifted his head, and their eyes met.

"You know, Tom, right now everybody in Friends of the Redwoods is in danger. And that includes—" *me*, she was going to say, but that wasn't her strongest argument—"your wife."

Chapter 19

Claire's stomach was churning with frustration, but she was too tired to hang on to it. And too tired to call Paul. Tomorrow. For now there was bed. She had earned it.

Her room was like a kiln. Maybe she should have Will put in another window when he did the paneling, she thought, dragging a quilt out to the back deck. The sun was low, but the day's heat lingered there, so she staggered back through the house to the front, north-facing deck, ringed by blood-red manzanitas and pleasant in the early evening. She spread her thin bedroll and sprawled, head toward the door. After a moment she noticed a pile of gray pellets two inches from her nose. Maybe she had missed them when she last swept, she thought hopefully, and looked harder. Fresh. Shit!

Too tired for disgust, she rolled over and was asleep in five minutes.

Some hours later she woke in the dark. Through the screen she heard the click of her answering machine and then the murmur of her own voice reciting its polite message—the ringing telephone must have awakened her—then another voice, no louder than the mosquito buzzing her ear, but the familiar cadence and timbre jolted her awake. As she scrambled through the dark corridor she could hear Sam saying ". . . anything I can do. Bye."

He had hung up by the time she reached the desk. Her heart was pumping and her hand unsteady as she replayed the message, which was an expression of concern for Marcy. She looked forward to the time when she wouldn't respond to that voice like a lab animal.

After that she never really got back to sleep. The day had been too packed with events to be comprehended as they happened, so now they reenacted themselves at a level of detail so thorough that it seemed it would take exactly as long to remember them as it had to live them. The weight of the sky as she hiked toward the sequoia ridge. The smudge and tang of smoke. The coldness under her ribs as she approached the "fallen log." The unnatural heaviness of Marcy's arm as the indigo flowers spilled from her limp hand—

Claire's mental camcorder halted, whirred, rewound, and replayed this scene, and she studied that bouquet of monkshood. There was something important about it. Of course it showed that Marcy had picked the flowers in the meadow, that she'd been coming *up* the trail when she was attacked, but Claire had already established that to her satisfaction. Something else, then . . . but the camera rolled on.

Finally at about four she dozed, only to wake at six exactly where she left off: atop the ridge with Andy, his broad, humorous face suffused with the green light that sifted through the canopy of fir and sequoia. This was kind of a nice scene and she wanted to linger for a moment, but her remorseless director shouted "Action!" and the cameras rolled. Weary as she was, she realized the only escape from memory was to rise and begin to accumulate new memories.

But when she struggled out of bed she discovered that her body remembered yesterday, too: her arms were so sore she could barely lift them above her waist. Definitely too sore to make her own breakfast. Besides, she needed company. But not Katy's Koffee Kup—Sam and the gang from work—not that much company.

A red California Conservation Corps truck was parked in front of Ma's Donuts, and just beyond it, a faded silver Trooper. Ma's smelled like a damp ashtray; the CCC kids had carried the fire with them, on their blackened faces and hands, in their hair, streaked along their yellow protective gear. They crowded around the square gray tables and strung themselves out along the counter, their blue hard hats at their feet like cocker spaniels. On a normal day these adolescent males—and a few females—would have been spurting off the walls like kindergarteners with attention deficit disorder, but after twenty-four hours of strenuous fire fighting their voices were a subdued murmur punctuated by the odd laugh and barks of scorched coughs. In the corner booth—Marcy's booth—two of them had fallen asleep, mouths open, leaning against each other like children.

"You knock it down?" she asked a Latino kid sitting by the door as she scanned the yellow suits for Will, who always worked the fires, according to Marie.

"Eighty percent controlled," the boy rasped.

There, at the far end of the counter—was that him?

"What started it?" She was still looking at the back of the man at the counter. Something about the way he sat absolutely motionless while the rest of the row swiveled ceaselessly from side to side on their revolving seats said thirty-something instead of eighteen.

"Not sure. Suspicious origin, they said—" His buddy doubled over in a spasmodic cough, interrupting him in mid-sentence, and she made her way to that one still figure.

His forearms rested on the counter. He was holding a fork in his fist as if he'd never used one before, staring dully at a plate of scrambled eggs and hash browns. Greasy strands of hair that might have been blond under the soot fell around his face, hiding his profile.

"Will?" she said uncertainly, and his face, when he raised it to her, was so filthy that she still wasn't sure.

"Claire." And as soon as she heard that compelling voice, she couldn't believe she hadn't recognized him.

"Rough time?" she asked, moving in beside him.

"I've worked worse fires," he said tonelessly. "Though this one got bigger than it shoulda." Pause. "I guess you know about Marcy."

She nodded. "Haven't talked to anyone since last night, though. Is there any change?"

He shook his head. "Still in a coma," he said, listlessly raising the fork, then lowering it. "You found her?"

Again she nodded.

"Tell me," he said, and she did, though Will didn't seem to be paying attention. When she got to the part about the helicopter he interrupted.

"They think she fell down the cliff. Marcy was like a mountain goat. . . ." He trailed off, then said abruptly, "I think she was about to leave me." Just that; no nonsense about evolving to a higher spiritual plane.

"For Dustin?" she prompted.

"Dustin," he repeated vaguely; then, "Dustin. That Indian kid." Tears of fatigue and despair ran in glistening rills down his blackened face, like rain after a brushfire. He wiped his eyes with the back of a sooty hand, and they teared all the more. "Shit."

"Hold on." She dipped her napkin in his glass of ice water and dabbed at his face. It was like washing headlights: suddenly she received the full force of his clear blue eyes and was rocked backwards by the raw need she saw there. *That* was Will's real sexual power—not the cheekbones or the shoulders but that helpless urgency (although the cheekbones didn't hurt.) She was like a deer, hypnotized, and if at that moment he had asked her anything, like "let's fuck on the table" or, more likely, "give me money," she would have reached for her zipper or her wallet.

But Will wasn't interested in her. His eyes narrowed in concentration as he tried to retrieve some bit of information. "I get . . . addicted to people, that's my problem," he said uncertainly. Then, with more confidence, "I have to learn to . . . to uplevel my addiction to a preference." He nodded twice while her jaw dropped.

She had planned to visit Marcy at the hospital, but on her way through Riverdale she passed Tom's black-and-white Blazer parked on the street. At work on Sunday morning, she thought; well, well, and pulled over just beyond it.

A narrow concrete walk skirted the deserted fire station and led to Tom's office around the back; to the right of it was a sad little municipal park with mangy yellow grass rubbed bare under a rusty swing set, and two pink fiberglass horses on springs. A familiar little boy was swinging ecstatically, head thrown back, the sun catching his white-blond hair at the top of each arc and turning it to white light, like the foothill grasses in late summer. For a moment she thought it was Sam's younger son.

No, of course it wasn't Terry. This little boy was, oh, six or so, and Terry was eight—no, nine, nine now—and his hair might even be losing that childhood phosphorescence. They changed so fast . . . She felt a sharp sadness that Sam's boys wouldn't be a continuing part of her life, forgetting, conveniently and sentimentally, how they had driven her crazy when they had lived with her. When had Sam said they were coming? She'd have to call him after all.

The walk turned left at the back of the building. She looked over her shoulder, and the boy was gone, but she remembered where she'd seen him—at the hearing; he was the logger's kid.

Tom was staring out the window at a big Fremont cottonwood, wiggling a pencil between thumb and forefinger so fast that it looked like rubber. He jumped when she knocked.

"Have you rethought your position?" she asked.

"Nothing to rethink. Riverdale hasn't moved. Still not my jurisdiction."

"Oh. Well, how's J.T.'s investigation going?"

"Christ, are you and my wife going to ask me that question every hour? There is no investigation."

"Well," she persisted, "can't *you* do a sort of unofficial investigation? As a follow-up to that threatening note?"

The pencil stopped and reclaimed its inflexible nature. "You mean," he said, "on the side? In my spare time? Sort of like a hobby?" His voice was taut with sarcasm but Claire imagined it sounded wistful, and when he added, "I have no more responsibility for this case than you do," she chose to take it as a hint.

"Oh," she said, rising abruptly. "Bye."

"Claire." She halted at the door. "If I thought you and Marie were in any danger, it'd be different. But I don't," He turned back to the window, and Claire left.

She called Paul from her car. "Tom is not budging on this," she said. "He surprises me. He claims we have nothing to worry about; I don't know what that means, either."

"If it means he doesn't believe Marcy was attacked, then he's obtuse." Paul's heavy, adenoidal voice was scornful. "Or self-deluding, or on Gene's payroll." A pause. "Look, somebody is obviously trying to stop our activities, and I have to say it's working. I have a friend in San Francisco who's willing to take the salvage lawsuit pro bono, but I'm stymied, I mean, I don't feel right encouraging anyone to get involved with us if it means putting themselves at risk. So"—voice deepening as he summed up for the jury—"I think we have to find out what happened to Marcy, not just as matter of simple justice, but for the Friends of the Redwoods. For the forest." A pause. "How would you feel about investigating this?"

"*Me?*" She had known this was coming but nevertheless didn't have to feign shock. "Paul, I wouldn't know where to begin! Those other times, with Tom—they were just flukes, I mean, I got pulled in before I knew it . . . Why don't you do something? You're the lawyer!"

"Civil law. Torts," he said. "I don't know the first thing about criminal cases. But I would do it myself, except I've got the farm, and I'd be worried about Nayo and Hannah—" He stopped himself before saying the obvious; you don't have anybody; nobody cares if you put yourself in danger. But instead of being insulted or depressed, she felt oddly exhilarated.

"I'll help you," Paul was saying. "We'd all help you! We all have something at stake!"

"Look, I'll think about it. But I have a sixty-hour-a-week job, which I can't just suspend to hare off after some evildoer—" The last word slammed into her, and she faltered. *Evildoer.*

Paul heard it in her voice. "Maybe you're right," he said. "It's too risky."

Don't throw me into that briar patch. "I'll think about it," she said again.

Chapter 20

She walked back over to the park and, remembering the boy's rapture, settled herself onto the abandoned swing. It was disappointing: the canvas seat pinched her adult hips. Entirely appropriate, she thought, since my ass in a sling is exactly what Tom and J.T. will want if I actually investigate this case.

"We'll all help you," Paul had said blithely, and she *knew* what that involved: you figure it out, you take the risk, then tell us about it.

The risk. She made herself think about that, and not abstractly. Because in the abstract she wasn't afraid of death. But she was afraid of living with fear—the kind of fear she had breathed last week and a few other times in the past few years; the fear she had first learned when her father got sick. It didn't matter what you *thought* you thought, then; your lizard-brain, your limbic system, took over and buzzed your skull and iced your spine and churned your guts and numbed your body . . . Did she actually want to volunteer for, to court, that state? For Marcy Hobbes?

Of course she was upset about Marcy. But they hadn't really been close, and this was a lot to ask. Especially since she could just sit this one out. As a new and marginal member of the Friends she had been, she now believed, an accidental target last week. Maybe the whole incident would just solve itself.

Or maybe not. And in the meantime she would again be afraid to walk in the woods, and the chain saws would rip and the trees would fall, and no one would speak for them.

It was a measure of her faith in Tom that she took some comfort from his belief in her safety even though that belief made no sense to her. Despite what Paul had said, she had never known Tom to be either stupid or venal. Maybe she would feel even better if she could follow his thinking . . . which also meant further investigation. It was Hobson's choice—in other words, no choice at all: probe further. Be reassured or be terrified.

Was there a workbook for this—Unit One, Suspects; Unit Two, Alibis?

She began to panic, not at the prospect of danger this time but at the task, at the words: suspects, alibis—television words, to her. Corn-seed maggot, wireworm, fire blight—those were her words. She told herself that it was just like a scientific study: the suspects were the pathogens and the alibis were . . . were . . . The soothing analogy disintegrated.

What she needed was someone who knew a little about police procedure, and as she drove west toward Mercy Hospital, she began to get an idea.

*   *   *

She crawled through festival traffic, finally escaping at the dam. Here she swerved around a sticky mess in the middle of the road from which one immaculate fan of black feathers rose stiffly. It looked like the moment of creation—as if a bird were forming slowly, wings first, from the primordial soup—rather than the aftermath of turkey vulture versus, say, Wal-Mart truck.

Marcy lay in her darkened room. Her eyes were closed, and from the door she looked as calm and rosy as a nun in her wimple of gauze. But then you saw the double tubes up her nose, and then the far side of her head, the right side, which wasn't completely bandaged and revealed her scalp, stubbled like a clear-cut. Claire sat heavily in the tweed chair. And watched.

Claire knew how to watch. She had sat like this as a teenager while her father was dying; she had watched the clandestine progress of the lymphoma itself, the ordeal of "heroic" intervention, of surgery, radiation, chemotherapy, surgery; the brave smiles, the roulette wheel of hope, more hope, less hope, and finally, no hope.

She was so caught up in the memory of that other bedside vigil that she was dragged back into the present only when someone else entered the room. The visitor's stench preceded him: three packs a day, so caustic that she almost gagged. Then, beyond the half-open door, she saw a snakeskin toe. A denim knee. A felt brim between knuckles. And then Stewart Connor was there, fancy boots and checked shirt and creased jeans and tooled belt and Stetson and all, staring at his wife.

Claire shifted in her chair, and he whirled.

"Claire," she said, holding out her hand. "Claire Sharples. We met at Casey's the other night."

"Oh, sure. I remember. Happier times," he said, then

looked uneasy, as if wondering how much of that evening's happiness she had witnessed.

In the carnival turmoil of Casey's Stewart had struck her as grotesque, a visual mistake, and afterward in the lot she hadn't really been able to see him. But here in the cool gray hospital room she could take his measure. And to her surprise he was an ordinary-looking man. It was only his eyes that were strange—"winky-wonky," Sam's aunt Effie from Wawokie, Oklahoma, would have said— one brown orb aimed about thirty degrees off center, so that it was hard to know where in his face to look.

And the cowboy getup was a slight misjudgment, even here, where the cowboy gradient was generally high, dipping from extreme down in Bakersfield to still-right-up-there in Stockton. On Stewart, though, the tight cloth-ing emphasized the swaybacked parabola of his lean body. But he was perfectly okay—not a head-turner like Dustin and Will, but a good-looking middle-aged man, with the seamed, weathered face of a real cowboy rather than a real estate broker or whatever. (What *did* Stewart do to make the payments on that car?)

It was just that Marcy was, had been, extraordinarily pretty, and looks were currency, and people usually paired off with others of equal endowment. Unless there was a heavy hand on the scale. Like money.

Or devotion. Stewart knelt beside the bed, taking Marcy's hand between his own. He was completely ab-sorbed, breathing in time with her, reading her face. After a minute he whispered, without looking away from his wife, "Do you think she's dreaming?"

Claire had wondered this herself while she watched: did consciousness flicker and crackle through the globe of Marcy's skull? Or was she just *out*, a snapped filament? "God, Stewart, I don't know. The mind is mysterious."

"Especially my wife's," he said, his mouth twitching; then he covered it with his hand.

"What does her doctor say?" she asked after a decent interval.

"Says the longer she goes without recovering consciousness the less likely it is that she will." He aimed for matter-of-factness, wavered, leveled. "Says if she does, it's hard to tell what she'll be like." He paused, and rage ripped out of him. "But what does he know, this . . . this Mook—"

"Mukherjee."

"Mukherjee," he spat. "He's just a kid. He's not even an . . . a specialist." "An American," he had probably been going to say. "I'm getting a reputable neurologist from L.A. up here tonight." A moist cough burbled from his chest, and the saturated smell of smoke intensified as if puffed out of him. His metabolism has converted to it, thought Claire; you could tap him for nicotine. A slow brown drip, like maple syrup.

"I.V. drips, oxygen . . ." he was saying, gesturing toward the bed. "I know Marcy wouldn't want this. We talked about it. To be hooked up to life support forever . . . or even worse, to be damaged . . ." His voice unraveled, and a spasm of pain clenched his ravaged face.

Chapter 21

Claire was cruising Church Street, where Parkerville had obediently placed its churches, slowly, because she'd forgotten which was the right one. Something serious, neither as heavy-duty as the Vessels of Living Waters Christian Center on her right nor as staid as First Presbyterian on her left.

The visit to Marcy had left her hung over with grief, both fresh and ancient. It was the first time in many years that she had relived the terrible time of her father's dying. Terrible, but gradual, so that each stage had come to seem inevitable, and if at the end she was angry, she was too worn down to realize it.

But there was nothing gradual about what had befallen Marcy. The work of an instant, and all that was unique and wonderful and maddening about the woman was snuffed out, and they were left with this Marcy-shaped husk. It was outrageous—Freewill Baptist, that was it.

She pulled into the lot and parked next to an old white

Cadillac that had a homemade flatbed carved into the
back end and an impasto of Bible verse—strips of Scrip-
ture spelled out in shiny press-on letters—on the fender.

Claire rolled down her window.

"Oh, come, come, come, come. Come to the church in
the wildwood. . . ." The rhythmic chorus leaked through
the church's front doors, slammed against the heat of the
day. Baptists, even white ones, had better music than
Unitarians. Everyone did. She couldn't remember a single
finicky tune or talky verse from her childhood.

Even with all four windows open, she could have fired
pottery in her front seat. She walked across the blacktop
and sat on stiff grass in the mingy shade of a crepe myr-
tle. Nearly every car in the lot had a little chrome Christ-
fish stuck above its license plate, and momentarily the
fish-with-feet that said "Darwin" on the back of her own
car didn't seem like such a cute idea. She leaned back
against the tree's narrow dappled trunk.

All around her the sun popped like flashbulbs off
shiny fish, bumpers, grilles, windows; she closed her
eyes and could still see the irregular shapes on the red
screen of her eyelids. One by one the lights winked out,
until finally there was only darkness. . . .

Darkness and blood. Blood was running down her
arms, inside her elbows, through her fingers like river
water. . . .

She jerked awake. "Washed in the blood of the lamb,"
the congregation was singing, and she just had to slip a
hand under her slick arm. It came away glazed with
sweat. Thin, seawater sweat. Not blood. Not Marcy's
blood, which seeped patiently into black mud and soft
white gauze and filled the pink cavity of her cranium.
They had no right! Claire thought with incoherent anger.

They? Who? Who had smashed that delicate head?

Suddenly alert and agitated, she began to tick likely 'thems' off in her mind. Those two loggers, of course. She was tempted to stop right there, but went for a more exhaustive list. The two Genes, maybe. Someone from the forest service? Possibly, though it was hard for her to stretch paranoia that far.

Oh, and what's-his-name, she remembered, momentarily excited—Three-fingered Pete, Pelon. Geraldo Ramirez, the escaped prisoner.

But it seemed to her that she needed more than an off-the-cuff list of likely suspects. Surely she could devise a more scientific approach. Let's see, according to Tom there were four, maybe five, primary motives for violence: anger, greed, jealousy, fear, revenge—and all possible combinations and permutations thereof, a sort of multidimensional array. You could assign all suspects a value on each axis—the AGJFR scale. The GRAJF scale.

She was in the process of assigning each suspect a score on the Sharples JAFGR Scale of Homicidal Motivation—for example, loggers: 0, 10, 5, 10, 8—when a woman's voice startled her.

"What are you doing here?"

And there was Marie Martelli, respectable, beautiful even, in a celery-green linen dress.

"I visited Marcy," said Claire, scrambling to her feet, "and I needed to talk to you about her attack, so I came to find you. Could we maybe get a cup of coffee?"

"I guess I could leave the kids in day care for an hour."

The two of them walked along Church toward the center of town. It was a hundred degrees, maybe a hundred and two, and Marie was wearing panty hose and heels that hit the concrete like buckshot on a tin roof. Won't the Lord love a sinner in sneakers? Claire wondered.

"How is she?" asked Marie.

"The same—I mean, she looks fine, but she's just . . . *out*. Stewart was there." She dropped her voice when a woman joined them on the sidewalk at St. John's Episcopal and stalked past them, throwing Marie a frigid look that had no perceptible cooling effect on the palpitating air. She was a substantial woman, corseted into old-fashioned blameless curves.

"Donna Jean," Marie said after the woman had passed, and giggled like a teenager.

"Donna Jean who?"

"Donna *Gene*. Mrs. Gene Senior. When I worked at the bank she tried to get me fired." She paused. "I guess the timber issue does heat this town up pretty good."

"Of course it does!" Claire looked at her curiously. "You know that better than most people."

"Well, it's just that I was thinking . . ." They turned south on Main. Claire lifted her heavy hair off the nape of her neck and stuffed it into the rubber band that seemed to sprout spontaneously on her wrist. ". . . in church," Marie was saying. "Mike Taggart was sitting two pews in front of me."

"Who?"

"Mike Taggart. One of the loggers we saw in Ma's that day, the blond one. Anyway, I couldn't believe *he* would do something like this, and then I started to wonder if *any-body* would do it! It's . . . I mean the whole thing is completely incredulous! Maybe she did fall down that cliff!"

"Marie! You don't really believe that!" Claire was so dismayed by the defection that she didn't notice that Marie had led her into Katy's Koffee Kup, and then it was too late.

She was staring directly into Sam's startled eyes.

"Shannon, stop hitting your brother," he had been saying listlessly, as if the refrain meant as little to him as it did to his sons, but he broke off when he saw Claire. He

and Linda were sitting at a long table that seemed to un-
dulate with squirming boys—his two, her two—and he
looked every inch the paterfamilias in his white shirt and
sports jacket. She blinked. A *sports jacket*. On the *weekend*. And it was that horrible green one that she had hidden at the back of his closet. In the nanosecond's sweep
she gave Linda, she had a general impression of country-
print cotton and demurely covered but hoisted breasts.

Had they been to *church?* Was there no end to what
Sam, a lapsed and pissed-off Southern Baptist, would do
for his kids?

Tactfully, or prudently, Marie had kept walking, and
Claire tried to do the same, sending the barest of nods toward Sam and what's-her-name. But eight, no nine-year-
old Terry turned around to see what his dad was looking
at, and called out excitedly, "Hey, Claire!"

Greeted by her expressionless face, his smile wavered
and foundered as he tried to decode one more obscure
message from the grown-ups. He had broken a rule.
What was it? Wasn't he friends with his dad's old girlfriend? He was still friends with both his dad and his
mom, even though they didn't live together.

And Claire, seeing his anxious face with its explosion
of white-blond hair like dandelion thistle, found that she
too was willing to do things for the boys that she
wouldn't have done for herself. Like smile.

And walk over to him.

"Hey, you're here!" she said, taking in his older
brother, Shannon, with her welcome.

"Yeah, we're gonna be here *all summer!*" Terry
crowed.

And not in my backyard, thank God. "Great! When're
you going to come see the lab?"

None of the conversation that followed moved between the adults, but probably the kids, with the self-involvement of their kind, didn't notice. Claire made her escape, ignoring Sam's grateful smile, and breathlessly slid in across from Marie with her back to the restaurant. She held her glass of iced tea against her cheek.

Marie looked over Claire's shoulder. "They're leaving." A judicious pause. "Linda's put on weight," she said, good friend that she was.

By chance or by design Marie had chosen Katy's "conspiracy table," on which Katy or her curator had sandwiched memorabilia of John F. Kennedy and Abraham Lincoln under a slab of Lucite. Claire set her glass down on the centerpiece of this exhibit, a dumbfounding document headed "???Coincidence???" that faced Marie.

"Wow," Marie said, "did you know Lincoln had a secretary named Kennedy and Kennedy had a secretary named Lincoln? And that Booth and Oswald were—"

"Born a hundred years apart and have the same number of letters in their names," said Claire, who had drunk many cups of bad coffee at this table. "Is this your subtle way of telling me I'm being irrational about Marcy?"

"No," Marie said, staring at the table. "I just wanted to be able to see Sam and Linda—Lincoln was elected in 1860 and JFK in 1960—"

"And both men were shot on a Friday in front of their wives and John Wilkes Booth shot Lincoln in a theater and ran to a warehouse and Oswald shot Kennedy from a warehouse and ran to a theater. Marie, you saw her. There wasn't a mark on her except for her head. She couldn't have bounced down a cliff."

Marie's eyebrows lifted, bracketing her dark eyes with worry. "Well, Tom thinks it was an accident, and he's trained in these things. We might have been wrong, is all.

Tom thinks that when it comes to forest issues, Marcy's made us all paranoid."

"Well, it doesn't look like Marcy *was* so paranoid after all, does it? And anyway, I'm not so sure what Tom thinks," Claire said. "He might actually believe she was attacked, but he won't admit it. At least to me." She tried to open a packet of melba toast with her teeth. "He thinks I'll meddle," she said, smiling at her coconspirator. . . . *Conspirator.* That was why Marie had chosen this table! She was sending a message that she would help with the investigation!

But Marie didn't return the smile. "Uh, could be," she said. "But sometimes Tom can't even let himself think about a case because he gets so frustrated with J.T. If you're right about what he thinks happened to Marcy. Listen to this: their successors were both named Johnson—"

The melba toast having proved impervious to fingernails and teeth, Claire had unsnapped her Swiss Army knife. "And both were Democrats and both were from southern states," she said, stabbing wildly at the packet. "Okay, so you think I'm paranoid. But just humor me for a minute, okay? Assume for now that Marcy *was* attacked, and listen to what I was thinking about while I was waiting for you."

"Okay," Marie said after a moment, looking up from the table. Her voice was unaccountably high.

Claire recited her list of suspects and half humorously described the JAFGR Scale of Homicidal Motivation. "So the suspects each get values on this multidimensional array," she finished. "Is that kind of the way Tom would proceed?"

"Tom?" Marie looked nervous, and Claire wondered if it had just this minute occurred to her that all of the Friends might be at risk, too. "Tom would think of the obvious suspects and figure out if any of them could have done it."

"You mean psychologically?"

"No, actually. You know, check their alibis."

Alibis! thought Claire. A whole other variable for the model! Binary, no continuous, coded for likelihood.

"Claire, I don't even understand what you're talking about," Marie was saying, "about multiterrestrial arrests or whatever. . . . I told you yesterday I couldn't help you!" She sounded definitely panicky now. "I've gotta get the kids."

Oh, thought Claire suddenly, it's *me* that's making her nervous. Me, Dr. Sharples, Ph.D. She's afraid she's not smart enough! "No, wait, Marie. I'm sorry; that was all bullshit, forget about it. Please. Just listen to this list of people and tell me what you think. Okay?"

Marie stared down at the table. Claire was prepared to hear that both Johnsons were opposed for reelection by men whose names started with G, but Marie took a long breath and said, "Go ahead," on an exhalation.

"Okay," said Claire, involuntarily looking around her and lowering her voice. "The loggers," she said. "The Genes, the forest service, the wise-use people—"

"The loggers, maybe," Marie, calmer now, said, "if Marcy ran into someone in the field and there was a confrontation. Somebody might have just lost his temper. Not Mike," she added quickly, "but his buddy Randy Unsel, or somebody else. They were mad at Marcy, and worried about their jobs—"

"Zero, ten, five, five, eight," murmured Claire.

"What?"

"Their score. Zero for jealousy, ten for anger, five for fear, five for greed, eight for revenge. Twenty-eight total."

"Oh, I get it," said Marie. Then her eyebrows contracted. "But how do you come up with the numbers?"

"Totally bogus," said Claire placidly. "I told you."

"And there's Andy Nilsson," Marie said. "Marcy thought he was a . . . a gopher for the forest service."

A gopher? "Oh. A mole?" said Claire.

"Yeah, a mole. And Andy did show up right after you found Marcy."

"So?"

"Well, Tom would take a close look at whoever found the victim."

"But that's me!"

"*And* Andy," Marie said. "And you know the res is right over the hill from that meadow."

"You mean Dustin? But Marcy was the gravy train for him."

"Yeah, but he's an Indian."

Claire began to laugh, then cut it short when Marie turned red. She wasn't joking.

"You don't understand!" Marie said defensively. "I'm not saying there's anything wrong with Indians. But people here have always hired 'em for dirty work—especially illegal dirty work, like rustling or . . . or runnin' off somebody you don't like. Anyway, it's not just that. Dustin might have been jealous. Have a what-do-you-call-it, a J-score."

J-score. Marie was right. Marcy's men, i.e., Will, Stewart, and Dustin, must be added to the list. She was about to mention this when Marie jerked her wrist up in front of her. "Oh, Lordy, the kids! Oh, Claire, I got to go!"

"This is sort of fun," Marie said, as they quick-marched back up Church Street. "It's like a game."

"Yeah," gasped Claire; despite high heels and straight skirt Marie was setting a blistering pace. "If it wasn't so scary—if it wasn't about Marcy, I mean." If Marie wasn't frightened, far be it from her to suggest it. "But you

know, scores or no scores, you're right about alibis. We
have to check out what these guys were doing."

"You know," said Marie, stopping in front of the
church, "there was a wise-use meeting on Saturday. I can
find out from Cindy Taggart who was there."

"She'd tell you?"

"Oh, sure. I mean, she stands by her man and all, but
she's a good friend. You might be surprised at what these
women will say when they're away from their men." She
paused. "In fact, you all in the group would be surprised
at what a lot of people in church will say. You have this,
whadda-ya-call-it, jerk-knee—"

"Knee-jerk."

"Knee-jerk idea that all Christians are timber beasts—"

Claire held up her hands to say it wasn't Christians but
fundamentalist Christians, then looked back at the church
and decided that Freewill Baptists probably qualified as
fundamentalist Christians. But by this time Marie was saying, "No, no, you've got a point. Sometimes I wonder
how long I can hang in there. But a lot of people in my
church feel like that nature is God's handiwork and we
shouldn't trash it."

"Really? A lot of people think that?"

"Well . . . yeah. Especially considering it's some of their
jobs that are at stake. Of course, the other half think the
Parkerville Zoning Commission is in cahoots with an in-
ternational conspiracy to hand America over to the United
Nations." She giggled. "And Tom thinks *we're* paranoid!
Listen, stop by the house and we'll talk some more, if you
want." And she disappeared into the building.

At the Riverdale firehouse, where the volunteer fire-
men were either appeasing or invoking their own fiery
Sunday deities by polishing the chrome on the yellow

hook and ladder, Claire turned right toward Tom and Marie's.

Already the Martellis' house produced suburban weekend sounds: outside, shrieks of kids, barks of adults and dogs from backyard; inside, roar of vacuum cleaner.

The roar ceased. "Come on in!" said Marie, shoving the vacuum aside with one foot. Through the French doors Claire saw various children crammed into a plastic swimming pool the size of a laundry hamper. She wouldn't have taken Tom for much of a frolicker, but there he was in Tang-colored bathing trunks, swinging kids into the air, lifting them onto a green plastic water slide. In this he was assisted by a young blond woman in tank top and shorts. Two of the kids she didn't know, but Claire recognized the Martelli children, who were, in descending order, Matthew, Mark, Luke, and Brittany. Marie's commitment to the New Testament seemed to have extended to parthenogenesis: there wasn't a round, blue-eyed kid in the bunch. Delicate, brown-eyed, with black calligraphic eyebrows, they were all precise replicas of their mother.

"I'm only going to stay for a minute. Is this really an okay time to talk? Who's that?" Claire said.

"Yeah, it's good. The kids are happy for the time being. That's Betsy, our next-door neighbor. The other ones in the pool are hers."

Claire settled in a ruffled chintz sofa next to Marie, and they peered out the window at Betsy. At Betsy and Tom.

"So," said Marie abruptly, "what's your J-score?"

Claire gave her a sharp look. "You mean, do I have murderous thoughts toward Sam or Linda?"

"Yeah." Her eyes strayed toward Tom and Betsy.

"Not during my waking hours." (What had Stewart

said? "Do you think she's dreaming?") "I just hope Linda
gains weight and Sam loses his hair."

"He has nice hair," Marie conceded. "It's his best feature."

"With his clothes on," Claire said absently, remembering the feel of Sam's hair, which looked stiff and black
like the Indian teenagers' but was as soft as sable when
she ran her hand over the top of it. Sam in fact claimed
to be one-thirty-second Cherokee, just enough to be romantic, not enough to risk any of the kind of contempt
that Dustin, say, attracted.

Marie looked both scandalized and delighted. "So
what's his best feature with his clothes *off*?"

"Well, he has really nice skin. Everywhere. And"—she
laid her hand flat against her hip—"what do you call this
part? The part that goes in in men and out in women?
Flanks? Anyway, he had nice . . . that part."

The French doors banged open and Tom walked in.
He'd put on a T-shirt but still wore his wet swimming
trunks. "We can see 'em from in here, and anyway
Betsy's watching them," he said, anticipating Marie's
protest. He dropped onto the couch next to his wife and,
with a sort of defiant look, draped his arm around her.

She gave a little cry and moved away from him.
"You're sapping wet!"

"Sopping!" Tom snapped, and left the room.

Marie looked after him for a moment. Then she turned
to Claire. "If I find out about the wise-use meeting that
might establish wrought-iron alibis for Mike and Randy
and the Genes *and* Nelson Pringle in one fell swipe," she
said in a low voice so Tom couldn't hear, "can you check
on Andy Nilsson? And Dustin?"

And Will and Stewart, Claire added mentally. "How?"

"Oh, you'll think of something," Marie said airily, stand-ing. "This was all your idea, remember. Just tinker down and do it." And she flipped on the vacuum with her toe.

Oh, sure, tinker down, thought Claire grumpily as she drove home. It was easy for Tom to just start asking questions—he had a mandate—but she was going to need a pretext, and Dustin she didn't even know.

Maybe Hazel Batts knew him. She had lived here a long time. But Hazel didn't have a phone—or, no, maybe she had a phone. It was just plumbing and electricity she lacked. As uncompromising as her tight gray braid, she lived alone in a cabin leased from the forest service, way up on the river. Claire would have to contact her.

Stewart—she didn't have a clue how to begin. Maybe Paul could help out. But Will, now.

She could probably think of some pretext to investi-gate Will.

Chapter 22

If Claire had a secret vice, as opposed to her obvious ones, it was kiddie cartoons. Especially when she was overloaded, they cleansed the mental palate. So on Sunday afternoon she succumbed to the Disney channel, telling herself that the two animated classics from her youth would be somehow instructive.

And they were. "Johnny Appleseed," which she remembered as sweet and insipid, turned out to be about a walking ecological disaster, some nut with a tin-pan hat and a compulsion to replace the genetically diverse native forests of North America with a single European species, *Malus.* The apple. And "Paul Bunyan," who clear-cut his way across a continent and into the hearts of schoolchildren—well, enough said. What was astounding was that as recently as the fifties American pop culture had been close enough to the pioneers to see wilderness as a threat, a beast to be subdued—and also as endless.

When had it changed? The sixties? With Rachel Carson?

Whenever the break had come, it had been too late for men like Nelson Pringle.

But then maybe it was Claire who was behind the curve. Wilderness-as-Beast seemed to be coming back around.

"Hi," she said into the telephone on Sunday evening. "It's Claire Sharples."

"Oh, hey, Claire." Will used "hey" in that southern way, to mean "hi." His voice was warm and slightly breathy.

"Listen, that steel wool didn't do the trick; the bats are still here. Would you be willing to tack up some more?"

He said doubtfully, "You want to try more of something that didn't work to begin with?"

"Well . . . maybe they're roosting in the gaps. You could fill them in."

"Reckon I could do that. And I noticed a pile of oak that needs some splitting. I could do that, too. Tomorrow afternoon suit you?"

"Sure."

"Great. I sit with Marcy every day at three for about an hour, talk to her, sing to her, try to tune in to whatever place she's at. I'll come up after that."

She planned to visit Marcy on her way to work on Monday morning, but the prospect was too painful. At lunchtime, she told herself. Or maybe she'd wimp out entirely and simply ask Marie, she thought, unlocking the lab.

"Hi."

Sam's voice, behind her. He and the boys filled the doorway at three different heights, like a bouquet. "They really wanted to come. Is this a bad time?" he asked, noticing her scowl.

"No," she said, once again responding to the boys'

smooth, radiant faces. Terry was more or less the same skinny little boy he had been last year, but Shannon had thinned and darkened. Almost twelve, he was beginning to look like a teenager. He was beginning to look like his father. "No, come on in."

She did call Marie; "No change" was the report. And then for the next hour she dragged out whatever she had to amuse the boys. Gross molds were good; so were snazzy machines if they whirred or produced printout. Computer programs she had worked on for months and months were good for about five minutes, if they shifted shape and color. She didn't know how to behave toward Sam. She experimented with graciousness, but soon found that ignoring him was more gratifying, though a hoax: at all times she was peculiarly aware of his exact position. But the more completely she pretended to ignore him, the more charming and effusive she was with the boys. Was this one reason people had kids? So they could use them to conduct a silent argument with each other?

Sometimes the sex ran out of a relationship, as from a wrung sponge: you were apart for a while, say, and then when you met again all you could see was the way the hair grew on his shoulder blades or how ugly his toes were, and you wondered how you ever could have wanted him to put *that* in *there*, and so on. Then you could find each other endearing, or irritating, or boring, without that distortion of desire.

Claire couldn't wait for this to happen with Sam.

She had planned to continue her search for the rare *Calochortus* after work, but she didn't have the heart for it, and she had lost her nerve again. No wandering the mountains alone until this thing with Marcy was under-stood.

So there were still a good two hours of daylight left when she started up the hill toward home. It had been a clear day, and when she reached the dam and saw before her the yellow hills and blue mountains beyond them, her heart lifted. "My heart lifted," she said to her-self, realizing that this was an actual physical sensation, a lifting of the diaphragm, an intake of breath at beauty.

Since she now drove down the hill relatively sedately, she had taken to driving up the hill as fast as she could, which, in her still-nimble car, was fast. So at the National Forest, Land of Many Uses sign she came up on a black jeep, sporty but top-heavy, which pulled off at the first turnout. She gave the driver a friendly beep and was on her way, shifting down for Deadwoman's Curve, which still made her sweat every morning, then picking up speed again.

Suddenly someone was there in her rearview mirror, only yards behind her. She pulled into the turnout and he swept past. It was the black jeep.

Black car, she thought, but dismissed it because she was sure *that* black car hadn't had a jeep's too-tall silhou-ette. Nevertheless, when she came on him again after only a half mile and he promptly pulled off as if he'd been waiting for her, the base of her skull began to tingle with alarm. *That* black car or another, he was behaving very strangely. But she swept past—she had no choice—and at the very next turnout she pulled aside and waited to see what would happen. He passed her.

Two weeks ago she would have thought, I offended his manhood by passing him, or it's some sort of courtship game among the males of this tribe. But as it was, she thought, I wonder if that other logger—what's-his-name, Mr. Owl Hash—has a black jeep. As he swept past she tried to get a good look at his plate but made out only four characters. Then she proceeded very slowly up the hill.

But he was waiting for her around the next curve, where the stairs went down to the river, and he pulled out behind her. She tried to drive at a stately pace, hoping he'd become impatient and give up this game, if game it was, but he just hung on her bumper until *she* became impatient. She accelerated; he accelerated, staying exactly six feet behind her. And so they drove up the mountain in tandem, as if she were towing him. Claire drove faster, screaming around curves, searching for a turnout, seeing only that sheer drop down to the river.

Finally, past the flume, a turnout! She pulled off abruptly; he whipped past, and she managed to make out the rest of the plate. She thought about running to the uphill side of the road and crouching in the oaks.

But crouching for how long? And then what? Her inability to form a real plan, or to know how seriously she should take the situation—her body took it seriously enough: she was cold with fear—made her thumb in Tom's number on her phone, then feel half relieved to get his machine rather than be told she wasn't in his jurisdiction. She left a message with a description of the jeep and the license plate. Then she continued up the hill at seven miles an hour. Several cars passed her with irritated honks, and she felt safer for the buffers between her and him.

It took forty minutes to make it home, but she didn't pass the jeep again.

She was so relieved to see Will's Trooper parked at the end of her drive near the woodpile that she forgot en-

tirely that he was a hypothetical suspect in the hypothetical assault on Marcy. All she felt was safe and grateful.
She paused at the top of the drive to watch him.

Splitting wood was like playing baseball to Claire:
something she had done, not well but well enough to
have occasionally experienced the satisfaction of a perfectly executed move, and to appreciate a skilled practi-
tioner. And Will was a pro. He started the wedge with a
crisp blow, then stepped back a precise distance and
swept up the heavy maul straight overhead, letting its
weight extend him fully so that his back muscles
stretched over his ribs, then bringing it down with a
swift, powerful swing. A metallic *chunk* meant that he'd
connected cleanly with the wedge, but it jammed about
halfway down the log.

"Shit," he said, and started another wedge from the
side. Again, the windup, the stretch, the downswing like
a killer serve in tennis. *Chunk.* The log fell into two flam-
mable halves. He tossed them onto the stack and
grabbed another piece.

She probably could have watched him all evening, or
at least until he put his shirt on, but after the next log he
sensed her behind him.

"Hey," he called.

"Hi." She coasted down the drive and slipped out of
the car. The aroma of fresh-cut wood stirred a guilty
memory; that's how the whole cord had smelled when
the guys from the res had delivered it last month. Somehow she'd thought that they'd just bring a truckload of
last year's cut wood, but the smell had told her they'd received her phone call, gone out, and chain-sawed a perfectly healthy blue oak. It was like ordering a steak and
watching them shoot the cow.

Well, country living was supposed to put you in touch with the consequences of your actions.

"Almost done," Will said with a grunt as he brought down the maul again. She jumped back; somehow she'd ended up a scant foot behind him. She could see the tattoo on his right bicep now: On the sweat-slick skin "Semper Fi" seemed to melt into its wreath of twining non-native leaves.

"Ain't got but a half-dozen pieces left. Oh," he said straightening and running the back of his forearm along his forehead, "and I crammed about a bale of steel wool into your eaves. Just let the little critters try to find a foothold!"

"I thought you liked bats!"

"I do, but a job's a job."

"Oh. Well, thanks. Come in for a . . ." A shower, she was going to say, but suddenly remembered that she was supposed to be interrogating him, to be considering seriously whether or not he had bashed in his girlfriend's skull. At the moment the idea seemed totally absurd, but nevertheless, no sweet-smelling naked bodies. "A beer," she finished.

There was a message from Andy Nilsson on her machine: did she want to botanize with him after work some night this week? He'd heard there was a rare Dudleya on some limestone outcroppings near her place, and he'd like to find it before it fried in the sun. Andy was supposed to be a possible suspect, too, but frankly she could not believe a man who was interested in Dudleya capable of violence.

She'd call later with a polite demurral. She walked onto the back deck with a pile of computer output that she had to transform into an article in the next week, and had barely begun to flip through it when the front screen banged.

"The beer's in the fridge," she called, and in a moment Will came out onto the deck clutching a can of Dr Pepper.

"I don't drink beer much anymore. Used up my quota in seventh grade," he said, popping the lid with a sharp *cushhh*. (You had to open things with caution at this altitude.) "That stack oughta keep you warm. Sure warmed me up."

"Wood warms twice," she said mechanically. Will was wearing something around his neck—a string of blue trade beads that matched his eyes, and a small buckskin pouch—and she smelled the sweat on him. Not rank, like old gym clothes or stewed Dacron, but fresh, tangy.

"Warms you four or five times, if you count cuttin', haulin', splittin', and stackin'," Will was saying. "And that's generally in summer, when you don't need warming. It's like it stores all that heat and lets it go in winter."

Engaging, garden-variety vernacular. Why couldn't he speak it all the time?

Maybe he can talk however he senses you want him to, she thought. Maybe he can *look* however you want him to, like one of those alien life-forms from *Star Trek*, though she wouldn't have guessed that her heart's desire was an aging surfer with an earring and a tattoo.

But he was educable. If Kirsten or whatever her name was could teach him NewSpeak, maybe she, Claire, she of the exquisite sensibilities, could unteach him.

"You were in the marines," she stated, eyeing the tattoo. "I thought you said you hated guns."

"I do," he said, sliding down the wall till he was settled about six inches away from her.

"Why'd you join?"

"Well, I was only eighteen. And the judge suggested it," he said, deadpan, and she laughed; it was the first sign of humor she had ever detected in him. His scent was as distinctive and powerful as Stewart's nicotine but more pleasant, making her think of salt skin, sweet saliva, bitter semen.

"How's Marcy?" she said abruptly, and took a swig of cold water.

"The same. She looks a little pale, but except for that and the hair . . . I keep thinking she's just gonna pop right up and pick up where she left off, start layin' into the forest service, you know." He gulped the soda, tipping his head back against the wall, then closed his eyes.

After a moment of sympathetic silence she said, "I ran into Stewart there yesterday."

"Oh, yeah," he said, not moving, "he comes every day, just about the time I leave."

"Isn't that kind of awkward?"

"Why? Oh, no, Stewart and I are basically cool. He knows you can't be possessive about Marcy. It's just a hard lesson, and we all lose it sometimes." With chunks of granite in our hands? she wondered, but had to admit that Will and Stewart seemed to be behaving with admirable civility. Will stared up at the mountain, and she waited for him to mention upleveled addictions or some damn thing, but all he said was "Today I thought I saw her eyelids flutter."

Claire felt an answering flutter under her own ribs, then a shock of guilt, as if she had just caught herself hoping . . . what?

Hoping that Marcy wouldn't recover consciousness?

Frantically she sorted through her as always opaque emotions. Jealousy? Did she want Marcy's boyfriend that much? She didn't think so, and anyway Will appeared to be as free as he wanted to be in these matters. Fear? Was she afraid of what Marcy might be like if she recovered? No. It didn't feel that altruistic.

She was re-creating the JAFGR Scale of Homicidal Motivation, she realized, so she went back and picked up A—anger. She tried it on: yes, that was it.

She was angry.

"Excuse me, Will," she said, and went indoors to refill her glass. She stood at the sink for a long time, staring at the wall. But instead of the careful loops and crosses of Don's scrawled instructions for replacing circuit breakers, what she saw was her father's stick of an arm lying on the sheet, his transparent face stretched like a death's-head into a painful smile that was meant to comfort but only frightened her.

What right did Marcy have to live when her father hadn't?

Whoa! What fulminating brew of neurotransmitters had spewed *that* one? Talk about deranged! Talk about irrational! Talk about . . . talk about . . . Don's letters blurred and swam, and she wondered why the hell he had written in purple ink.

"You okay?" Will's voice, from the deck.

"Yes."

"Just wondered"—approaching—"because the water was running for a long ti— Hey!"

She had turned toward him and he saw the tears. He drew his thumb under her eye and said softly, "Hey. It's okay. She's going to pull through," and she leaned back against the sink, undone by the unexpected gentleness and by shame, because he thought she was grieving for Marcy, and that was so far from the truth.

"I'm all right," she said, sniffling and wiping her nose with the back of her hand, but he was already pulling her against him, into muscle and sweat-smell and warm skin. Thought ceased, unless "other animal feel good" was a thought. He ducked his head and blindly nuzzled until their mouths connected. His was syrupy with Dr Pepper. She got used to it.

What about Marcy? she thought to say at some point, but she knew what answer she'd get: Marcy and Will didn't own each other, it was wrong to become addicted to anyone, blah-blah-blah. And in any case it turned out she was too upset even to make out with Will Brecker, so the question of Marcy was academic.

She pulled away. Will seemed almost relieved, as if he hadn't really had the heart for this either.

"What's in the pouch?" she asked, rubbing her breast-bone where the buckskin sack had pressed into her.

"Medicine bag," he corrected. "Some sage, some to-bacco—tobacco's strong medicine, you know. But there's one really magical thing." He loosened the drawstring of the pouch with his thumb and forefinger. "See, last sum-mer this Native American shaman from Montana visited Marcy, and we walked up to a sequoia grove," he said, then added slowly, "Marcy and I were . . . well, it was a good day." He swallowed, and she thought he was going to have to stop. But in a moment he went on: the three of them were hiking this trail the shaman had never seen before, when suddenly the visitor stopped by a granite boulder, bent down, dug into the earth with sure fingers, and came up with something in his closed fist.

"He handed it to me, said it belonged to me." Will pulled something through the opening of the bag. It lay on his palm like a heavy lump of light. "And it was this incredible crystal."

"It's beautiful," she said, picking it up.

"Yeah. It almost looks as if somebody was trying to

work this face. See? Right here?" tracing a rippled pattern of striations. "Maybe an Indian, a long time ago." She looked closer.

"But Will—" she began, then stopped short. As far as she knew there were no big, showy crystals of quartz like this in these mountains. And this hadn't cleaved like a crystal; it had run, like a supercooled liquid. Like glass.

It was, she was sure, a piece of glass. A chunk of an old Coke bottle, say.

"It's amazing," she finished.

She walked him to the front door, where he pointed to his neat stack of oak and said "Lots of good fire there."

Fire!

She was supposed to ask Will where he was during the fire! She was supposed to be checking his alibi!

"Do you—do you wear your medicine bag when you're fighting fires?" Lame, lame!

"I wear it all the time," he said, surprised. "Even during . . . even in bed." He grinned. "Especially in bed."

She felt an answering tingle but forged ahead. "Aren't you afraid it'll get scorched? During fires, I mean," she added hastily as he started to laugh. "Like the other day, Saturday. You must have been out there for a long time—I remember you said the fire was bigger than it should have been."

"Oh, yeah. Some moron set a backfire about six miles to the south. Didn't make much sense. Even so, it was knocked down by Sunday morning—well, you saw me at the restaurant. And at that point I'd been on the line for about eighteen hours. I've done thirty-six, like during the Stormy fire a few years ago."

Eighteen hours. So that rolled back to noon Saturday, more or less. About the time she'd found Marcy.

If he knew the details of that backfire, he had definitely been fighting the fire at some point. But a story like his would have to be checked and cross-checked, with his fire crew, Cal Fire, the CCC; it would take the manpower and connections of the sheriff's department. Of experts. Of whom little Claire Sharples, with her highfalutin theories of homicide, was definitely not one.

And if she couldn't check even Will's alibi, she certainly couldn't check Stewart's. Not to mention Dustin Gomez, whom she'd probably never even see again. Maybe if Marcy died, J.T. would investigate her case.

At this thought tears of shame once again flooded her eyes, and Will once again moved to comfort her. She couldn't stand it. She pulled away.

"I should be comforting *you*," she said.

"I don't need comfort," he said firmly, " 'Cause I know she's gonna be all right." He smiled.

When he'd gone, she called Paul and enumerated the last two days' worth of activities, editing the last few hours. "But there's so much I can't do," she said. "Shouldn't we have some sort of group meeting?"

She could hear the indecision on the other end. "I'm not sure," he said, and she thought, Marcy would've known what to do. "See, the thing is, I think some people haven't realized the implications of this. They're not scared yet. So why frighten them?"

"Well, I need help," she snapped.

"What? What can I do?"

Make Tom take over. "Stewart," she said. "Can you find out anything about Stewart?"

"Stewart!" he repeated; then, incredulously, "Jealousy?"

"Mmm. Seems unlikely, but I figure he would have just had time to get from the mountain to L.A. before Marie called him."

"That hardly matters. Rich men like Stewart don't do their own dirty work anyway."

"Oh. But then . . . but, Paul," she said, voice rising, "if we're talking about hired hit men, that's way beyond my capabilities!"

"Hey, you're doing great," he said soothingly. "At some point we'll have to haul in the professionals, but at least for now something's being done! Listen, call me tomorrow and I'll tell you what I've found out about Stewart. But call before seven-thirty 'cause Naomi and I are actually going out. Got a sitter and everything."

Later, when she was dropping off to sleep, she remembered she hadn't paid Will for the wood or the batproofing. No doubt he would send her a bill.

Chapter 23

A fifteen-inch pileated woodpecker can sweep an eight-inch arc with its head and spew wood chips over a two-foot radius. It can drill a nest cavity six inches in diameter and eighteen inches deep into a solid tree trunk. Storer and Unger compare the noise of a woodpecker at work—that is, excavating a nest or searching for grubs or ants—to the sound of someone pounding with a hammer. At dawn.

Claire was awakened at 5:30 A.M. from the first pleasant dream she'd had in months, involving her and Will Brecker and a common household utensil. With the desperate inspiration of the sleep-deprived, she came upon the solution to the woodpecker problem. Shoot the damn thing. Simple, permanent, satisfying: she would buy a .22 that very morning. And on a related subject, she staggered into the kitchen, opened a small can of Whiskas Liver-'n'-Chicken, set it inside the steel trap under the house, and snicked the catch. She'd worry about what to do with the skunk when she caught it. This was war, goddammit!

At nine, full of insane purpose and strong coffee, she drove straight to Wal-Mart and marched to Idaho—the gun counter.

Idaho, she saw now, was subtly trying to secede from the rest of Wal-Mart. They had lined the wall with dark wood-grain paneling, draped camouflage cloth from the acoustic ceiling, and turned down the OR lighting to create a sort of rustic-hunting-lodge-cum-survivalist-enclave atmosphere. Claire advanced to the glass counter skittishly, as if approaching Lenin's tomb. There they lay in state: the Colt .45 Regulator, the 9mm Gluck, the Smith & Wesson 659 9mm automatic.

Neat little tools, and so harmless-looking—less lethal in appearance than, say, a handheld blender or a Nikon with a zoom or even a first-class hammer. It seemed entirely unlikely that out of all the objects under the vast roof of Wal-Mart, these were the ones equipped to kill. Now, the rifles lined up behind the counter, that was another story. Their long bores and polished stocks and scopes and sights proclaimed function; they could only be what they were.

The clerk eyed Claire curiously; she was the only female in Idaho, except for the woman narrating an informational video in the calm but cheerful tones of a flight attendant explaining the safety features of the 747. Her modulated voice was punctuated every so often by a loud *blam! blam-blam-blam!* Claire moved west, past the Russian SKS rifles, the Remington bolt-action Savage 110. The rifles diminished in firepower. Now she was at the Remington .22 Viper, Semi-Automatic, $124.99; then the Winchester 12-gauge Turkey Gun, $329.99, which looked like a space shuttle compared with Sam's old shotgun. Then the Marksman Biathlon, $39.99.

"Why is this one so cheap?" she asked the clerk, who was attempting to convince a very short man with thick glasses of the merits of something called a P39. The jargon was the point, she thought; a P39 microprocessor or camera or drill bit or spray rig probably would have made them all just as happy.

The clerk broke off long enough to say, "That? That's an *air* rifle," scorn divided equally between Claire and the wimpy weapon. He turned back to his customer. "You won't be sorry," he said, but he was losing the little guy.

An *air rifle!* She hadn't heard that phrase in years, not since her brother's Daisy Repeating Rifle, which he had coveted for most of his childhood, ordered from the pages of a Spider-Man comic book, and abandoned to her eight months later when he got his driver's license. She had happily plinked cans from the back porch for a year, until . . . what?

Until her father got sick, that's what.

She passed the other air rifles: the Pumpmaster and the Western Style 2100 Classic and the RepeatAir Semi-Automatic CO_2 Rifle—interesting; the technology had progressed. This last used little CO_2 cylinders instead of a manual pump. The pellet speed varied, from 590FPS to 725 FPS (the Western Style 2100). Enough firepower?

Enough for what? she suddenly asked herself. What exactly was her purpose here? To plug a woodpecker? Or to protect herself?

"What's this?" she said, half to herself. A huge-bore snub-nosed handgun lay between the long barrels.

"CO_2 pistol," said the clerk, who had decided that a wimp sale was better than no sale. "You fill it with these cartridges 'stead of pumping it. Good for target practice, that's about it. Maybe pot a chipmunk, if you get lucky."

Pellet speed 400 FPS, low end of the scale. But it would fit inside her day pack. It looked real and lethal. It made a loud noise. It required no waiting period.

"I'll take it," she said, but on the way out she eyed the Remington .22 Viper again. Maybe next time.

At work there was a message from Andy, which she returned with guilty haste. But he was out in the field, which was where she should be, right after she started this article. But first she made her morning call to Marie.

"How's Marcy?"

"No change," Marie said.

"Oh." Yesterday's ambivalence had passed entirely, at least from her conscious mind. "Listen, Marie—did you happen to find out anything about that wise-use meeting?"

"Oh, yes, I ran into Cindy. It started at ten and didn't end till two, and both Genes and Nelson Pringle were there. And Mike and Cindy, of course. And some other people I don't really know; I made a list—"

"How about that other guy from the restaurant?" she asked, remembering the black jeep. "Roger, Ronnie?"

"Randy Unsel? Uh-uh. He's kind of a loner."

As in Sirhan Sirhan? "Thanks," she said, and turned to her computer.

Hull rot is a serious disease of almonds, she wrote.

But between the first and the second sentence, adult onset attention deficit disorder struck: Will. Will Brecker.

She so wanted to cross him off her list of suspects— she wanted to cross anyone off, but especially Will—that she mistrusted her judgment. Nevertheless his remarks about not owning Marcy had disarmed her. They might have been wishful thinking, New Speak, but even so, could a man obsessed by jealousy even talk like that? Be pals with Marcy's husband? She made herself consider other motives. Greed? Financially speaking, Will had every incentive to keep Marcy alive and funneling Stewart's money, in the form of posh accommodations and posh cars, his way.

Dustin Gomez, same thing. Silver necklaces . . .

Necklaces that chafed like dog collars. No, Dustin, she guessed, wasn't altogether happy with his arrangement with Marcy. And he belonged to a group to whom, according to Marie, locals had traditionally turned to do their dirty work.

"Hi," said a deep voice behind her, and she jumped out of her seat to see Ramón Covarrubias, the Small Farm Adviser.

"Oh!" she said. "Ramón. Raymond."

"You can call me Ramón; I like it. I'm interrupting you?"

"I'm writing an article that I've been putting off for weeks."

Most people wouldn't have interpreted this as an invitation, but Ramón said, "Article? On what?" and dropped into a chair.

"Uh, hull rot," she said, remembering with effort. "A study of the relationship between late irrigation and hull rot in almonds."

"Is there?"

"Is there what?" No wonder he was called "Raymond"; he had almost no trace of the lilting accent and sibilant *s*'s of even second-generation Chicanos. Claire missed it.

"A relationship."

"Yes," she said patiently. "If you stop watering three to

four weeks before harvest, the incidence of hull rot drops significantly."

"Oh. What else you doing these days?"

Okay. She resigned herself; unless she wanted to be rude, they were going to chat. "I'm investigating some alternatives to MBr. Methyl bromide."

"Anything look good?" His eyes roamed the laboratory as if he were as lightly tied to the conversation as she was.

"No single treatment," she said, "but in combinations. Tea tree—you know, neem—looks promising. And I personally am rooting for marigold, *Tagetes*, at least as a nematocide—"

"*Cempasuchl.*"

"What?"

"*Cempasuchl.* Marigolds. That's what the Aztecs called 'em. They cultivated them, you know. That's why Mexicans put 'em on Day of the Dead altars."

"Really. I didn't know they were a New World species."

"Apples," he said. "Know anything about 'em?"

"Um"—she was knocked off conversational balance again—"I know what I like." Bushel baskets of red McIntoshes—early crop, before they got mealy—under a brilliant New England sky. "But professionally speaking, not much. They're not a major crop around here, they take cold weather. Why?"

"Were you serious about helping out on the Small Farm Project?"

"Absolutely." She wondered why he couldn't seem to field a question cleanly.

"Why? I thought you were a hotshot in the lab."

"I like both. That's sort of why I left MIT; you know, head in the clouds, feet in the mud"—the biologist's

motto—"and I served my time in the clouds. Now I'm enjoying plunging both feet—"

"And hands," he said, holding up his own blunt,
stained fingers for inspection. The gold band, she noted
with mild interest, was gone. Divorce? Dermatitis? Or just
too much mud? Most people here didn't wear rings—
practical, but also convenient for those intending to cheat
on their spouses. Was Ramón intending to cheat on his
spouse? An interesting idea.

"Could you commit some time to these particular small
parcels of mud?" he was saying.

"I could make time. I really like the idea of the Small
Farm Program."

"You could start with that woman from the reservation
I mentioned at the meeting. She has a couple of acres of
apples. They're at about a thousand feet out there, so
they get enough chill days. But nobody's cared for the
trees in years, and she's got little brown holes all over the
fruit."

"Codling moth," she guessed, picturing abandoned orchards in the Berkshires.

"What do they coddle?"

"What? Oh. No," she said. "Only one *d.*"

"Oh. Cod. Little cod?" he muttered. "Codpiece—I won-
der where *that* comes from. Middle English, probably."
Her mouth fell open. No comment had ever surprised
her more, except his next: "Sorry. In a former life I taught
Chaucer to college freshmen. Anyway, codling moths.
Apples. Think you can help Daisy Gomez?"

"I'm not sure— What's her name?" she asked, interrupting herself. "Your client?"

He repeated it.

"*Gomez!*" she said excitedly; then, when he looked at

her curiously, "Everyone I've met from that reservation has the same last name! Is it some ceremonial title?"

"You mean like Singh for the Sikhs? Naw," he said, a grin animating his serious face. "Just a big family. Like the Covarrubias."

"We don't have a real pomologist at the station," she said slowly, thinking that an entrée to Dustin's family, and maybe to Dustin, had been handed to her on a plate, "but Kate Dolmovic worked in Washington State for years. She knows apples. If she helped me, well, I could at least check out the orchard."

"Good," he said, suddenly brisk. "Daisy's expecting you today at two," and left so abruptly that she found herself staring at the door for several seconds before she wailed, "Today?"

At least the codling moths had smothered her wayward thoughts under their powdery wings, and she was ready to wade into the article for the next—she checked her watch—three hours. She read what she had written so far: **Hull rot is a serious disease of almonds (prunus dulcis)** . . .

The phone rang.

Andy, returning her call. "You up for some botanizing at the Craig Ranch?" he asked. "Like after work today?"

She grimaced and guessed that Andy was lonely; the Craig Ranch, a preserve on the west side of the valley, lay in dry, bleak, hot, boring terrain. But she felt she couldn't refuse again. Especially since, technically, Andy was also a suspect. "Sure," she said brightly. "Late, though. After it cools off. Say six-thirty?" She hung up and turned to her computer.

. . . caused primarily by _monilinia fructicola_ or _rhizopus stolonifer_. Three other . . .

"Hi."

The gamine face of Kate Dolmovic was at the door. "Word on the street is you want to know something about pests of apples." Her wiry arms cradled a two-foot stack of Xeroxed articles, and she blew a strand of salt-and-pepper hair away from her mouth. "Codling moth, orange tortrix, apple scab—that's not a big problem down here—rosy aphids. Mostly codling moth, though. That's your primary pest."

Claire received the stack from Kate and dumped it onto her lab bench. "What does 'codling' mean?" she said.

"Oh. I never thought about it!"

. . . **three other organisms** . . .

Chapter 24

At two she checked out the station pickup and drove through the dry hills toward Daisy Gomez.

The reservation road followed the river's south fork, so Claire was looking at the back of the hills she knew. They swept in drapery folds down to the river, that thick corridor of pale green—sycamore, cottonwood, willow, elderberry—that joined the road and ran along her left; on her right were smooth, cattle-cropped fields. She braked as a couple of quails, stately and alarmed, motored across the road, and then began to relax into the rhythm of gray asphalt snaking through gold hills. Gray road, gray boulders, gray oaks, gold hills; gold and gray from Oregon to Mexico, as it was in the beginning, is now, and ever should be.

But that was a lie, Claire knew. This was a new landscape, even by human standards. Not the elements—boulders, oaks, hills—but the palette. Those oaks had sprouted in hills that were green and alive, not in this bright dead grass.

It was the Gold Rush that had killed the hills, imparting to them its color as a sort of funerary tribute. The forty-niners who poured into the Valley had brought something worse than Winchesters—seeds. In pants cuffs, grain sacks, the guts of stock: seeds from the Old World. The invasion of prolific annuals displaced native perennial bunchgrasses as quickly as Yankee and Irishman displaced Yokut and Miwok, though less violently—

She stopped herself.

What was the point of *knowing* this stuff? Why did she have this compulsion to spoil the landscape with facts? She had been happier thinking that clear-cuts were meadows and that the smog didn't come up this high and that the hills were golden because California was the land of opportunity.

The fence ran out and the houses took on a provisional look and the occasional dead car became a fleet, scattered through the grass like boulders. Or maybe those were boulders. Convenient that the rock here had coagulated into Ford-sized units instead of stitching the soil like gray tweed as it did in New England. She thought of her great- or maybe great-great-grandparents clearing a Massachusetts field, stooping, working a rock free, tossing it into the cart. But there was always another rock, and as the way before them cleared, the load they dragged behind became heavier and heavier. . . . I wear the chains I forged in life—

Whoa! Jamming into the brake pedal, bracing against the wheel, fishtailing, screaming to a stop, because suddenly there was a *horse*, a gigantic white horse with wild eyes and flaming mane, sliding stiff-legged onto the road twenty—no, fifteen; no, ten—feet in front of her, where it paused, then bolted up the other road cut, shoulder muscles working, making for the river, and then there was another white horse and a bay and then a couple of Appaloosas pouring down the slope, a flash flood of horses. . . .

And then they were gone. The road was empty except for the fine dust settling into an ochre scrim against her windshield.

Her heart thudded like a sprung rabbit. Terrified as much by the abrupt beauty as by the close call, she just sat for a while, finally creeping slowly on, rumbling over a cattle guard and coming to the official reservation sign: You have entered, sixty thousand acres, 8-member Tribal Council, 1883, Fort Tejon, abide by tribal rules. The road spilled out into a wide, dusty circle, and she pulled up under a cottonwood next to a good-sized building of yellow brick.

Still shaky with unspent adrenaline, she slid down from the truck and looked around her. Where was the town? She had been expecting some sort of mercantile center, a couple of knickknack shops at least, but there was nothing—just that pool of dirt. Beyond it was a corral and a small church bell tower and a road of sorts, disappearing; behind her was the ugly structure that must be tribal headquarters.

The emptiness was unsettling, as if she, the alien, were being watched by hostile eyes from behind drawn curtains. She locked the truck and walked across the plaza toward the hills, past the empty corral, and up a rise to the small wooden chapel, which was deserted. Mater Dolorosa, said the peeling sign, and underneath, hand-lettered on cardboard: Childrens Clothing Help Yourself. The doors were wide open; small stained trousers hung over the backs of pews like a row of *W*s, and pink plastic carnations slouched against the altar.

She returned to the cinder-block building and walked to the end of it, skirting a new Ford pickup—midnight blue with silver detailing, evidence of human presence— and stopped at an empty blacktop where a mesh basket dangled from a backboard in the lifeless air. Slowly she came back along the side of the building, peering into each shuttered window in turn. Nobody lounged in the lounge. Nobody racked 'em up on the pool table. Nobody clicked the remote.

But the last window opened like a refrigerator door on the fluorescent lights of bureaucracy. Claire stepped inside.

An old woman with a strong nose and sparse *Caltrans*-orange hair looked up from her telephone and pressed her palm against the mouthpiece. Her hands were clotted with blue veins like Stilton cheese. "Can I help you?"

"Daisy Gomez?" asked Claire, distracted by the words "Loose Horses" that floated at eye level before her.

"Beyond the church, next to the sawmill," the woman said, while Claire learned from a bulletin board by the door that loose horses were rounded up into the communal corral on Saturdays. "White trailer. Can't miss it."

"Thanks."

Outside, the air was still and hot, sliced by the snarl and whine of a buzzsaw. She homed in on that whine. Behind the church the road curved and rose toward the first of the yellow hills that stepped up to the mountains. On her left were two small houses and the carcasses of cars, not rusted—nothing rusted out here—but bleached and collapsing, the tires mummified. The lichen had probably already established a beachhead.

Now she saw the metal tip of the sawmill's incinerator, and then the rest of it—a ribbed wooden silo, archaic-looking and sepia-toned like a da Vinci drawing. She smelled charred wood.

Before the mill was a white double-wide trailer with green gingerbread trim. "Gomez," said the mailbox, and she gave the door two smart professional raps.

"Ms. Gomez?" she called brightly, then suspiciously, then resignedly, because getting stood up by a client was all part of the job. She trudged up to the sawmill.

"Have you seen Daisy Gomez?" she shouted at a fat shirtless man who was pushing a board into the circular saw, ripping it lengthwise. The wood bled its sweet hot smell into the open yard. Claire, trained by Marcy, wondered where it had come from and what it was. Sawdust coated the man's stiff black hair and sweat-slick breasts and belly as if he'd been floured for frying. He fished a green cigarette filter out of his right ear when he saw her mouthing at him.

"Daisy?" he said. "Try Uncle Robert's. Back up the road, just outside the res."

"How far?"

"Half, maybe three-quarters of a mile beyond the cattle guard, on the right-hand side you'll see a dirt road. There's two crummy trailers about fifty yards along it. That's Robert's place." He screwed the foam earplug back in place.

She took a long drink at the dirty hose bibb outside the yard and walked back down to the plaza. Nothing moved across the landscape but Claire. The baked hills rose on every side around her, focusing the heat until she floated on the fat air like a fly in a soup bowl. On the wooden steps of the church a black-haired woman now sat instructing a little girl.

"Blessed art thou . . ." the woman prompted, while the five-year-old writhed across the stairs in an agony of boredom; even from the grave the mission fathers cracked their whips.

Back in the truck, back over the cattle guard. Someone honked loudly behind her and she swerved to the right to let the shiny blue pickup tear past, then stared after the small elderly man at the wheel.

What business would Gene Senior have on the reservation?

A dirt road, possibly *the* dirt road, opened off to the right; she turned onto it, and in a few hundred yards she passed a faded blue Pinto from one of the fireball years, and saw an old Airstream sitting in the tall grass. Beyond it was an even older trailer, Lucy-and-Desi vintage, like a canned ham balanced on its edge. They were parked on the crest of a hill above the braid of green river vegetation, and they were deserted—abandoned, she would have said, except for the Pinto and the three pairs of ragged Jockey shorts that hung on a line strung between the canned ham and a blue-leaved Kellogg oak.

She smacked the Airstream's screen door. "Mr., uh, Mr. Gomez?"—taking a guess at the last name—"Daisy?" No answer. Shit. She peered through the dirt-filmed window.

It was dark in there and filled with things that didn't make sense even when her eyes adjusted. Junk, no doubt, but from her mid-thorax view into the silver caterpillar, she could imagine bug lungs, bug guts, bug kidneys.

Canned ham—same thing. Stuff and more stuff, no room for a human. She was straining at the window to see as far to the left as possible when suddenly there was a thump behind her.

From inside the Airstream.

"Mr. Gomez?" She trotted back to the other trailer and tried the door. It creaked outward and she hoisted herself up the steep grooved metallic stairs into the belly of the beast.

With awe, and some disappointment, she stared around her. Just junk after all. But what junk! It was like a mail-order catalog entitled "You Never Know": a peach crate of vacuum tubes, because you never know, tube amps might come back. A dozen old Bakelite radios, because you never know, TV might not pan out. Ten TVs, because it might. A tower of plastic reels for reel-to-reel tape recorders. A dozen curved objects of specific but obscure purpose, like oversized chess pieces, covering a flip-down shelf.

Claire was finally deciding that the chess pieces were chair legs, when there was a loud crash behind her. The tower of tape reels was toppling, slipping disks in all directions. She darted to catch them and suddenly the chair legs were rolling off the edge of the shelf in a ponderous, deafening cascade. She knew she hadn't even brushed them; probably her weight on the floor, or her breath, was enough to disrupt the equilibrium of Uncle Robert's collection, but it was hard to escape the sense of a malevolent intelligence. The haunted Airstream.

Through the tiny screened eye of a window, she saw something dark flick by outside the trailer.

"Hello?" she called, scrambling for the door, dislodging five or six fishing rods so that they formed a hedge behind her. She stumbled down the stairs, ran around the blunt nose of the trailer, and saw something slide over the crest of the hill.

"Hey!" she cried, to the sarcastic echo of a crow.

Might have *been* a crow, she thought, shrugging, and decided to take a look at Daisy's orchard. Guessing, she started for the river, then saw what looked like an orderly row of trees on the next hill.

But when she approached, she realized that they were not fruit trees but oaks, and that they appeared orderly because everything around them had been scraped away. Someone had been busy with a bulldozer, leveling, shoving, widening.

At first that was all she saw: the trees, the broad avenue between them. Then, under the trees, the cars. Three—or three and a half, depending on how you counted—mid-70s Malibus/Cutlasses/Monte Carlos; a Chevy Biscayne; a mid-1950s Buick; an old Checker cab; a gutted Morris Minor; and a right-hand-drive Post Office jeep. Variations on the ordinary: everyone out here accumulated junkers, and why not, if you had the land? That first year you just might get around to fixing them; later they might be worth some money, and finally it was too hard to haul them to the dump.

Then she began to make out shapes in the dappled patterns of light and shade under the trees. Long white tubes lying in the grass like ruined columns . . . Oh. Water heaters. Many. *That* was alarming; one or two, sure, because you never know, but *eight*?

She zigzagged slowly past the washing machines, the washing machine *agitators*, stacked pagodalike, the snails of tubular sheet metal, function unknown, and stopped at a boxcar—an actual whole boxcar, how had he towed it here?—stuffed with hubcaps. The litter of the twentieth century under dusty trees created a powerful mood, like Stonehenge, only more complicated—an unsettling mixture of the solemn and the comic, Ozymandias in a funny hat—

Something flickered behind the trees.

Squirrel? Crow? she thought, suddenly uneasy. It was

time to find the apples or leave. She walked briskly back the way she had come.

Again, movement at the edge of her vision.

"Hello?" she called, wishing that she'd bought that .22, then wishing that that concept had never entered her repertoire. It was all too easy to become a person who carried a gun.

There it was again. Big, bigger than a squirrel. By the water heaters, a hole in the gray oak shade.

"Daisy? Mr. Gomez?"

And suddenly it darted into the sun, swift and dark like the shadow of a plane passing overhead. Tall, black—

"Hey!" she called again, and at that exact moment a woman's voice cried "Jason!" and the figure resolved itself into a man—Claire blinked—no, a boy, in black T-shirt and jeans.

He stopped dead and they stared at each other.

It was the little ninja.

"Jason!" the woman's voice demanded again.

The boy's eyes rolled like the horses', and he bolted down the hill. And this time Claire didn't need to look elsewhere; there was no mistaking what he was afraid of.

He was afraid of Claire.

Chapter 25

"I see you met my son."

The plump flushed blonde stood at the lip of the hill. Claire joined her, and together they watched the kid bound down the slope, holding his arms straight out from his sides and running like a child, scared, exhilarated. He turned upriver, toward the high country, and for a minute his black figure was silhouetted against the soft riparian green; then he disappeared into the forest.

The woman shook her head, then turned toward Claire. "Sorry," she said. "I don't know what gets into him. You're Dr. Sharples?"

"Yep. Daisy?" Claire said doubtfully. The woman's hair was the color of the bleached grass around them; she was pink and blue-eyed. Claire was a more convincing Indian.

"That's me. Sorry I'm late—I was down in the orchard." She wiped her brow with a pneumatic forearm and gave Claire a curious look. "You're not what I was expecting."

"Neither are you," Claire answered without thinking.

"No? Oh. Paler, I bet." Daisy grinned. "I'm only half Indian. Irish and German on my mom's side. Listen, let's go back to the trailers and see if we can round up my uncle. He's supposed to be helpin' me out on this, and I want him to hear what you got to say." They tramped back toward the first hill.

"You got kids?" Daisy asked, halfway up.

"No," said Claire, defensive and apologetic by reflex. She was thinking that since she herself was not a particularly terrifying presence, Jason's flight probably meant a guilty conscience. And that scared *her*. What could that soft-faced kid have done to make him terrified of a complete stranger?

"You're smart. I reckon I lose ten years off my life every time one of mine hits adolescence. Now Jason, he has been so spooky lately, I just don't know what's going on."

They had come up on the Airstream. "Robert!" Daisy roared, so suddenly and enormously that Claire flinched. "Yo, Robert!"

"I didn't see anyone around."

"Yeah, his car's not here," Daisy said. "But let's just see . . ." and she opened the door. The fishing rods clattered halfway down the steps. "Jesus," she said after a minute, "it's worse every time."

"I'm afraid I knocked some things over."

"How could you tell? Sometimes I wonder about Uncle Robert! And the other trailer's exactly the same."

They stepped gingerly inside. The smell of petroleum by-products was asphyxiating, and the trailer was, if possible, hotter than outside. Daisy strained to click on a fan in the kitchen porthole, and it clattered into a lazy spin.

"Let's sit under the tree," said Claire, backing down the steps.

Daisy filled a plastic thermos top full of greasy water from the trailer's sink, and then joined Claire outside, where she settled under the oak like a stack of inner tubes. Her round legs in white shorts stuck straight out in front of her; her big shoulders strained at the ribbed pink tank top. She was built like a Channel swimmer: cushiony subcutaneous fat, plenty of muscle underneath. Out of the glare Claire could see her face better: high cheekbones, yes, and vaguely Asian eyes. But they were blue eyes, with a careful line of turquoise under each to reflect their color, and with that pink skin she looked Slavic or Finnish. She lit a cigarette and looked down on the river.

"It's good to be back on the res," she said, flicking the match into the cellophane-dry grass.

"You've been away?" Claire's eyes followed the match.

"You might say that," she said dryly. "I've lived in Galena, Nevada, for the last twenty years. Moved there when I got married." Claire's eyes kept straying to that hot match. "But I finally left. . . ."

Was that smoke or dust? Claire barely followed the thread of Daisy's tale of twentieth-century entrepreneurial woe: the failed print shop, the failed packaging-and-mailbox store, the failed frozen yogurt parlor, the failed frame shop, the failed convenience store, the bankruptcy, and finally, the husband and the Wal-Mart checkout clerk.

". . . right there on my fucking—excuse me—my daybed! On my new comforter, the son of a bitch! I didn't say a word, just packed everything into the Pinto and grabbed Jason and come back here. That was last October . . ."

Dust, Claire decided.

". . . my daddy's apples. But nobody's took care of those trees since Junior—that's my daddy—died. And they've got little brown holes all over 'em; Raymond must've told you."

"Let's take a look," Claire said, though what she wanted was to stretch out for a short nap—after dousing the match. Daisy hauled herself up, dropping her cigarette at her feet, and Claire managed to refrain from diving for it, but she stepped on it as she passed.

On the far side of the trailers they struck a rough dirt road that led down toward the river. "The trees are down there," said Daisy. "For the water."

Claire hoped this didn't mean she was tapping the river directly, a straightforward solution to what Ramón had called her "water problems"—but also, unfortunately, illegal. On their left a citrus-yellow backhoe was frozen in a crook-elbowed gesture next to a gash like a new grave in the pale grass.

"You putting in a crop here?"

"Uh-uh," Daisy said. "Robert must be making another trailer pad."

"Needs to expand, huh?"

"Naw, he just likes to scrape the pads."

They passed a low mound of green waste and chicken shit. Ramón's got her composting, thought Claire; maybe I should collect my bat guano and bring it out here— though there had been no bat sightings for two days. Maybe Will got them this time. She could see the trees now, silver leaves shivering in the hot wind, small green fruit.

"I thought this was the right thing to do for him," Daisy was saying. "Jason, I mean. Jenny and Jimmy Junior, the older ones, they're staying in Galena till they finish high school. But Jason, he's got menfolk here—uncles, cousins. I thought they might make up for losing his dad, a little."

"He having trouble adjusting?" Claire said absently, lifting the hand lens on its string from around her neck.

"I think it's *me* having trouble," Daisy said. "See, Galena's a small town. I know that may sound weird—like, what could be smaller than the res?—but the kids here, they have a hard way to go and they grow up fast. So Jason's backward. Not in school, in school he does good, but he's fourteen, and next to his cousins he seems like a baby. Only all of a sudden I got to deal with that teenage stuff."

"What kind of stuff?" Meaning what could have sent him careening down the hill like that? They were in the shade of the trees now, and the temperature had dropped maybe half a degree.

"Oh, you know, smart mouth. And the hair, my god, he's worse than any woman! You notice the hair?"

"What is that? Kind of a ninja style?"

"Beats the shit out of me. All I know is all his friends have it, that silly little ponytail. Or else they have it short, with a little braid in back. They think they're Indian warriors, you know?" She snorted. "And if one of 'em gets a normal haircut, the other ones rag on him, call him a Meskin. 'Course, Jason's so white he's gotta be extra bad to make up for it. See what I mean about the fruit? It's almost all ruined." She pronounced "ruined" like a southerner making it a diphthong: "roo-eend."

"What do you mean, 'extra bad'?" Claire asked after a minute. She had picked two fruits, one riddled with holes, the other lumpy, misshapen.

"Oh, nothing really heavy, not yet. I'm just waiting, you know? 'Cause his cousins, they're already messing with some shit. Nothing big-time. Stealing cars. Growing pot."

What was big-time? Claire wondered as they walked the rows. Assault with a hunk of granite? She tried to give some attention to Daisy's trees. "Where does your water come from?"

"Well, Junior dug a little ditch from the river until somebody downstream noticed and complained. Then for a long time the trees didn't get no water at all. Robert and Dustin was digging me a well—"

"Dustin!" Claire said sharply. "Dustin Gomez?" Stupid, how could there be two?

"Yeah," said Daisy. "He's my . . . my ex-brother-in-law, I guess you'd call him, my ex-husband's kid brother. Jason's uncle, anyway."

Claire let that subject lie for a moment and frowned at the fruit through her hand lens. "The little holes," she said, "those are the codling moth that Ramón said he talked to you about. Looks to me like about forty percent of your fruit is affected. And you've got some aphids, too," she added, holding up the lumpy fruit.

"Oh, Jesus," said Daisy, distressed.

"I think we can solve both problems. You're committed to staying organic?"

Daisy nodded. "If I can do it without going broke. And if I can corral the labor. Seems more natural, and Raymond says in the long run it might even save me money, 'cause my inputs could be cheaper, at least the fertilizer. And I can sell my organic produce for more. Raymond thinks I should direct-market at farmers' markets, play up the Indian thing. People are into that right now." She touched her hair and grinned. "I might have to go brunette. Or get me somebody who's more exotic-looking. Maybe Jason."

"Or Dustin," Claire said casually.

"Dustin!" She screwed her face into an unreadable expression. "I don't know what I can get out of Dustin. He don't think farming is *manly*. Not worthy of a warrior, you know." She paused. "He's living with us, and he's supposed to help me out. That's the deal. But I swear it's like havin' another teenager. I mean, I ain't seen him in a week—"

Her robust voice broke off abruptly, but it wasn't till she spoke again that Claire—who was thinking, A week; that means no alibi for Saturday—realized she was crying.

"This whole move has been one big disaster. I ain't got no help, the trees are spoilt, my kid is spoilt—at least I knew what I was in for, with Jimmy!"

Uncomfortable and helpless, Claire looked at Daisy, then away. Sometimes she felt like a social worker instead of a farm adviser. Did this happen to her male colleagues?

She should be taking advantage of Daisy's vulnerable moment to probe about Jason and Dustin, but what she said was "Well, I don't think there's any cure for kids; that's why I stick to plants." Daisy gave her the ghost of a grin. "And I do think we can solve the problem with your apples. I'll have to get back to you with more details, but I think there might be a pheromone treatment for your codling moths—it doesn't actually kill them, but it disrupts mating behavior and keeps their population under control. And there's a parasitical wasp that kills the eggs, and a virus you can spray. As for the aphids, if you get a good cover crop between the rows, you'll have beneficial insects that will control them."

Daisy rubbed a round hand into her eye and her knuckle came away stained blue like a bruise. Claire wasn't sure how much of this Daisy had followed, but she said, "That stuff that stops the bugs from mating. What did you call it?"

"Pheromones. Doesn't actually stop them, just confuses them."

"Maybe I should slip some into Dustin's coffee. He's just like his big brother there," she said as she dug in her purse for another cigarette.

It occurred to Claire to wonder what kind of rental agreement Dustin and Daisy had worked out.

Chapter 26

Claire was supposed to meet Andy at 6:30 P.M. at Craig Ranch, and she was late and not making any effort to remedy that. For one thing, the earlier she was the hotter it would be; for another, she wasn't sure why she'd agreed to meet him; she hated this part of the Valley. Wide open, hot, monotonous: if you rolled a ball from the Coast Range to the west or from the Sierra to the east, this is where it would come to a stop—the Valley's dead center. Once upon a time this was where the rivers ran out. Now it was all cotton.

She could see the dim shapes of the Temblors, which were themselves foothills of the Coastal Range, when she saw the little white sign: Alton, Population 5,034.

Marcy's hometown, she remembered with a little shock, and immediately afterward saw a weathered wooden sign, a duck-shaped arrow, that said Duck Club. In spite of her lateness, she followed it, sure that these must be Marcy's ducks. On her right a bright white bird, probably a heron, settled into the glittering leaves of a young cottonwood. She hit a dead end where another ancient sign said Thigpen's Duck Club.

Thigpen. She could understand why Marcy had married Gilbert Hobbes for his name. Despite Andy, Claire pulled over under the sign.

But Thigpen's Duck Club and the environment that had once supported it were both long gone. The Army Corps of Engineers' dams upstream had finally done in the last of these wetlands. The sign for Thigpen's was adjacent to what might have been the margin of a marsh but now was only a puddle of irrigation runoff. In this little ecosystem a thicket of tule had sprouted; beyond were what looked like high tension lines. Or oil wells— not the local rod pumps, rocking and sucking, but Texas-style oil wells, the classic derricks they called Christmas trees.

Claire backtracked to the main road and passed through downtown Alton—two churches, a school, twenty houses, a general store, so poor, so ramshackle, that she was surprised that the kids walking or biking along the shoulder of the road were all Anglo. No wonder Marcy had longed for the mountains.

She made a screeching U-turn just past the store, then stopped and went in for a soda.

An old swamp cooler rumbled ineffectually in a high window above the Spam and stewed tomatoes. Two blond girls bought popsicles. An old geezer had placed a single beer on the counter and was talking to the dark young man behind the counter.

". . . death penalty. What I mean," the geezer was saying, "you gotta pay for something like that!"

"Yep."

"Death penalty's the only thing."

"Yep."

"I mean, some of these here criminals—killing people and eating human flesh—"

"Jeffrey Dahmer." The proprietor looked bored.

"Whatever. Eating human flesh," the geezer repeated with relish. "That ain't right. I mean, I ain't no angel, but you gotta draw the line. . . ."

Claire suppressed a snort of laughter and set down her Dr Pepper, and the clerk turned to her with relief. His brief expression at her automatic "*Gracias*" made her realize he wasn't Latino and left her feeling silly, but she asked him about the duck club anyway.

"I've seen the sign," he said with an absence of accent that was in itself an accent, "but it's before my time."

"What you wanter know, missy?" rasped the geezer, who was right behind her, holding his beer. "I know all about Thigpen's, useter hunt there. Closed mebbe twenty years ago. Closed the bar. Closed Juanita's. Closed every damn place in this town. These nowadays ways ain't worth a damn—"

"Are those oil wells?" she interrupted. "Behind the old sign?"

"Hell, no," he said. "There ain't no oil around here. Lost Hills, Kern River, that's where you got your oil."

"Oh," she said, obscurely disappointed. "Thanks." She paid for her Dr Pepper and left.

The geezer was on her heels, still talking. "Now, there was a little excitement twenty, twenty-five years ago," he said, taking her for a historian of petroleum engineering. "Found some oil-streaked sand out by Thigpens'. But it never did amount to nothing."

She nodded, fingering her key impatiently but hearing him out, calculating how many woman-hours she had lost in her life because she could never bring herself to be rude to these old guys. Apart from the green cotton field behind her, the dusty town had no more color than a sepia photograph. So when the vertical streak of lipstick red suddenly appeared on the left-hand shoulder of the road she squeezed her gritty eyes and refocused, and the geezer stopped in mid-anecdote.

At fifty yards the blaze of color resolved itself into a woman in a scarlet sari, as exotic and unexpected in this Okie landscape as a giraffe. She was headed for them. She walked gracefully past the gas pumps, jingling faintly, not young but erect and perfectly composed in the breathtaking heat. When she disappeared into the store a whiff of sandalwood lingered.

The old man watched her until the screen door slammed. "Nope," he said, shaking his head sadly. "No oil."

"I think I've got it," Claire said, geezered to the max. "There wasn't any oil!" She slipped into her car and started to slam the door.

"Nope," he continued, unperturbed. "That there's gas. Natchel gas."

"Natural gas?" Reluctantly she squeezed out the next question. "Is that worth money?"

"Ohhh, yeah! Brung in a hundred thousand dollars a year. Don and Ethel got out of ducks in a hurry, you bet. 'Course, Ethel got the cancer the next year, and Don, his heart give out in 'seventy-three. I hear their daughter got it all. And she always was a wild un!" He leered. "Purty li'l gal."

It was now six-thirty. Following Andy's directions, she turned north at the duck club dead end, then right again. Why had she assumed the money was Stewart's? Sexism?

Or because she couldn't figure out why else Marcy had married him?

She was now north of the land she had just looked at. In a quarter of a mile she saw the forest service van parked on the shoulder.

"Andy?" she called. "Andy, I'm sorry I'm late . . ."

There he was, pistachio shirt on brown grass, black Baltimore Orioles cap beside him, stretched out in the shade of the van.

"Andy!" she snapped. Finding Marcy seemed to have made her permanently disconcerted by prone bodies, and she released a whoosh of breath when he jerked and sat upright.

"Sorry," she said again and squatted beside him. "You looked very peaceful."

"Yeah. It was a good nap. Mmmm." He flopped back down and pulled his cap back over his eyes. His attenuated limbs landed at odd angles. He looked as if he came from a low-gravity planet. "I love to sleep," he murmured.

"It's about the best thing to do in this weather," she said, kneeling beside him.

"Any weather. I really, really love to sleep. Especially falling asleep: when I was in college I used to set my alarm to go off every four hours, just so I could enjoy going back to sleep again."

She snorted with surprised laughter. "Andy, you're a sensualist!" she said delightedly. "I never would have guessed!"

"There's a lot about me you might not guess," he said coyly, then reddened under his fine-textured skin. He was like a mood ring.

"So," she said, "how'd it go? It's all pretty standard stuff out here, nothing exciting—"

"Hey," sitting up, "you'd be surprised what excites me. You're talking to a man who wrote his thesis on lichens. But I did pretty well; knew more than I thought I would. There was a grass I couldn't identify, though. I'm not too good on grasses, and in my opinion neither is Jepson." He picked up his two-ton *California Flora* and opened it on his lap.

"You really are a botany nerd!" Claire said, pointing to the book's custom-made Gore-Tex field case with convenient handles.

"Of course!" he said with dignity. "Did you take me for a . . . a poseur?"

Pretentious? *Moi?* "No, just somebody who's studying French."

"What? Oh. No. Peace Corps. I was in Togo a long time ago. It's just an unconscious habit." He reddened again so that Claire didn't quite believe him. But it was a quaint affectation.

Anyway, she was impressed by that magic phrase, Peace Corps. She herself had been on the verge of a two-year stint after college, but had gone straight to grad school instead, and had always regretted it.

But down to business. "Let's see this grass," she said.

Andy laid the sprig on his knee and they alternated their attention between it, the book's botanical key, a decision tree written in code—"Glumes 0 or vestigial OR Glumes 2, well developed; Lemmas rigidly awned OR lemmas awnless," and so on—and the glossary, because neither of them was very familiar with the arcane terminology specific to grasses. Very soon they were completely obsessed, enraptured even, by what was, after all, a homely little sprout, thin and knobby like Andy. Claire had entirely forgotten to compose hard-hitting questions about the day of Marcy's attack.

She glanced up from the flora, and in a gap between two sycamores caught sight of a skeletal tower, rectilinear as only the works of man could be. Nature abhors a right angle. It was one of the Christmas Trees, the natural gas wells she had seen from the south. If Marcy was an heiress . . .

"Did you know that some lichens only grow two millimeters a century?" Andy was saying, while she thought about what the geezer had told her of the fortunate-unfortunate Thigpens.

If Marcy was an heiress, if the money was hers, not Stewart's, it changed all the equations. All the scores on the JAFGR Scale.

Especially Stewart's. "Do you have a mobile phone?" she asked abruptly, because she had suddenly remembered she was supposed to call Paul about Stewart Connor *now*. "Mine's in my own car."

"Not in this thing, no. But I think I saw a pay phone back in town."

"I need to make a call. And I should be heading home anyway," she said.

"Ow!" Andy was disengaging himself from a large and tenacious tumbleweed. "Son of a bitch! Okeydoke; I think the plants are starting to turn on me, anyway. Want to stop somewhere for dinner?"

"Um . . . sure. But I need to make that call first."

Andy followed her in the van until she screeched to a gravel-ripping stop in front of the phone.

"Man, you always drive like that?"

Ignoring him, Claire walked to the phone, dialed the Weissbergs', and got their answering machine. But she thought maybe Paul had left her a message before they had gone out, so she called her own machine. Her own voice always surprised her: from inside she was crisp and confident, but from the outside she sounded sweet and slightly hesitant, so which was the true Claire?

And then suddenly there was Marie on her machine, telling her that they had operated on Marcy for a blood clot at 4:00 P.M. and she wasn't expected to live.

She walked slowly back to the car.

"That was fast— Hey! What's wrong?" Andy said.

She told him, and saw the color drain from his face.

"Oh, my God. . . . I'll meet you at the hospital!"

They leapfrogged all the way to Parkerville, where they pulled into the lot within seconds of each other and parked among familiar cars: Will's Trooper, Tom's Blazer, Stewart's Mercedes, a Honda with a UCSB bumper sticker. Claire wondered briefly who would get Marcy's Jaguar. Will? Dustin? Was that a motive for murder?

Stewart was standing at the entrance, smoking a cigarette; he shook his head when Claire passed, which could have meant no news or bad news. In the waiting room, Paul and Naomi and Cheryl and Hazel sat on one side of the room; on the other side, apart from the others, Will rested elbows on thighs, electric eyes closed. Claire settled next to him; he might need some comfort tonight. Laurie sat to their left, next to Marie, who held her hand, and beyond Marie, to Claire's surprise, sat Tom. She wouldn't have expected him to turn out for this.

And where was Dustin? she wondered, looking around. With his long-haired girl? But then, maybe no one had told him.

After a half hour Laurie wandered restlessly to the candy machine. The ashtray was already a jumble of Snickers wrappers. Stewart stuck his head in and disappeared again, and Claire thought about him. If the money was Marcy's . . . well, Stewart's motive was obvious: it looked very much like Marcy was about to divorce, and therefore disinherit, him. But he seemed so distraught!

He entered again, gave Will a wide berth, and sat beside Andy.

"Anything?"

"Nothing"—a desultory exchange that was repeated over the next two hours, until they were sick with not knowing.

And then there was something, and they were sick with knowing.

At 8:13 P.M. a doctor—not Mukherjee but Stewart's "real" doctor, some gray-faced patriarch—entered the waiting room. He was sorry, he began, and maybe he was, but the speech was practiced: they had done everything they could do, but Marcy had died at 7:50 without recovering consciousness. Laurie's wail—a thin, desolate siren—rose over the room.

In fact, there was an explosion of small noises: a single "tsk" from Tom, who began striding up and down the hall; a strangled sob from Marie, a soft "fuck" from Will, then "God." Claire looked over at him. He was wiping his eyes with the heel of his hand, first one eye, then the other: "fuck," the left eye, "God," the right, over and over again. She laid her arm around his shoulders. The others, in one of those exquisitely uncomfortable moments that death creates, had grouped around Stewart. Later they would stop by Will and mutter, "Sorry, man."

As for Claire, she sat with tight throat and dry eyes, wishing, as usual, to feel more than she felt.

She wasn't ambivalent about Marcy's death: last week's inappropriate feelings had sputtered out as quickly as they had appeared. Wasn't surprised by it: she had known a week ago, when Mukherjee told them Marcy probably wouldn't recover, what that "probably" meant— although there was nothing vaster than the difference between *one-in-a-billion* and *zero.* That was the zone of hope. That was where humans lived.

She just didn't believe it. Or rather, believe *in* it. For the moment her reason was rejecting the whole notion of death as totally preposterous.

Life she believed in. As a biologist she routinely, daily, acknowledged the profoundly inexplicable fact of life. But the equal mystery of death . . . Marcy Hobbes had lived forty-four years, accumulating a brain full of unique experience and memory. And now they were supposed to believe that it was all gone. Gone where? Huh? Answer me that!

Some people left. Paul made a hoarse speech in the parking lot. They would miss Marcy's passion, he said, but they had to go on, not only for the forest but for Marcy. That's what she would have wanted. Marcy had lived for the forest.

Naomi looked at Paul, and Claire figured she was thinking what Claire was thinking: that that was all very well, but what if Marcy had died for the forest? What if a vengeful logger was stalking them? Was that worth it?

The red light on her answering machine blinked at her when she walked in. Andy's high voice—ragged, rapid, verging on hysteria: "I've got to talk to you about something, it's really urgent, but we shouldn't talk about it over the phone. Call me so we can meet."

She did call, twice. But there was no answer. And then she wanted to call Will, but she wasn't sure where he was. At Marcy's? Or had he been evicted by Stewart or Laurie? She dialed the number and shivered at Marcy's sweet, calm voice on the machine.

"Will," Claire said tentatively, "if you're there . . . I just wanted to tell you how sorry I am, and if you need company or anything, just call me." She hung up, not knowing who, if anyone, would receive the message.

She tried Andy again, with no luck. With touching optimism she prepared herself for sleep, brushed her teeth, washed her face, put on her nightshirt—then lay rigid in bed, thinking about Marcy and the world without Marcy.

At four she got up to make herself warm milk, caught sight of herself in the mirror, and remembered Naomi's stricken face under the blue lights of the parking lot. She thought about the number of men in the waiting room that night, and it occurred to her that Naomi's look might not have been fear at all, but something very different.

Her last conscious act before she drifted into a fitful sleep was to wonder whether every man in Riverdale had had strong feelings of some sort about Marcy Hobbes.

Chapter 27

At five in the morning Claire sat bolt upright in bed, having remembered—in her sleep, evidently—the trap that she had baited so many hours ago. Oh, no, she thought, grabbing a flashlight, what if the skunk had wandered in? What if what had awakened her was the sound of the trap clanging shut? She crept out the door and around to the crawl space with trepidation.

But the trap was empty, the cat food untouched. She unbaited the cage and set it outside.

She was tremendously relieved, but wondered why the skunk hadn't eaten the bait. Vegetarian? Finicky? Was he even there at all? She hadn't heard or seen him, only smelled him, and maybe her nose was deceiving her; maybe it was the septic tank, or maybe she had one of those brain tumors whose first symptom was imaginary or distorted odors.

This was a job for Bisquick. She sprinkled a thin line around the crawl space, smoothing it as best she could with a ruler so the little skunky footprints would show. Then she drove to work.

Between six and eight o'clock she was alone in the office and actually managed to forget about Marcy and make significant progress on her article, finishing the introduction and plowing into the conclusions, the two sections for which she was responsible. In fact, so thoroughly did she forget that at eight-thirty she automatically reached for the phone to make her ritual call to Marie—then remembered about Marcy again, and felt sick. Instead she tried to call Andy at the forest service, but he was already out in the field.

"I'll call later," she told them, declining to leave a message in case she was on somebody's list of personae non gratae, and dialed Tom's number. She had to tell someone about Marcy's fortune, and maybe Tom would be a little more receptive this morning.

"So that gives Stewart a motive—" she was saying, when Tom interrupted her.

"Look, don't tell *me* this," he said. "I'm sorry Marcy died, I really am. Marie's a basket case. But nothing's changed. Maybe J.T.'ll take this a little more serious, is all. Step up the manhunt for that escapee, what's-his-name. Pelon."

"Pelon the felon," Claire said absently, too tired to fight.

"Like I said, if I thought you all were in danger I might try to work on J.T. But I don't."

"What the hell do you mean by that, Tom?" She aimed for righteous outrage, but her voice was unsupported, like a newspaper over a pothole, and collapsed under the weight. "How could that be true? Everybody in the group is at risk!"

"You got any evidence for that?"

"No evidence, just a hunch," she said with heavy sarcasm. "Maybe it's just this sustained campaign of terrorism against the Friends of the Redwoods, culminating in the murder of one of its members!" Then, in a normal voice: "Did you get my message about somebody trying to run me off the road the other day?"

"Yeah. I already knew whose black jeep it was, but I checked it out for you."

"Don't tell me. Randy Unsel." The toothless logger.

"Yup." Silence.

"So?" Claire said.

"So you want to press charges?"

"Well, yeah!" she said.

"For what? Passin' you on One-seventy?"

"No, for . . ." Nailing the owl and tampering with my brakes and sending threatening notes and slashing tires and maybe bashing Marcy. But she could anticipate Tom's response: You got any evidence? "No, I guess not."

"Okay."

As she started to hang up, she heard his tinny voice crackle: "Claire. Unsel may be an asshole, but he didn't kill Marcy."

"No?"

"No. Think about it." And Tom hung up.

Well, she did think about it. All day, as she plodded through her article, she thought about it. And finally, reluctantly, she decided she was going to have to revisit the scene of the crime. Definitely not eager to venture back into the mountains alone, she called everyone in the group, but no one was available to accompany her.

So at five-thirty she stopped at home, stuffed her little popgun into her pack, and once again rattled up the road toward the flatiron ridge.

Somewhere to her right a chain saw was snarling. Marcy would have tracked it down, thought Claire. Alone in the middle of the wilderness, Marcy would have checked it out. But look what had happened to Marcy! I won't get too close, she thought as, half scared, half angry, she turned right, once again following the paper plates toward the salvage lot she and Marcy had explored the other day. Soon the air smelled like her fresh-cut woodpile, and she rounded a curve, pulled off the trail, and walked through the brush toward the sound. It was hard to be discreet with a chain saw.

In a moment she saw him: one guy in a Grateful Dead T-shirt "falling" an orange ponderosa. His mouth opened and closed rhythmically in what she guessed was song— impossible to hear over the bite of the saw—and when it opened she saw black where teeth should be. Oh, great. Randy Unsel. Mr. Owl Hash. Mr. Black Jeep. But she kept watching.

Back home she had seen people take out trees, dropping them with precision between house and garage and lilac and forsythia. But not much finesse was required of Mr. Unsel: working in from the road, he had already cleared a swath. He had a wide simplified space to play with.

Even so, his aim was sloppy. When the hundred-foot giant tipped, then toppled with excruciating slowness to crash through the edge of the clearing and explode against the earth, it took a lot of saplings with it.

The whine of the saw decrescendoed into idle and Claire heard "Gotta whole lotta love, uhh, uhh, gotta whole lotta love, uhh, uhh . . ." She grinned in spite of herself and felt her upper lip stretch across her own orthodontically perfected middle-class mouth. She had the fleeting realization that Unsel's missing teeth were not simply a way of making himself a sinister joke, but that he couldn't afford to fix them. Then the chain saw revved, and he moved in to shear off the ponderosa's smaller lateral branches.

He was the obvious suspect, she thought as she marched back to her car. What was Tom talking about? Unsel was the guy whose alibi they should be checking. He had worked himself up to murder through the petty stuff, finally bashing Marcy under circumstances . . . well, circumstances very much like these, she realized, abruptly bending double and creeping through the ceanothus.

Unsel, either acting for himself or as a hit man, of the kind Paul described, for the Genes. Her interest in Stewart and Will and Dustin suddenly seemed simply expedient, like the old joke about looking for your keys on the porch because the light was better, even though you had lost them in the driveway. She was investigating Marcy's men because she *could*, because they happened to fall within the small spotlight of her own knowledge, whereas Randy Unsel was beyond her field of vision.

But not Tom's. Tom could find out all about Randy Unsel, or anyone else. Why was he being so blind?

She turned the car around, careful not to land in the ditch this time, and headed back to the main fire road. When she passed Unsel, she slumped down to make herself as inconspicuous as possible, but he didn't even look up. Nevertheless when she finally parked, about a quarter mile from the ridge, the first thing she did was pull her absurd little gun out of her pack and load it with a cartridge and pellets—450 feet per second. Well, she could always throw it at him.

She walked to the ridge and started up the trail, listening so hard it was like clenching a muscle, and then her attention was absorbed by the descent toward the meadow. Near the bottom she stumbled at the same place she, and later Andy, had tripped the day Marcy was hurt; the root of a white fir snaked across the trail. Tom and J.T. were right, she admitted: it was a steep trail. If Marcy *had* also stumbled right here, she might possibly have caught her temple on—well, on that sharp elbow of rock, say, and plunged to the bottom.

Not plunged—skidded and bounced, and wound up scraped and bruised and battered.

Which she had not been.

Not to mention the now-vanished bouquet of monks-hood, which meant that *if* Marcy had simply fallen, she had been on her way *up* the trail, without downward momentum, which made it even less likely that she had stumbled.

In fact, it was ridiculous for anyone to persist in believing that Marcy had fallen.

So ridiculous that Claire stopped where she was, a couple of feet beyond the treacherous root. What if she was misinterpreting Tom altogether? What if Tom meant that he knew, or thought he knew, the identity of Marcy's assailant—no, her killer—and also knew that this person represented no threat to the other Friends of the Red-woods? Because . . . because—because the attack *had* been purely personal! Something to do with Marcy and only Marcy!

One of her men after all, then? Stewart, Dustin, Will, and who knew if that list was exhaustive? Who knew if there wasn't another Mr. X, or a whole roster of them? Marcy seemed perfectly capable of juggling a couple of people simultaneously, and of grooming a farm team so she could bring somebody up in case of injury or retire-ment.

Claire could see it: someone—some faceless Mr. X— hands Marcy that MIA bouquet. Marcy's favorite wild- flowers; she buries her face in them. And then—whack! Yes! Because Marcy hadn't defended herself; that's why Tom asked the doctor if she'd had wounds on her arms!

Think about it, Tom had said. He had known that Marcy had trusted the person who'd attacked her.

Which did seem to rule out Randy Unsel, or anyone like him, and did seem to suggest a friend—no, let's be realistic; this was Marcy—a lover.

And did seem to place the rest of the Friends of the Redwoods, including Claire Sharples, out of danger!

That's what Tom meant, she thought, almost whooping with relief. She stowed her popgun back in her pack and continued to do what she had come to do, following the trail down to where it spilled into the meadow, bending low to examine the long grass. No trace, no impression, no stain remained of Marcy, but there were plenty of po- tential weapons. Rocks. Hundreds, actually, piled in a layer of scree at the bottom of the cliff. Was one of them bloodstained?

After an aimless inspection of four rocks she realized this was a job for a forensics team, just as the establish- ment of alibis was a job for Tom or J.T. . . . She palmed one last chunk of granite from beside the trail and saw yellowing stems, strewn like pickup sticks beside the path, in clear view.

Claire lifted one of those stems. Four days of hot Sierra sun had sucked away every drop of moisture, and the papery leaves and brittle flowers came apart in her hand. But those leaves had been deeply lobed like the feet of the frogs for whom the family Ranunculaceae was named, and the flecks of petal that clung to her sweaty fingers retained a hint of midnight purple.

Monkshood.

First she thought, Here's proof for J.T.! Marcy *was* in the meadow!

Then she thought, Why didn't Andy see these? Either he didn't look very hard or he hadn't identified them. Maybe he wasn't much of a botanist after all . . . but no, he had been very good on the riparian species yesterday. He would certainly know monkshood.

And then, against her will, the blurred features of the anonymous Mr. X assembled themselves into Andy's ski-jump nose and droll mouth. What if he too had succumbed to Marcy's charms? What if he had handed her the bouquet that day? And what if Marcy had laughed at his fumbling overtures, and he . . . and he . . .

Andy, who had written his dissertation on *lichen*? Impossible!

"Impossible, impossible," she chanted as she trudged back up the trail. But she remembered that other woman, Andy's not-girlfriend. She was killed in an avalanche, he had said. "There's a lot about me you might not guess," he had said.

No. Impossible.

The wind had been rising, and on top of the ridge it roared like the tide. Once again she felt the sky not as a two-dimensional ceiling tacked somewhere *up there* like a blue dish towel but as the whole deep, heavy ocean of air, a tsunami of air that surged above her. She stepped into the hollow sequoia for shelter and looked up, watching the wind stir the upper branches of the other sequoias and set the lesser trees swaying like sea plants.

The triangular opening framed the meadow, and she imagined someone watching from that very spot last Saturday, only a hundred yards from her—straight up, but still—watching while she dragged Marcy across the meadow.

Someone like Andy, who had appeared so fortuitously.

Who would have known how to find *Calochortus in-venustus* subspecies *westii* and pull it up to save his employer a whole lot of trouble.

She squatted in the duff and pulled her popgun—which had become a sort of talisman, like Will's "crystal"—out of her pack again. Inevitably, previous refugees had carved their initials into the tree wall, RW, at nose level, JB + TS. Only initials, nothing elaborate; the sticky pitch, residue of an old fire, wasn't a good medium. Over her right shoulder was a scratchy heart surrounding DG + KM. Dustin Gomez? Where had Dustin been when Marcy was killed? And where was his little nephew Jason?

The wind was like a slipstream inside her, compressing her heart, upping the pressure in her head. She was digging into her pack for her bottle of Advil when the back of her left leg stung fiercely, and in her present over-revved state she swatted so hard that she bruised both her hand and the back of her knee. The sharp toluene smell of formic acid filled her nostrils, and she pulled up the crinkled corpse of a huge carpenter ant.

Meanwhile, the bottle had squirted out of her hand and rolled somewhere. She scrubbed in the dirt and came up with more ants; a used condom, its sticky residue of pleasure coated with powdery duff; a big black beetle, moving with complicated gait on jointed legs; a roach, if that was what they still called the stained, too-small end of a joint, if that was what they still called marijuana cigarettes. But no bottle. This was a big tree; you could have parked a car inside it—a VW Bug, not a Cadillac—but it was a simple space: round dirt floor, hollow trunk. No place to hide, she would have said. But the bottle was gone. She pulled her Maglite from her pack and investigated.

For the first time she noticed that at the back of the hollow there was a gap between the floor and the wall—that is, between the ground and the tree. When she peered at it closely, she discovered that it was a surprisingly large gap, like the opening to a cave—which it in fact was, she realized. The tree straddled its own small personal hill, and the hill's slope fell away from under the tree's massive base. The topography created a space beneath the tree, she saw, just as the slope of her canyon created a lower level to her cabin. Fascinated, she lay flat on her belly and aimed her light through the hole, scanning from right to left, and saw that there was indeed a whole other low-ceilinged chamber below the main hollow. She was in a split-level bear den!

Suddenly the flashlight picked out a long, dark shape up against the left-hand wall. Oh, God, she thought, scrambling to hands and knees, the master is in. Then she stopped. The light had glanced off something shiny, and when she flopped down again she saw white rubber soles.

The bear was wearing sneakers.

The air whoofed out of her, and she scrabbled out of the hollow and edged around to the east side of the tree, where she pressed herself against the big trunk. This somehow made her feel safe, though there seemed to be a rhythmic booming inside the tree. Presently she realized this was her own heart pounding under her ribs. The figure, the bear-in-sneakers figure, wasn't moving. If he had been lying in wait for her, he was playing it a little too cool. By the time he struggled out of that chamber, she could be halfway to her car.

He hadn't moved, even when she played her light down there. Maybe he was hurt.

What would Marcy have done?

Marcy! Marcy was, had been, a self-destructive megalomaniac. Marcy was a danger to herself and to others. Marcy was . . .

Oh, hell.

She ducked back inside. "Hello?" she called timidly, aiming the flashlight down into the lower chamber. In the narrow beam of light it was hard to make sense of the figure. If those were sneakers, then okay, those were feet; and the dark green must be trousers. Beyond that, the figure cast its own shadow. But whoever was down there, it wasn't Smokey.

Well, I'd better go down, might be hurt. *Marcy* would have gone down, God damn her. But the prospect made Claire cold with fear. She surveyed the low opening; it was certainly big enough, she realized, dismissing the image of herself stuck halfway through, like Pooh, with no Eeyore to rescue her. After all, he or she had made it through. Feet first, she began to wriggle her way down. Almost immediately she wished she had started on her belly, because it was bad to be on her back and helpless, waiting to be grabbed by the ankles at any moment. But it was too late to turn over. The last few seconds were the worst, sensing that whole living obelisk swaying above her as dirt and sawdust filled her mouth.

Then she was through.

The cave smelled damp and earthy, like the forest's subconscious. Like a fresh grave. The figure hadn't moved during her clumsy exertions, and her heart bumped again. The tiny flashlight drew a narrow light-stripe from sneakers to dark green trousers, glowed on a pistachio-colored shirt, and nestled in the pink hollow underneath the chin. A black-and-red Orioles cap lay over the upper part of the face, hiding it but revealing the wide, comical mouth.

He really will sleep anywhere, was her first loony thought as she lifted the brim, expecting those amber eyes to snap open once again.

But under the cap his eyes were already open. The cruel needle of light stabbed right into them.

Her stomach lurched, and she fell back onto her heels, landing on her wayward Advil bottle. Then she wrapped her arms around her knees, and for a moment she just rocked—back and forth, back and forth, humming Unsel's stupid song and nodding her head as if agreeing to an irrefutable argument. She felt sick with guilt, as if she herself, by thinking unkind thoughts about Andy— absurd, irrational thoughts, she saw now—had somehow contributed to this.

Presently she stopped rocking and, despite all common sense, felt for a pulse, this time going straight for the carotid. When she touched his neck, his head lolled sideways at an angle too acute for even a loose-jointed skeleton like Andy's. His fine skin was almost cold, and at this indisputable physical fact tears, hot with life, spilled from her eyes and she rocked and nodded, rocked and nodded. *Gotta whole lotta love.*

Help, she thought dimly. She had to get help. Andy was beyond help, but she was not. On elbows and knees she struggled back up through the birth canal into the hollow and blinked in the blessed light of day. Then she began to run down the trail, fast and crazy so she wouldn't have to think; but she had to slow for rocks and switchbacks, and then the thought fragments came like bursts of static: hurt himself and crawled in there to . . . couldn't crawl with a broken . . . if she'd been right about him and Marcy . . . killed himself because . . . you

couldn't break your own neck . . . you could hang yourself but not in a four-foot cave . . . if someone else had
killed him . . .

Someone had killed him.

This last shard of thought took a long time to work its
way to the surface. Strange, given Marcy's fate and
Claire's beliefs about that event, but merciful, since she
was suddenly terrified, and still ten minutes from her car.
And now, no matter how fast she ran, she couldn't stop
thinking.

Thinking about a jack-o-lantern grin and a chain saw,
right up the road.

"I don't understand," Tom said over the phone. "A tree?
Or a cave?"

"It's sort of both," said Claire from the floor of her
house. Her CO_2 pistol lay on the rug beside her, and she
had a shawl draped over her shoulders. Halfway home
she had started a convulsive shiver that had just sub-
sided. "You'll see when you get there."

"And you're sure it's Andy Nilsson?"

"Oh, yes."

"And you're sure he's dead?"

"Yes." Pause. "I think his neck was broken." She began
to shiver again. Maybe she had malaria.

"Oh, my God," Tom said—shockingly; it was the
strongest expression of emotion she'd ever heard from
him. There was a long silence. "Was he . . . Never mind.
I'll have to come up. With J.T. We'll stop by your place
and you can lead us to this tree-cave."

"Oh . . . Tom?" she began, but he'd hung up. Bring a
skinny deputy, she finished in her head.

They did: Enrique Santiago, broad in the shoulders and

narrow in the hips. Claire reckoned he could get down into the lower chamber.

As J.T.'s Cherokee bounced up the fire road Claire began to imagine that Andy's body would be gone, leaving no trace. Or, as they trudged up the trail, J.T.'s breath like a breaching whale as he labored behind them, that somehow she'd been absolutely wrong and they'd find Andy peacefully munching gorp beside the tree. Oh, God, she thought, filled with a huge, mindless hope, let me be humiliated, let me wonder about my sanity, let me be wrong!

But Andy wasn't sitting by the tree. And when they squeezed into the hollow and Tom aimed his enormous policeman's torch into the lower chamber, the white sneakers gleamed like two crescent moons. Claire's throat ached with despair.

"Well, he's down there, all right," Martelli said, as if he had entertained the same fantasies as Claire. He and J.T. seemed to look at their bellies, then, simultaneously, at their slender companions.

"*She* can't do nothing," J.T. said. "I got to call for some people. Shit, should've brought the phone up. Ricky," he told the young man, "go down to the car and call George and Henry. Explain the situation so they know what to bring."

"Maybe a generator and some lights," Tom called to Ricky's retreating back. "It's black as a butthole in there."

Claire hadn't smoked since her sophomore year in college, when she had paid for one semester of looking cool with a bout of bronchitis. Otherwise she would have sat under that tree and smoked till she smelled like Stewart, but as it was, all she could do was remember Andy, and shiver in the cold wind. Tom and J.T. muttered inside the hollow, contaminating it with their speculations and notebooks . . . No, that sacrilege was committed by whoever had snapped Andy Nilsson's neck.

And by the sheriff's men, who showed up a half hour later and actually wrapped yellow police line around the tree, like a Christo installation.

Eventually she popped her head in, to try again to emphasize to Tom the importance of Randy Unsel. Light played high up in the blackened chimney and shifted in the lower chamber. "Here he comes," said a strained voice, and the white sneakers appeared, followed by the rest of Andy, strapped to a board. Somebody had closed his eyes. They kept pushing him until he was clear of the hollow, and Enrique had to dive for the stretcher to prevent him from tobogganing down the slope toward the meadow in one last wild ride. She followed the crew that carried his sheet-draped form down the ridge, and then the deputies took her home.

Claire called Marie, who already knew about Andy through marital radar. "Oh, Claire, this is so awful," she said in a wobbly voice. "Tom's beside himself, I've never seen him so upset, and he didn't even know him. Andy, I mean. He seemed like such a sweet guy. Andy, I mean. He called me last night, you know, only I wasn't here. He said he had something to tell me but he couldn't talk about it on the phone."

"Yeah, he called me too."

They were both silent, wondering what sort of information Andy might have had to impart so urgently.

"Tom told me not to go out of the house alone," Marie said. "He didn't say that when Marcy was attacked. I don't understand why he's so freaked out now."

Well, of course he's freaked out, Claire wanted to shout. This changes everything! Andy was probably killed by someone in timber biz, so Marcy was, too. And that means we're all in danger after all!

"Oh, and Claire," Marie was saying, "Paul knows about Andy, and he wants us to meet at his house. Tomorrow night, seven-thirty. All of us."

"What's left of us," muttered Claire.

Chapter 28

At 6:30 P.M. on Thursday Claire was driving south—foothills left, valley right—from Fresno when she began to shiver uncontrollably in what was probably upper-nineties heat. Yesterday's malarial shakes had continued to afflict her throughout the day, like ague, she thought, whatever ague was—a good Old English word, anyway; she should run it by Ramón Covarrubias—or like Hodgkin's, for that matter. She had read that Hodgkin's disease was not genetic, but you never knew, and she had been exposed to some mighty dicey chemicals in the last few years. She should get some tests. But probably this was nothing but nerves and shock—post-traumatic stress disorder, as Sam had once called it—and would pass.

It would pass, but it was an intimation of mortality, or at least morbidity, a reminder that her body could surprise and betray her, that it had lost the infinite resilience of youth.

But the grow must go on, and she had just spent two hours talking to a pomologist up at the Kearney field station about biological control of codling moth. There she had learned that (1) the moth was introduced as early as 1747; (2) it laid its eggs on developing fruit; and (3) larvae entered the fruit through the calyx end, moved to the core to feed happily on seeds, then exited to pupate.

She didn't learn (4) what "codling" meant.

"I never thought about it!" Dan Tripp had said. "Want me to look it up?"

No, she said, not important. Some other time.

Her throat ached as if scraped raw by the words she had forced through it. She yearned for bed, and she looked longingly at the turnoff to the mountains as she whizzed past it on her way to Paul's.

The cars of the usual suspects were strewn in the dirt yard surrounding the Weissbergs' little house. If someone wanted to take out the Friends of the Redwoods, Claire thought as she pulled up beside Will's Trooper, this was the time to do it. Car bomb, Molotov cocktail . . . She shivered again and wondered what kind of shape Will was in.

When she walked into the room her eyes found his almost immediately. Wordlessly she settled next to him on the dark green Mission-style sofa, leaning against him more for warmth than affection.

"How are you doing?" she whispered almost noiselessly, because the room was silent.

"Not great." He shifted his weight, and Claire straightened and moved apart from him.

There was no small talk, no big talk. Claire saw Paul pick at the cheese and crackers, scan the room as if taking inventory, and then glance involuntarily at the door.

Then she saw Cheryl do the same, and after a moment she found herself also staring at the door.

They were all waiting for Marcy.

Paul cleared his throat. "I guess everyone's here but Mar . . . Marie."

The door banged open, and everyone gasped as if Marcy's spirit had in fact appeared, white and ghastly-eyed. But it was Tom Martelli, rosy and corporeal, followed by Marie.

"Oh. Tom wanted to say a few words before we leave tonight," Paul said, which simply made everyone more nervous so that when the door banged *again*, everyone jumped.

And there, stiff and self-conscious in the doorway, stood Dustin Gomez, whom Claire had thought never to see at these gatherings again.

Marie said to Dustin, "Oh, good. You got my message," and shot Claire a sly glance from under her eyelids, as if to say, I may be the bigot, but I was the only one who thought to call him.

"Yeah," he said truculently, and strode to a chair in the corner. His boots hammered the old hardwood floor that Naomi had refinished on hands and knees with Q-Tips. His neck was bare of his heavy silver collar.

"Well," said Paul again, "now we really are all here." *All that's left of us* lingered in the pause, so Paul hurried on to the next sentence. "I'll get right to the point. Andy Nilsson tried to get hold of some of us on Tuesday, the night Marcy died. We were still at the hospital, so he never did talk to anybody."

Will made the small, aimless movements of a man in pain. This meeting must reek of Marcy for him, thought Claire.

"But today I received this letter," Paul continued, hand-ing it to Hazel on his right. "It's postmarked yesterday. I figure Andy must have written it that night and mailed it yesterday."

"The day he died," murmured Marie.

"Right. And I assume it's what he wanted to talk to us about. I'll tell you what the letter says while it's going around," he continued. "Basically, Andy overheard Nelson Pringle offer Sierra Wood Products a quarter-million board feet out of a new green sale in Mint Meadow."

Claire didn't have the feel for a board foot that she did for, say, an ounce or a cc, but she knew from the general hissing of breath that this was dramatic news. Will groaned softly, and Hazel said, "That's a hell of a lot of trees," flipping her iron gray braid behind her.

"I know that land." A deep male voice, slightly slurred and lightly accented, almost Chicano, not quite. She looked into the dark corner of the room from which it had issued and realized with amazement that the speaker was Dustin Gomez, whom she had never heard utter a word. "It's next to the res. I'd say it's forty percent rock. You can't *get* a quarter-million board feet out of there."

Marie was looking at him placidly, but Claire suspected that the inner Marie, like the inner Claire, was sitting with her mouth hanging open.

But she didn't have time to dwell on Dustin's unexpected depth, including voice, because after a startled moment Hazel said, "Well, sure, unless they shave off every single goddamn tree right to the ground—"

"Which is a clear violation of the Memorandum of Understanding!" Paul said.

From the corner Dustin cleared his throat as if to add something, but Tom broke in.

"Paul, excuse me," he said, "but exactly who got a message from Andy Nilsson that night? Marie and Claire, I know. Anybody else? You and Naomi? Cheryl? Hazel?" he asked, going around the room. Everyone but Dustin and Will nodded assent.

"I don't know," Will muttered. "I haven't listened to Marcy's messages."

"But he didn't leave anyone any hint of what he wanted to talk about?" Tom said. Heads shook.

The actual letter came across Claire's lap, passed to her by Marie. It was handwritten in a script as twitchy and attenuated as Andy himself. "*Cher* Paul," it began, and Claire smiled.

I've been waffling over whether to pass this info on to the Sequoia group but I guess Marcy's death decided me. This probably means my job once again but like you said tonight Paul Marcy lived for the forest so this is the least I can do.

We've all known for a long time how cozy Sierra Wood Products and Nelson Pringle are, how Nelson lets the Genes take salvage that isn't salvage, take way more than their quota out of the Red Box green sale, make secret deals on green sales. But its just like at my last job, theres no way to prove it. Only last week I got lucky, I *happened* to be passing Nelson's office while he was on the phone discussing the details of a new green sale—at least that's what it sounded like to me. Naturally I stopped and listened! But I couldn't hear enough of the conversation. Then I got the brilliant idea of listening in from the phone in my office (just call me James Bond!). It worked! Well, to make a long story short Nelson is telling Gene Doughty about a new sale that's coming up, a forty-acre parcel near Mint Meadow. How about if Nelson asks for bids on a quarter-million

board feet? he says to Gene. Gene's quiet for a
minute, then he says, kind of shocked, A quarter-
million? (Well Paul he ought to be shocked—we
both know that's way too much timber to take out
of that parcel!) And Nelson says, that's what we
agreed, right? Can you believe it Paul? Nelson is *per-
suading* Gene to violate the Memorandum of Understanding! So finally Gene says Sure. Those assholes!
(Pardon my French.)

Andy went on: He had thought about telling somebody
in the group, but until now hadn't been able to decide.
He thought he could still do good things from within the
forest service, but if word got out that he'd blown the
whistle on Gene and Paul, he'd be back teaching seventh
grade general science. It ended, "Yours for the Forest"
and "*Au revoir.*" Claire's throat tightened and she quickly
passed the letter on to Will, who looked at it briefly and
laid it aside, fidgeted, then stood and crossed the room.

In a moment Dustin Gomez did likewise, and together
the two restless young men disappeared through the door.

"So," Paul was saying, looking at Tom, "seems pretty
straightforward to me. Andy wanted to blow the whistle
on the deal, to alert us so we could file suit before it was
too late. And then he was killed. Pretty convenient."

And then he was killed is right, thought Claire. Like
twelve hours afterward. In fact, there was something very
weird about the timing of all of this. Andy had heard
about the Mint Meadow sale a week ago; if he had been
killed because of it, why had the killer waited until yesterday? It suggested that someone had known that he
was about to blow the whistle.

But if the only people he had called were Friends of
the Redwoods—

"Well," Tom said slowly, "this murder is the county sheriff's case. Officially. Just like Marcy Hobbes's . . . death. But I don't know how, uh, how . . . appropriately!" happy with the word, "how appropriately J.T.'s following it up. And seeing as how my wife and you all may be at risk"—one loud communal heartbeat here—"I'm going to do what I can, and if any of you have any information or ideas that you want to communicate"—his voice dipped suddenly and he looked at the melting Brie, at the satiny wood floor, at his fingernails, anywhere but at Claire— "give me a call."

Claire was not surprised by this speech, but she was immensely relieved, even though part of her wanted to snarl, Oh, sure, *now* you're on board!

"Now, this letter," Tom was saying, "is news to me. So let me see if I have it straight. You all have been planning a lawsuit, is that right?"

"Right," said Cheryl.

"Now, if I've understood Marie over the past year, that suit is over . . . salvage logging?" Marie looked at him with amazement.

"Right," Hazel said. "Sierra Wood Products has been cutting more than they should on the national forest—"

"In other words, they've been robbing the taxpayer," Paul broke in, unable to resist the opportunity for rhetoric.

"Uh-huh. And Andy's letter is evidence of that?"

"No," Paul admitted. "The letter is about a whole other issue: secret agreements between the forest service and the timber industry, without due process or public input."

"And," Hazel said eagerly, "that's way more timber than they should be taking out of that parcel. Just like, um, Dustin, said. So that's a violation of the Memorandum of Understanding we signed with the forest service after our last lawsuit."

"So you'd probably initiate a lawsuit over this, too?"

"Probably," Paul said.

"So that would make how many times you've sued the Genes?"

Hazel and Cheryl, who'd started it all, looked at each other. "Four times," Cheryl said finally.

Claire thought she knew what Tom was getting at. Gene Doughty had weathered three lawsuits, each resulting in temporary restraining orders and eventual minor restrictions, each a royal pain in the ass for Sierra Wood Products. But would one more lawsuit constitute a motive for murder?

"Andy did the same thing at the last place he worked, in Idaho," she said, "and they just reassigned him."

"Mmm," said Tom, rising. "Well, like I say, anybody gets any information or bright ideas, let me know. I'll pass 'em on to J.T."

"J.T.!" his wife said scornfully. "J.T. and the Genes are hand in spoon."

"Glove, and that's the best I can do, Marie. Oh," Tom said, pausing at the door, "it might be a good idea if you all took some precautions over the next few weeks. Avoid deserted places, lock your doors, that sort of thing. Those of you have guns, keep 'em handy. Those that don't might think about acquiring one." And he was gone.

Claire rushed after him.

"Tom," she called. "I just wanted to mention something."

He halted, and the Weissbergs' porch light showed him arrested in a posture of resignation. "Yes?" he said, polite and resentful, waiting for the I-told-you-so.

"The timing of Andy's death bothers me," she said.

"Yeah," Tom growled. "I already figured on finding out exactly who else Nilsson called Tuesday night."

"Oh. Well, if you find out, could you let me know?"

"Be delighted." He lifted himself into the Blazer and backed out.

Claire was shivering again. How could I be cold? she thought, and then remembered how cold Andy had been. And she had never even touched him, not once, while he was warm and alive. Abruptly she had a wild need to touch all her friends *now*, this night, before she went to sleep—to brush their hands, smooth their hair away from their faces, anything—because you never knew.

This is kind of a New Age idea for me, she thought as she walked back toward the house. Must be contagious; what's next? Crystals and shamans? She peeked through the small window in the front door.

They were all there, her friends, what remained of them. The Rembrandt lamplight flowed over them like golden oil. So she stepped back inside and took Naomi's small cool hand between hers, and then Paul's, and then Marie's, moving through the group as if down a receiving line. Paul was startled, then seemingly understood the impulse and pressed back. Cheryl crooked an arm around her shoulders in a half-hug.

Missed a couple, but that will have to do, Claire thought, slipping out into the starless Valley night.

Chapter 29

Along the mountain road gray leaves of manzanitas gleamed briefly in the sweep of her headlights like dollops of wet snow. Claire had to blink and think to remember it was summer. Amazing that crops which had evolved halfway across the globe kept track of the seasons, blooming and leafing and fruiting and seeding and going into dormancy like living clocks. Because Claire herself occasionally lost track of the time of year, at night, when the heat had abated. Or flying back to the East Coast, when she would look down on the Bonneville Flats or the beaches of one of the Great Lakes and think, snowdrifts—and then remind herself that no, it was August, and even in Michigan it didn't snow in August.

At home the Bisquick perimeter around the crawl space, a sprinkling of hoarfrost, was smooth and unfootprinted.

*   *   *

Tom called her Friday morning, flabbergasting her with a request that she stop by. So on the way to work she pulled up behind his Blazer and walked around to the back of his office.

He was studying a familiar-looking blurry photocopy. "That's the guy who escaped from Corcoran," she said, studying it upside down.

"Geraldo Ramirez," Tom agreed. "Kern County Sheriff's Department picked him up by Lake Isabella yesterday afternoon, and J.T. went down to question him."

"To *question* him," she echoed, dropping into the gray plastic chair. "You mean, about *Andy?*"

"Andy, or Marcy Hobbes. Prob'ly both, I reckon." The pencil was out again, vibrating between thumb and forefinger.

"Can I see the flyer?" she said suddenly.

"Sure." He shoved it in her direction.

"Alias San Luis, Pelon," she read again. "Controlled substance . . . 21 to life . . . missing two fingertips—Wait a minute. This guy weighed two hundred and fifty pounds!"

The pencil came to a halt, pointing straight down. "Yep," he said.

"So how could he . . . I mean, he couldn't, there's no way he could have moved Andy into the cave! He wouldn't have fit through the opening!"

"Don't seem like it."

"What does J.T. say about that?"

The pencil began its slow arc again. "Well, I did point it out to him. But he said Ramirez could have just pushed the body through, that he didn't have to go through himself."

"That's ridiculous! He was all stretched out like—like he was taking a nap." *So white, so cold, so fair . . .*

"Pelon could've lost some weight since the circular," Tom was saying. "But anyway, that ain't why I called you. The reason I called you . . . see, Marie tells me . . ." He trailed off, looking uncomfortable. "Marie tells me you been lookin' into this," he said firmly. "So if you got any information that might help, I'd surely appreciate it," this said in a rapid mumble like a kid delivering a speech at the 4-H banquet.

No gloating, she told herself sternly. "I didn't get very far, so I can't help you much. At first I was going on the assumption that whoever *attacked* Marcy"—she stressed the word slightly; that didn't count as a gloat—"was somebody from timber biz. They had the obvious motive." Can I tell him about the JAFGR Scale? she wondered. "But Marie probably told you that the major timber players had an alibi for the time of the attack. Except for Randy Unsel, and you know he—"

"Was working up where Nilsson was found. Go on." His eyes had strayed out the window.

"Well, later I was thinking about Marcy's men. Because I knew them better and because I was trying to follow your line of thinking." Flattery had no impact on Tom's round bland face, but his eyes had swiveled in her general direction again. "And it seemed to me you were looking at the attack on Marcy as a crime of passion."

He nodded. "I think of violence as hot or cold"—his own sort of JAFGR scale, she thought—"and I thought this was hot."

Cold. There was that word again.

Tom, too? Tom was a friend—probably against his wishes, but still . . . Did she have to touch Tom?

That was a daunting thought. But yes, even Tom.

But she'd have to ambush him. "Because of the bouquet. Because she didn't try to defend herself," she said, rising from her chair.

"Right."

"You figured she knew and trusted her assailant," moving around behind him.

"Right again. It wasn't only the physical evidence; it was the kind of woman Marcy— What are you doing?" She had laid a casual hand on his shoulder.

"Nothing," she said. "I just wanted to look at the circular again."

He shrugged violently and shoved off from his desk like a swimmer. "Well, just *ask*, okay? You're gettin' to be like Marcy, always *touchin'* folks!"

"Sorry, I'm sorry," she said rapidly, face hot. "I didn't mean . . . It's just that . . . Andy was so cold, and I . . ." *Like Marcy.* "Oh!"

"Oh what?"

"You . . . you and Marcy . . ." was all she said, but Tom jumped to his feet.

"No!" he said, and then, for the first time in their acquaintance, Tom overdisclosed. "I didn't do nothin', okay?"

"I—"

"I love Marie! I would never, never . . ."

"Look—"

"Blowin' in your ear was just Marcy's way of sayin' howdy!" He was practically shouting now, and she had to wave her hands like a referee to get his attention.

"Tom, I don't really care what happened with Marcy!" she said. I'm amazed, I'm incredibly curious, but I don't really care. "I'm just wondering if it could've affected your judgment—"

"Nothin' happened, and that's God's truth," he re-

peated without hearing her. "She made me feel like it
had, but it was all her."

He sat again, slowly. "She was in here one day, to ask
about how she could get an injunction enforced, and she
come around behind me—just like you"—he said bale-
fully, "and then I feel something kinda tickling the side of
my face. Her hair. And then she *kisses* me. Real quick.
Right here," he said, rubbing his temple as if his head
hurt. "I look up, thinking I imagined it, and she's smiling
like a cat. In front of the window, with the light behind
her.

"I don't know what it was about that woman," he went
on, gazing out the window as if seeing her again. "To my
mind she wasn't as pretty as my wife, and she had that
silly frizzy hair. Christ, Marie even went and curled her
own nice hair so's to look like Marcy. And she was wearing this dress that wasn't nothing special, like a white
nightgown"—a three-hundred-dollar nightgown, thought
Claire—"but she was . . . she was . . ."

Formidable, thought Claire, remembering Andy's word.
But "seductive" was what she said. "She even seduced
me. Oh, not literally," she added hurriedly, seeing Tom's
face. "She just made me want her to notice me. She'd pay
attention to me and then snub me. It's an effective technique."

"Yeah, well, it worked on me. 'Sorry,' she says, just like
you." Tom aimed a nasty blue eye at Claire—"'Sorry, but
I've been wanting to do that for a long time.' Well, I
knowed that was pure bullshit. She wanted somethin' out
of me."

"Why?" Claire interrupted. "Maybe she just wanted to
make a little contact." She paused. "Like me, just now."

"Bullshit," he said again, roughly. "I don't know what
touchy-feely crap *you're* up to, but Marcy didn't make

contact with no paunchy middle-aged policeman. Nossir. This was strictly business." His voice ended in a little sigh.

"What business? What could you have done for her?"

He gripped the pencil and brought it down in a short chopping movement. "Christ, I don't know. I don't think *she* knew. It was just sort of a reflex, an investment that might pay off sometime. Quid pro quo. I mean, after that she pretty much ignored me. Like you say."

Claire didn't know what to think. Marcy had liked men, and maybe she just couldn't resist Tom's baby blues. But if her approach was calculated—business, as Tom said—if Marcy wanted to take him out of the game in case he lined up with the Genes sometime, then she had played him perfectly. If she'd come on to him in a really blatant manner, well, Tom was no fool, she would have pissed him off. Turned him on, maybe, but pissed him off. But that little kiss, sweet, ambiguous . . . it was perfect.

"Well," he was saying, "I got to say I did think about her. Some. And," he added pleasantly, looking at Claire, "if you tell Marie I'll rip your lungs out."

"There's nothing to tell. You behaved like a gentleman."

"Yeah. I did."

"Just like with Betsy," Claire blurted.

"What? Betsy? You mean my neighbor? What's she got to do with anything?"

"Nothing. Only if you love Marie, you might tell her sometime."

He ignored her. "Anyway," he said, "as far as my judgment goes, I don't know exactly what you mean. But I do know that's why I figured the assault on Marcy for a crime of passion. 'Cause me, I'm a sweet guy, but she was playin' a very dangerous—"

"Assault! You knew it was an attack all along!" Claire exclaimed.

"'Course I did! I ain't J.T."

"So why didn't you tell me?"

"Claire, I got no obligation to let you in on my inner thoughts. About *anything*. But now, with this other murder . . . well, it looks like I might have been wrong. Like it might have been some timber business after all. And like I said, I would be, um, grateful"—he gargled the word—"for any more information you got."

"You'll let me know when you find out about the calls Andy made?"

"Delighted," he said sullenly.

She told him what she knew about Will, Stewart, Dustin. "And then there's Jason," she said reluctantly.

"Who?"

"Jason Gomez. Dustin's nephew." She told him about her encounters with Daisy's son, regretting every syllable as it escaped her.

Chapter 30

She felt that she'd put in a full day of work by the time she got to the station, but in fact it was only 8:30. But there was already a fax on County Ag stationery lying on her desk. Something about codling moth, she thought, starting to move it to the appropriate pile. Then she read more closely.

8:00 A.M. Claire, it's not the moth, it's the apple!

Codling: a cooking apple of a long tapering shape; formerly any hard or unripe apple. From *querdlying*, "hard." Middle English, derivation unknown—possibly *coeur de lion*. "A codling, e'er it went his eys in / would strait become a golden pippin." Swift, "Midas."

Ramón

P.S. Cod: a bag, or the scrotum, Old English.
Hence *codpiece*.

It was a delightful morning greeting, and she called
Ramón to tell him so. But he was already out in the field,
and so she moved Andy and Marcy to the bottom of her
stack and set about making her own field calls. Botryo-
shpaeria blight, pistachios, Tierra Buena. Brown rot, nec-
tarines, Lemoncove. Brown rot, almonds, Richgrove
(which wasn't). Something mysterious, peaches, Famoso
(which wasn't). Back to the station by three o'clock.
Ramón had returned her call. Returned *his* call; he was
gone again.

So. Look up weird stuff on peaches. Could it be an-
thracnose? Hadn't been seen out here in twenty years;
could put Famoso on the map. Definitely get an article
out of it, anyway. *Article!* She cringed and started typing.
Ramón still not in at six.

But he called just as she was packing up to leave, and
she was surprised by the bump of anticipation and pleasure she felt at the sound of his deep voice.

"Hey," she said. "Wearing your codpiece?"

"Hell, yes. Never go out without it. The other fellows
would laugh at me. Listen, you want to go out to see
Daisy Gomez tomorrow?"

"Tomorrow? Tomorrow's Saturday." It was not unprece-
dented to work on a weekend, but neither was it desirable.

"Only day I could schedule it, and I've got to help her
with some weird BIA funding. And I know you talked to
the pomologist, so I thought you might want to come
along."

She thought about it. The various Gomezes were certainly a draw, as was Ramón himself. They could talk about word derivations—

"We could make it early," he was saying. "I've got a softball game with my kids."

Oh. Kids. Married. Of course. She had forgotten. "Sure."

"It's my weekend," he said, then hesitated. "Miranda and I are trying out this arrangement."

"I talked to Dan up at Kearney for a long time," Claire said. It was nine on Saturday morning, and she and Ramón were winding up the long gold-and-gray canyon to the reservation. Claire was driving. "He said it was really hard to get rid of a heavy codling moth infestation without spraying for a year at least. Ideally you time the applications to egg hatch. Oh, sorry." She had brushed his knee as she shifted down around a sharp curve.

He straightened his leg. "But if Daisy sprays, she can't sell to organic markets. Even after she stops, she has to wait two years." He looked out his window at the lumps of houses, lumps of cars, lumps of granite. "How about pheromone confusion? Disrupt the little buggers' sex life?"

"Not as effective in the San Joaquin as along the coast, according to Dan," she said, "especially if there's a heavy infestation."

"Shit." He drummed his fingers on his thigh. A biologist's hands: deft, articulated, a little grubby. "Things looked so good. I was going to have her put in some Fujis; they're really hot right now."

"It's too late to save this year's crop in any case," Claire said. "But there is one thing she could do next year. It's really labor-intensive, though. Three person-hours per tree."

"What?"

"Bag 'em."

"Bag 'em? The fruit?" said Ramón.

"Mm-hm. Thin the trees and put little paper bags around the remaining apples. Dan showed me an article; it's amazingly effective—for a small orchard, of course."

"Bags," he muttered. "Bags, cods . . . Cods! Cods on the codlings!" he said happily. "Why not? Get the whole Gomez clan out there! That's the point of a big family." Claire couldn't quite imagine Dustin Gomez bagging apples, but she took his point. "That's a great idea, Claire! Maybe keep that kid of hers out of trouble, too."

Was Jason in trouble? Did Ramón know something she didn't? Before she could ask, he said abruptly, "You miss the East Coast?"

"Yes," she said, startled. "How did you know? I mean, that I'm not a native?"

"Accent," he said briefly.

Claire was deeply insulted. *She* had an accent? These Californians had accents—or anti-accents, like antimatter; a real accent was just too much trouble for them. They drawled their vowels, slurred their consonants. They had lazy tongues . . . She suddenly tasted Will Brecker's mouth.

"Plus I asked Kate Dolmovic about you," Ramón was saying. "Anyway, I suppose you miss the seasons."

"I do. This place is exhausting, I mean, the growing season never stops, there's no downtime. You get people through dormant sprays and bud and bloom-time rot and fruit-set and summer pests and harvest panic and post-harvest pruning and discing"—her voice rose in mock hysteria—"and you go back to your office and sharpen a pencil and the damn trees are blooming again! You know those experiments where they wake people up every fifteen minutes so they can't dream, and they gradually go insane? That's what it's like out here. Whereas in the East, the land sleeps. Snow," she said. "Snow is like sleep. Like dreaming."

Ramón was laughing immoderately. "How did you end up as a farm adviser?" he said. "You sound like my old crowd of dyspeptic poets."

She loved that "dyspeptic," and turned to him with a smile, but they were coming around the curve of wild horses and she had to pay attention. "Me!" she said. "I'm not the one who taught Chaucer. I've always wanted to be a biologist! How did you end up here?"

"My spelling was bad."

"What?"

"I set out for the etymology department but wound up in entomology. No," he added over her dutiful laugh, "not really. Business school to please my parents, comparative lit to please me. Then I started to feel the tug of my campesino blood, I guess, and got a second degree in agricultural economics.

I could have told him, thought Claire, that with those hands he was doomed.

"Anyway," he went on, "this is the perfect job for me. I feel like I'm genuinely helping people—helping to create a community, really, if that's not too corny. And the work uses a lot of me."

"Really?" Claire sometimes felt that her job used only about a demitasse of her, of the essential Claire, and the rest got into trouble.

"Sure," Ramón said, and counted off on his fingers: "My ag training, obviously, and my business background, to help people get loans and to organize co-ops. And my Spanish, which was pretty rusty; I'm third-generation, and my parents didn't really speak it except with my *abuelos.*

And I'm always introduced to new cultures, too, and new languages, which I love, obviously. And then there's the food," he said, rubbing his solid gut. "My clients feed me. Weird shit, some of it, but good."

It all sounded like the Peace Corps. Sign me up, she thought. "Listen," she said hesitantly, but then the car bobbled loudly over the cattle guard. They were there.

Daisy's Pinto was on strike, so they picked her up at the community center and took her back out to Uncle Robert's trailers. As the three of them walked down the hill to the orchard, a sturdy figure came tramping up toward them.

"Yo, Robert!" Daisy hailed him.

Uncle Robert wasn't what Claire expected, any more than Daisy had been. She had imagined a stringy old desert rat—leather face, week-old stubble, the gleam of a gold tooth. Robert in the flesh was pink and seal-sleek, like his niece. With his silver-rimmed aviator glasses he looked like an aerospace engineer.

"Hey, Petunia! Who's this?" he said, walking straight to Claire and taking her arm.

"She's a farm adviser, you old goat! She's here to help with the apples! Claire, Raymond, this is Robert Cinders, my uncle. King of the Airstream."

Claire extricated her arm and stuck out her hand. Robert took the hand between his two and adroitly tucked it back into the crook of his elbow. "Let me show you what I'm building up here." She cast Ramón a pleading look, but he just grinned at her.

Actually, she was curious to see what Uncle Robert had added to his junkyard Ozymandias. "Sure," she said. "I'll catch up with you folks down at the trees."

But they passed the trail to the equipment graveyard, hugging the hill, climbing a ridge. As they picked their

way down the other side, Robert seized the opportunity
to clamp her arm tightly to his side.

"Puttin' in another pad over there," he said, waving toward a little hump that had been sliced off like the tip of
a thumb. "And down here"—he guided her into a shallow bowl—"I've got some major earthmoving to do. See,
the water collects in this little hollow, so I've kinda filled
it in." He indicated the hard froth of dirt, shiny with mica,
that had been piled in the middle of the path.

"Why?" asked Claire.

"Why? That water would flood the road!"

"What road?"

"Oh, see, I'm gonna put a road through here so I can
get up to the new trailer pads. And over here," he said,
dragging her toward a tangle of greenery, "I'm kinda di-
vertin' this streambed." A little seasonal watercourse,
marked by elderberry and willow and alder shoots, now
slammed into a dike of raw earth and gravel and slash
pile.

"Why?" she said again.

"For my *road!*" he exclaimed, dropping her arm and
looking back up the hill, his eyes receding behind the silver rims as if he saw a four-level interchange instead of a
cattle track. Or maybe not; it was hard to know whether
he was the Robert Moses of Kaweah County or just a
major league putterer, or if there was a difference. In any
case, Claire felt she was in the presence of some fundamental male mystery.

"Well, this was interesting, Mr. Cinders," she said, "and
I wish you luck with your projects"—as in I hope you
jump clear when your backhoe falls of a cliff—"but I'd
better get over to the orchard."

"I'll walk with you. I'm puttin' in another pad up
here. . . ."

A hawk cruised overhead and she followed it into the tender morning sunlight, tuning back in when she heard him say, "Dustin told me. Funny, I went to school with Gene Doughty, Sr., and I would have said—"

"I'm sorry Mr. Cinders," she said sharply. "What were you saying?"

"Robert, call me Robert. I've filled in that little marsh over there."

Filling a wetland, thought Claire: violation of Section 404 of the Clean Water Act. But what she said was "I meant about Gene Doughty."

"Oh. Well, Dustin, he's my nephew—or nephew-in-law, or . . . hey, you know what? I don't think there is a word for it, you know, when somebody's the brother of the jackass your niece married."

"English is funny. Did Dustin tell you something about Gene Doughty?"

"Oh. Yeah. Dustin. He's a strange one, ol' Dustin. Likes to party, likes his sex, drugs and rock and roll. 'Specially his sex," he said, leering. "But he's got this thing about trees. I mean, to me a tree's *for* something—for firewood or lumber or even shade, for God's sake. Otherwise, take 'er out. But Dustin, he did one of those, what do you call it, vision quests, or some damn Indian thing, up in the mountains, and he come back talking about the trees like they was his relatives. Damnedest thing. Now, over on that little rise—"

"But Dustin talked to you about Gene Doughty," Claire said desperately.

"Oh. Yeah. Told me he heard Gene bid on more board feet than he can take out of a parcel up the hill. And what I said was, Gene must be losin' it, must be gettin' old. I've never known Gene to make a bad deal in his life. Hey, Petunia!" he called as they joined Ramón and

Daisy. "Well, nice talkin' to you. I got to get back to work."

"So," said Daisy with a grin, "how was Uncle Robert?"

"Um." She wanted a moment to sift through what Robert had said; she felt she had glimpsed something useful somewhere in that whole trailerful of conversation. But Daisy and Ramón were waiting for interaction. "He certainly has a lot of energy," she said. "Maybe you could enlist him to help you bag. I don't know if Ramón talked to you about that?"

"Yeah. I think we could manage it, but I don't know about Robert helping. It don't have enough . . . enough . . ."

"Scope?" suggested Claire. "Vision? Glamour?"

"Toys," said Daisy. "It don't require hardly any time on a big machine that goes *vroo-ooom*."

"None at all," Claire agreed solemnly. Ramón looked puzzled, and finally laughed.

They circumnavigated Daisy's little orchard, pushing through the thigh-high thickets of lacy vetch and clover that flourished between the rows and planning where to put in the Fujis, then walked downslope to her vegetable plot, which was right on the bank of the river: Japanese eggplants, tomatoes, orange and purple peppers, specialty squash, all looking good. . . .

Claire kept staring off toward the mountains, where the midmorning sky had flattened to a matte blue. Dustin and his vision quest. It appeared Dustin actually had a commitment to the forest and wasn't just an adjunct of Marcy. This was *interesting*, but was it important?

The three of them drove back to the reservation, where the plaza dozed in its eternal airless heat and dust. Claire imagined a pond-sized high-pressure system stalled forever overhead, like the rain cloud that followed the black-mooded character in Li'l Abner. Li'l Abner, Pogo, Nancy and Sluggo—slow and quaint and ancient, not part of the universe of RAM and virtual reality, and yet she had learned to read from their thought balloons, sitting on her father's lap. Her sense of humor, of politics—hell, probably her intellect and moral sense too—had been formed by those antediluvian characters.

She was standing in the shade of the cottonwood staring at the community center bulletin board; inside, Ramón and Daisy plumbed the mysteries of BIA loans. From the far end of the building came a rhythmic thumping. *Whump. Whump-whump.* Pause. *Do-iing!* *Whump-whump. Whump.* Pause. *Do-ing!* Someone shooting baskets. And missing.

Dustin had said you couldn't *get* a quarter-million board feet out of the Mint Meadow parcel. So was that old horse trader Gene Senior finally losing it? Had his business sense finally deserted him?

And how could this have anything to do with the death of Andy Nilsson?

She had read all three bulletins three times, and was trying to decide between walking up to the church and seeking out Daisy and Ramón, when the thumping stopped. "Shit!" she heard, and looked up to see a tall young man approaching along the concrete walk. It was a second or two before she realized it was Jason Gomez.

His exclamation had not been for her; he was trying to palm a basketball and it kept squirting out of his hand, forcing him to run a few steps and retrieve it. Because of this he didn't see her, at least to recognize, until he was almost on her.

She expected him to bolt, and obviously he thought about it, tensed, poised. But he hesitated, searching her face. Then the ball dropped, rolled a few feet, and stopped in the dust. He went after it and didn't come back.

Chapter 31

When she dropped Ramón at his car at the County Ag office in Parkerville, he said, "I gotta run off right now, but maybe we can converge somewhere in the tri-county area next week for lunch."

"Sure," she said, and was pleased by his warm parting handshake.

Since the day was mostly shot, she went on into the office and finished her goddamned article at 5:20. At six she wearily took the last curve and coasted down her drive.

The red light on her message machine blinked at her from across the room: Sam. He was taking the kids on a picnic up to the fire tower tomorrow afternoon. Did Claire want to come? Linda, he added, was visiting her folks.

Well, of course she wanted to go! But she forced herself to be severe when she returned the call. "Aren't you the teeniest bit nervous about taking the kids into the mountains when there's a murderer on the loose?"

"Murderer?" he repeated vaguely. "Oh, Andy Nilsson. No. Tom said they caught him."

"What?" Her stomach plummeted. Had something happened in the last twelve hours? "Caught who?"

"Ramirez. The escaped prisoner from Corcoran; they found him in Nevada today. So there's nothing to worry about."

"Tom said that this guy was the man who murdered Andy Nilsson?"

"Um . . . I can't remember. I think all he said was they caught the escaped prisoner. Period."

"Sam, Tom knows damn well Ramirez didn't kill Andy. There's no way he could have—"

"Look," Sam said, with that exasperated click of the tongue that she remembered so well, "I'll take my forty-five if that will make you feel any better. The kids haven't been up to the fire tower since they were little."

"They're still little."

"Do you want to come or not? It's your decision," he said, then paused. "I . . . we would all like your company."

There was a long silence while Claire sorted through various thoughts, some pleasurable, most uncharitable. Such as: You son of a bitch, you dumped me for your kids and you won't even take care of them! Finally she said, "I'd better come."

"You'd *better* come?" he echoed, mocking the grim decisiveness of her voice. "Why? To protect us?"

"Maybe."

"Guess what these are."

It was Sunday afternoon. The four of them, Sam and Claire and Terry and Shannon, were taking the long way to the fire station trail, circling counterclockwise from the trailhead. This route took them through a shaded saddle that lay between the fire station's peak and its more spectacular twin, the Needles, and also through a grove of giant sequoias. Claire had stooped to snatch up a mature cone and tap it against her palm. And now she held her hand out to the boys, displaying the tiny brown flakes like fish food.

"Those?" said a bored Shannon. "Those are sequoia seeds. Dad showed us a long time ago, when we were little." He hitched himself up and intoned, "The wonder of nature," in as deep a voice as his eleven-year-old-larynx could produce, "These tiny seeds, no bigger than a baby's fingernail, grow into these"— gesturing stiffly— "majestic trees."

Terry was doubled over with hysteria, and Claire giggled. "Okay. Mr. Wizard," she said, "do you know how much they weigh?"

"How much they *weigh*?" he repeated, saving face by a show of incredulity at the lameness of grown-ups.

"Yeah. There are ninety-one thousand of these in a pound." She had looked this up one day.

Terry looked suitably impressed, but then his brother said with heavy sarcasm, "Ninety-one thousand? Not ninety-one thousand and *two*?" and so of course Terry smirked and said, "Not ninety-one thousand and *three*?"

A smart mouth, Claire remembered Daisy saying, was a sure sign of male puberty. Sam better watch out: adolescence loomed. "Nope," she answered with dignity, "ninety-one thousand. I'm a scientist; I'm paid to know these things."

"Come on!" Sam urged them from a hundred yards up the path. "I'm ready to eat!" He had stopped at a spot no better or worse than any other on the trail and was opening his pack. "*Zauschneria!*" he exclaimed.

"Gesundheit!" Claire muttered, but she looked for and found the patch of scarlet California fuchsia, *Zauschneria californica*, like flames licking the base of the white granite.

The boys settled in the middle of the trail itself, having immediately realized that this was the only level surface, while Claire shifted her bottom on the steep slope in search of an angle of repose. "We passed some flat boulders that would make a better table," she complained.

Sam shook his head. "I want to stop here."

"Why?"

"It's a very special place," he said.

She couldn't disagree. It was just that all places were special at that moment, on that trail. They were in an open dry forest of lodgepole pine, fir, and sequoia, and at eight thousand feet the air was almost chilly in the shade—an exciting sensation for those enduring a Valley summer—and, in the sun, warm and aromatic, smelling of pine needles, duff, and artichokes. The artichoke smell was mountain misery, *Chamaebatia*, the lacy, dense brush they had been kicking through for the last hour.

Aromas and birdsong. Once the sandwiches were distributed there was almost complete silence—even the boys were quiet—except for the birds. Sam began to identify them by their calls—dusky grouse, wood pee-wee, solitary vireo—to Claire's mixed feelings; she was a sucker for this Mark Trail stuff, but she didn't want to notice Sam's charm. She wanted to notice that he was always late, and always walked fifty yards ahead of everyone, and made arbitrary and dictatorial decisions about where to stop for lunch. Anyway, soon their ears learned where to tune in, and there were too many birds for him to name.

Then suddenly, as Claire and the boys were unwrapping Power Bars, there were two loud, melodious *whoo-whoo*s, one right after the other, from just behind them. They all whirled to see Sam, looking mighty pleased with himself.

"That was you, Dad!" Terry said accusatorily.

His father pursed his lips and emitted another liquid *whoo-whoo-whoo*, and then a long ascending whistle. Claire was impressed, despite her resolve.

"I knew it was you!" Terry said, and Sam nodded.

"That one was me," he said, "But the next one—"

Whoo. Whoo-whoo. Whoo! No mistaking this; it had a certain presence and authority that Sam had lacked, not to mention that it came from twenty feet above them. Chins shot up as they all searched the branches.

"There!" Shannon whispered excitedly, pointing to the lowest branch of a young sequoia directly behind them.

Claire squinted. In the foreground a spiderweb twisted and glinted, spanning the space between branches; beyond that . . . Yes, there it was, buried among the needles: a pale, eared ovoid. She thought of the owl on Marcy's door, then of Marcy, then of Andy, then of the nameless killer in the woods, whom she'd totally forgotten after ten minutes at this altitude, and then of these tender young humans. She felt behind her for her pack: the barrel of her CO_2 pistol poked up between the trail mix and the space blanket. Absurd.

When Sam laid something heavy and cold in her hand she flinched, thinking it was his service revolver. But it was binoculars, so she focused and scanned the world, which became a stack of two-dimensional screens, one behind the other, like vaudeville scenery. She was looking for villains, but what she finally caught in her sights was the big white bird. He looked demoralized and unkempt, like a sick pigeon.

"Southern spotted owl," Sam whispered from behind her. "I saw him earlier this week. That's why I wanted to eat here. He's still a fledgling."

That accounted for the rumpled look—baby down amid the grown-up feathers. A teenage owl. While she watched him, he twisted his head like a lid on a jar and looked straight at them. As if made uncomfortable by the unblinking gaze, Sam moved a couple of feet away from Claire.

"He's looking at me!" Terry cried excitedly.

"Shhh!" scolded his older brother, while the bird flapped its wings in alarm. "Do you know why they have to move their whole head to look to the side?" Shannon asked, then said, without waiting, "Because their eyes are so big they fill up the whole skull! There's no room for eye muscles! Right, Dad?"

"Right," said Sam, and laid a hand on Shannon's shoulder.

They sat watching the owl for a good forty minutes, Sam and the boys waiting for him to fly away as a signal for them to continue their journey, Claire listening tensely. Where before there had been only the chatter and warble of birds, now there seemed to be a continuous shuffle of underbrush.

But the owl stayed put and so did the hypothetical stalker, and eventually Claire said, "It's six-thirty. Shouldn't we go on to the fire tower?" High ground, she thought; easy to defend. Then she felt ridiculous.

"Yeah!" the kids chorused. So they shrugged into their day packs and continued their upward spiral, striking the official trail again after about twenty minutes. The forest was full of branches cracking under feet not their own, and Claire looked back over her shoulder at every switchback.

But then they came to the iron stairs and began their ringing ascent, and she began to relax. She had a three-hundred-sixty view.

"Will Lainie let us come in and listen to her short-wave?" Shannon asked between strenuous breaths.

"Sure," Sam said.

But by the time they had climbed the multiple flights of steps—fifteen, twenty, ten, twelve, the kids trudging and whimpering up the last flight—the lookout was deserted. Sam rattled the door handle and said unnecessarily, "I guess Lainie's skedaddled for the day. It's already seven, but I thought she might stick around longer on the weekend."

They all pressed their faces up against the north-facing windows and wished themselves in the cozy-looking room, but in the end they were still on the outside. Deflecting the boys' disappointed whines, Sam pointed eastward. "Look! There's somebody climbing the Needles!"

Claire leaned her forearms on the wooden railing and scanned the ragged spire from bottom to top, picking out dark seams, shadows, a stunted tree growing out of sheer rock.

"About twenty yards down from the top—see?" Sam handed the binocs to Terry and stood behind him to help him focus. "In a blue shirt. He better move it if he's going to make it before dark."

Now Claire had him—a spider on the west face, moving so slowly it was not movement at all, except that now he was even with the tree, and now he was above it, crawling up the black thread of the fracture. "What do they do when they get to the top?" she asked Sam.

"Oh, there's a perfectly good trail that runs down the ridge and brings you right back to the saddle. Takes about fifteen minutes." He grinned. "Rock climbing is not what you'd call an efficient sport."

"Dad, can Terry and me go rock climbing sometime?" Shannon asked.

"Sure. When I'm safe in my grave."

While Shannon and Terry wrangled over the binoculars Claire and Sam moved around the corner of the catwalk and sat facing south, with their backs against the lookout. A swirl of high haze approached from the far horizon, led by four parallel linear clouds that looked as if a claw had raked the blue fabric and the stuffing was spilling out.

"Must be some moisture coming up from the Gulf," Sam said.

"Did you bring your gun?" Claire said abruptly.

"That's a hell of a question coming from you!"

"Did you?"

"No. I forgot. Anyway, you're being ridiculous."

"*Ridiculous!*" she repeated, wondering whether this was in fact true. "Sam, there have been two murders up here in the last two weeks!"

"Marcy Hobbes was not murdered. And they caught the other guy."

"Yes she was, and no they didn't, and you didn't pay any attention to what I told you! That's what's *ridiculous!*" she hissed, her conviction increasing with her anger. "Though I guess it shouldn't surprise me!"

Her overheated whisper was perfectly audible. The boys were unnaturally silent, probably listening avidly to every word.

Shannon poked his head around the corner. "I'm hungry. Can we go now?"

"Not right this minute," Sam said. "I'm talking to Claire."

"When can we go? There's nothing to do up here!"

"I said in a *minute*, Shannon! Read the comics you brought!" and Shannon retreated.

"How could you bring them up here?" Claire resumed.

Ominous silence. Then, "What are you saying? That I would put my kids in danger?"

"No," she said recklessly. "I'm saying you *have* put them in danger. Just because you didn't respect me enough to take my information seriously!"

The attack on two simultaneous fronts halted Sam's momentum, and in the instant it took him to regroup they both heard a metallic ring, like a giant marimba. Then another.

Someone was climbing the stairs.

Sam said, "It's probably other hikers. Everybody comes up here on the weekends."

"Yes."

"Or Lainie. Maybe she forgot something."

Ring. Ring. "Maybe."

He rose to his feet. "Shannon, Terry," he called, "why don't you come around here? The light's better."

"Can't we go down, Dad?" Terry's voice.

"In a minute." Sam was reaching up under the eaves for something that hung hidden there, wrestling with it, finally pulling down a long pole with a little basket at the end, like a miniature fruit-picker. "Lainie uses this to change the lightbulb up by the flagpole," he said in a puzzled voice, staring at it as if he couldn't imagine why he was holding it.

The boys came around from the east to the south side of the catwalk while Claire moved around the east side to the north, where the stairway ended. She delved into her pack and wrapped her fingers around the butt of her little gun, which might actually be useful here. It had enough kick to knock him/her/it off balance.

Ring. Ring. Pause. That was the next-to-the-last landing.

"Hello?" she called. No answer. Sam had come up behind her, holding the lightbulb-changer like a quarterstaff, and the boys crowded behind him.

"What's wrong, Daddy?" Terry said. "Why are you holding that pole?"

"Nothing's wrong. Shannon, take your brother back around to the other side."

Ring. Ring. He was on the last flight now. Claire could hear his breathing, not harsh and desperate like her own, but little rhythmic grunts. "Hello?" she called again. Twelve steps, she thought. Ten. Nine. Eight. Any second now they'd be able to see him.

Chapter 32

A head poked above the top step. Eyes the color of a High Sierra sky regarded them blankly. Seafaring, or rather, skyfaring eyes.

"Will?" said Claire.

"You know this guy?" Sam said, relaxing behind her.

"Yes, of course. It's Will Brecker." The fact that she knew someone in Kaweah County that Sam didn't would have pleased her under normal circumstances, but she was angry that Will had scared her. "Why didn't you answer me?" she demanded of the yellow head.

"I guess I didn't hear you in the wind." Will leapt lightly onto the catwalk. "I was climbing on the Needles," he said, swinging an arm to the left, "and I just wanted to say hello to Lainie."

"We saw you!" Terry squeaked, coming around the building, then remembered to flatten his voice into casualness. "Hey, man, we were watching you climb."

"Oh, yeah? Through the telescope in the lookout?"

"The lookout's locked," Sam said. "Lainie's gone."

"Oh. Well, then, it's lucky I wandered by," Will said. "Because . . ." —he reached above the door and pulled down a key—"Ta-da!"

Terry was now wholly his. "Climbing is so cool! Do you ever fall?"

"Sometimes. But the ropes catch me. So far." He fiddled with the lock. "This thing always sticks—ah! Got it!"

He and Lainie must have been lovers once, thought Claire, as Will pushed open the door. Another "first boyfriend." The boys rushed in, followed more slowly by Sam, who paused at the threshold. "Thanks," he said to this other male who had captured the attention of his son and his ex-woman, and coolly studied him. Claire did likewise.

A layer of gray dust blurred him, making him look half materialized, or half erased. Dust had settled into the fine lines around his eyes, muted the bright tattoo on his right biceps, and seeped into a long scrape down his right forearm. He lowered himself wearily to the wooden walkway, facing the Needles. Claire sat beside him in silence.

"Haven't seen you in a while," he said eventually.

"Not since the meeting." She was acutely aware of Sam and the boys watching through the windows.

The sun was setting, and the tip of the Needles began to glow like a live coal. After about ten minutes Sam announced from the door of the lookout that he and the boys were going to start down. "You coming?"

"Already?" She had a sense of unfinished business with Will. "Maybe you could wait for me in the car for a few minutes."

"How long are you going to be?" Sam said ungraciously. "Because the boys need some dinner," laying a

slight stress on the words, as if to show her he was taking care of them. "Maybe Bill here—"

"Will."

"Will, could give you a ride home."

"Um . . ."

"Sure," Will said quickly. "I'd love to."

"Thought so," Sam said nastily.

"No." Claire scrambled to her feet. "No, I'll come down
with you all."

But Will reached up and touched her hand. "I could
really use some company," he said in a low voice, and
she looked at him indecisively, torn between sympathy
and an ill-defined separation anxiety.

Sympathy won. "You and the boys go on," she told
Sam, settling back on the walk. "Bye, kids."

"Bye," said the boys, but their father merely turned and
started down the steps. As their musical footsteps
dimmed she felt both nervous and relieved.

"I didn't really talk to you at the meeting," she said.
"How have you been doing?"

"Okay, I guess," he said, stretching a little. "Right now,
too tired and sore to feel anything but my body, which is
the way I want it. I've been climbing almost every day,
like eight hours a day, since that night, you know. You
can't think about anything but the rock, and where your
fingers and toes are . . . It's real basic. Real centering. And
I look up at that ocean of sky and down on the trees,
and I feel like she's with me." Pause. "You ever read *The
Tibetan Book of the Dead*?"

He had turned toward her, his face the color of fever
in the long rays of the sun.

"Uh-uh. Read about it."

"I don't know what I'd do if Kirsten hadn't turned me
on to it. See, it explains everything. About reincarnation,

THE SHY TULIP MURDERS

about how after you die you spend thirty days—or is it ninety? Anyway, you spend some time just sort of . . . recovering and choosing a new form, and then you come back to planet Earth." He paused. "I figure Marcy's choosing a big ol' sequoia."

"In a protected grove, I hope."

"Well, that's *our* job," he said and circled his sleeveless arm companionably around her knees, smearing her bare thigh with dirt and blood. She exclaimed and recoiled.

"Oh, wow, sorry," he said, whipping away his arm and examining the wound. "I didn't even feel that." He dabbed at her leg with the tail of his damp shirt. Now she was marked with Will's sweat as well as Will's blood and Will's grime. Not too many juices left.

The dark was rising from the east. Not black—black was the serrated mass of the high range off to the north, like surf rolling toward Nevada—but a deep luminous purple. Like monkshood, she thought, feeling uneasy.

"Starting to get chilly," Will said. "Let's go inside."

The only real furniture in the lookout was the bed—high, ample, soft with pillows and thick down quilts, Lainie's only luxury. Will prepared to scramble aboard, but Claire looked at his dusty limbs, at that creamy quilt, remembered Jimmy and the Wal-Mart clerk on Daisy's new comforter, and forced him to wait while she spread her solar blanket—scrubbed since Marcy. Then they clambered up like little children in an oversized world, and leaned against the thick bolsters and each other.

It was as if they were already lovers, thought Claire, or amiable ex-lovers—or like kids, who flung themselves together naturally, unself-consciously. Will was probably easy with any body, just as he was with his. But she was not, and she sorely missed access to legs, arms, hands, a beating heart other than her own. Contact, warmth; why was all touching in this culture sexual? she thought, as her pulse accelerated and she admired the swell of Will's biceps and thigh.

"This is cozy," he murmured, rolling toward her. His breath was warm in her ear. His arm tightened across the small of her back.

Okay, whispered the primitive lizard-brain at the top of her spine, now just relax. Looks like there's going to be a little sexual activity here, it's no big deal. I bet it will feel really good. . . . What's that sound? A gentle soughing, like quiet surf.

Will was asleep.

Claire smiled. It was hard not to feel tender toward someone sleeping in your arms, but under the circumstances it was also hard not to feel disappointed, slightly insulted—and more than a little relieved. Relieved? she thought drowsily; that's strange. Alone with Will in this incredibly romantic aerie, on this incredibly soft bed, but I'm not . . . ready . . . incredibly . . . soft . . . She drifted off.

And woke from a voluptuous dream of Will to find Will leaning over her and running his hand up her leg.

She jerked in panic. She wasn't ready! It had been too long! She needed a bath! But his face, inches above her, was as familiar, as well studied, as the face of a lover. I want this, she thought, and *Yesss*, said lizard-brain. Don't worry, it'll all come back to you. It's just like falling off a bicycle.

And it was. In an instant she was falling, falling into a well of pure sensation. Wet mouths—his sweet, even without the Dr Pepper. Weight—his pressing down on her, theirs pressing her down into the stiff blanket underneath them. Hands—hers, his. Layers of clothes shucked from smooth warm skin.

He was moving too fast, rushing toward his own pleasure and oblivion. Next time she would slow him, instruct him. But not now. Now was a religious experience. Love, significance, reservations, consequences—all irrelevant: the moment existed outside history, a bubble in time in that bubble of a room. "Will," she murmured as he started to slide inside her.

"Yeah," he said and rolled away. A rip, a grunt, and then she felt the cool, dry latex—all in a matter of seconds. A pro in this as in all else.

"Where did that come from?" she whispered.

"My pack," he whispered back. "You never know, you know." She clasped him again; he rocked, bucked, gasped, and collapsed. His breathing changed, and she knew he was asleep.

All ri-i-ght, hissed ol' lizard-brain, that was more like it! Not great, but who knows? He's young, might even get a second round out of him. . . . For a long time she lay under him, perfectly empty-headed, perfectly content. She stroked the top of his head, sweaty as a baby's, and looked out at the black sky all around them. But eventually she began to want to have thoughts again.

Will seemed like an appropriate topic, but nothing came to mind, other than Well, here he is, and then, That goddamn medicine bag is drilling into my collarbone. She shifted; he woke with a long, ragged intake of breath and eased out of her, gathering together the condom and dropping it on Lainie's nightstand, then falling back on the pillow. In seconds he was asleep again.

Claire inched out from under him and walked around the central podium that held the tools of the fire watcher's trade—radio, map, binoculars, compass. It was now deep night. She turned on a cheap china lamp on a low shelf in the corner, and her breath hissed as a white face, hollow-eyed, lit from below, loomed in the window. Oh. Her own face, reflected against the night. And the rest of her, still naked: bony sternum, hanging breasts, striated ribs. She looked ghastly, a white corpse floating there; she scared herself. Without waking Will she retrieved her underwear, pulled on underpants and fastened bra, then walked back to the bookshelf.

No Leopold or Dillard or McPhee here, but plenty of King and Koontz and Cussler; Lainie must be a hell of a woman, or else entirely without imagination, to read them with that hostile blackness, vast and heavy, pressing in on every thin pane— Claire clamped down on panic. She suddenly felt like a diver in a bell, held precariously in light and warmth.

The wind began to keen around the corners of the cabin. She had a small, possibly spurious, epiphany: King et al. were absolutely right, and a whole shelf of literate, lyrical nature writers dead wrong. The darkness, the wilderness out there, *was* terrifying, the stuff of nightmare; it *was* the windigo with talons and beak, and the cruel, alien face of the owl; it *was* the eternal adversary. And for a moment she understood Johnny Appleseed and Paul Bunyan and even Nelson Pringle and Gene Doughty.

Nelson and Gene. She turned her face from the night and clutched at that puzzle. Why, she wondered, would Gene pay for more than he could get? Why do that?

"Unless that *was* the deal," she heard herself say, and wondered what the hell she had meant. It was like a sort of polite Tourette's syndrome.

The wind was now shrieking like a teakettle from hell.

"God, that wind," Will muttered sleepily. "I used to think it would tear the roof off this place and suck us right out of bed."

"Like shucking oysters," she said, crossing to him and perching on the bed. So she had been right about Will and Lainie. Her intuition seemed to be surer about sex than violence, she thought. And why not? She certainly knew more about sex than about violence, though that ratio had been disturbed of late. Will grasped her by the wrist and drew her down toward him. Lizard-brain stirred: Okay, maybe you got another chance here. Slow him down this time, get him to do that thing with . . . Shit! Can't you turn off Ms. Motormouth Higher-order-processing?

Andy's letter, she was thinking. "A quarter-million board feet," Gene had said, shocked. And Nelson had answered, "That's what we agreed." Gene and Nelson, arguing behind the blue karaoke booth; she had forgotten about that. . . .

Maybe Will noticed her inattention. Because he sat up in bed, picked up their sticky balloon, and tossed it into the wastebasket, where it splatted against the side.

"Won't Lainie wonder about that?" she said.

"It's not the first time," he said. "Marcy and I . . ." He pulled on his shorts and scooted along the silver blanket toward the foot of the bed.

So much for second rounds. "I've been trying to think of a reason why Gene would make that deal with Pringle," she said coolly.

He had dropped below eye level, and when she looked over the edge of the bed he was on his hands and knees, searching for something.

"You know, the Mint Meadow— What are you doing?" she asked.

"Looking for . . . Oh, there it is!"

He hauled something out from under the bed: a little wooden platform, about two by two, mounted on four glass insulators. It was like a crude stationary skateboard. "Lightning," he said, stroking an insulator as if it were his crystal. "We used to stand on this when there was lightning. Should have seen the two of us trying to balance on it." He stared across the room at his reflection in the window. "Tell me something," he demanded abruptly. "Why doesn't anyone ever like me *better* after they get to know me?"

So Lainie must have evolved to a higher spiritual plane, too. After all, it wasn't for Will that she rode her bicycle up and down that steep trail twice a day. Maybe if you applied some of that delicate rock-climber's dexterity to foreplay, she thought, but what she said was "Maybe if you didn't talk about two other women quite so soon after making love with a third."

"What?" he said, startled. "Oh. Oh, God." He rushed to the bed and began to knead her shoulders feverishly. "I'm really, really sorry, Claire."

"That's okay," she said good-naturedly, pushing his hands away. "It's not like I thought this was true love or anything."

"No, no, it was really magical, you felt so good"—not *that* good, she thought—"it's just that this thing with Marcy has me totally, like, not centered, like—"

"Distracted," she supplied. "I know. It's okay. I was sort of joking." She pulled her shirt on and located her shorts.

"No, I mean, you really are a good person. You were the only one to call me that night. When I came home to that empty house it was really good to hear your message. Made me feel not so alone."

At that moment she was in the process of stepping into her shorts. Suddenly the floor of the whole lookout seemed to tilt and she would have fallen if Will hadn't grabbed her hard by the upper arm.

"You okay?"

"Mmm." But she felt distinctly queasy. Delayed vertigo? Too long on her back at a high altitude?

He picked up the lightning board and walked to the far window. "Sometimes I think Marcy never got over Gilbert," he said quietly. "You know, her first husband. It's like he killed her—killed her spirit, I mean."

"I think she was a wounded person," she agreed, then flinched at her own word choice. Her sense of discomfort persisted; she was having trouble concentrating. "I mean, problems, she had problems with men. Trusting them."

"I know that. Don't you think I know that? But I did everything I could to heal her, everything, I was sensitive to her needs, I was there for her. . . ."

And it still wasn't enough—that was how his speech probably ended, but Claire didn't hear it. At "there for her" she flipped back to the subject of Gene and Nelson as abruptly as someone under posthypnotic suggestion to tune out the New Age. She replayed Andy's overheard conversation once again. "It almost sounds like blackmail," she said out loud.

"What?" The lightning board spurted from Will's hand and crashed against the wooden floor—a breathtaking explosion with overtones of cracked glass.

"Ouch!" She clapped her hands over her ears.

Will stooped to retrieve the board, then knelt to examine it, muttering, "Shit, I snapped off one of the insulators."

"I mean the conversation Andy overheard," she continued. "The wording almost sounds like Nelson was *forcing* Gene to bid on more timber than he could get. Like he was extorting him. Blackmail."

"Oh. That." He straightened, his back to her. He was holding the heavy glass insulator in his right hand, stroking it with his thumb, hefting it, revolving it, like a pitcher finding the seam on a baseball.

Suddenly she really felt ill. Maybe she had become allergic to semen. "I think I'd better go down. I'm not feeling very well."

A long pause. Then, "Sure, I'll take you."

They stepped out onto the walkway, Claire letting Will go first. Once she was out in the night instead of watching it, it lost its menace. It was just air after all, not some vicious medium. Only air, cool, kind, the moon smeared and the stars soft behind a gauze of cloud. Will's foot rang out on the top step, and after six rings Claire followed; even the stairs were less terrifying in the dark, except that she couldn't see Will at all, only an occasional glint of bright hair. So she listened, and when she heard him reach a landing she would stop, continuing only when she heard his steps again.

They rode silently in the Trooper. Presently his husky voice came out of the darkness. "It was magical, you know. Marcy and me, I mean. At first it was really magical, the way we connected at the heart level. I think we always did. But then it was like . . . like she *became* Gilbert." (*Sometimes I think Gilbert won*, Marcy had said that day.) "I'm not talking about the other guys; I didn't mind the other guys," he said rapidly. "Really, I mean, you can't own someone else, the other guys didn't matter . . ."

This time Claire made it through "magical" and "heart level," but lapsed into some sort of fugue state at "can't own someone."

"Stewart," Will was saying when she returned. "You

know, Marcy and him connected at a head level, I mean he's real smart, a professor and all—"

"*Stewart?*" she repeated, yanked out of her ruminations.

"Yeah. He teaches something at UCLA. I don't know, philosophy or something."

Stewart? Claire repeated to herself, but Will was still talking.

"And that Indian kid, I don't even think that was happening, I think it was some game of Marcy's. But . . ."

He trailed off and spoke no more.

Her stomach settled as they neared home. He stopped at the top of her drive, picked up her hand and carried it to his mouth.

"I'll see you soon," he said. "I promise."

Chapter 33

At an ungodly hour on Monday morning the telephone rang. A woman's voice, powerful, peremptory, vaguely familiar. "Claire, you got to come out here right away!"

Daisy Gomez.

"*Now?* It's"—Claire checked her watch—"five in the morning!" she blurted in bleary outrage, then added, fighting to keep her voice civil, "If you have questions about what we talked about yesterday, let's—"

"This doesn't have nothing to do with my apples," Daisy broke in. Some strong emotion was overriding her natural politeness. "It's my boy, Jason. You remember?"

"Oh, yes, I remember Jason. But—"

"He's got something he has to tell you. An' I got him sorta wedged into his room right now, but I don't know how long I can—"

"Me? He needs to talk to *me?*" Clearly she had missed some short but crucial segment of her sleep cycle. "Not to . . . to Tom Martelli?" J.T. Cummings, she was about to say, but had just enough wit about her to realize she didn't want J.T. Cummings talking to tender little Jason Gomez, no matter whose goddamn jurisdiction, no matter how innocuous, please God, the subject.

"No!" Daisy said loudly. The fear in her voice was so palpable that Claire felt she herself was generating it, that she was in the midst of a terrible dream. "Only you! He won't talk to nobody else! So can you come out here right away? I'm sorry, I know it's early. I don't have no right—"

"Yes, sure," Claire said. "Only, how long will it take? Because I have work—"

"Not long," said Daisy.

Claire's groggy torpor persisted as she drove down the mountain, at which point the coffee kicked in and transformed it to groggy agitation, and the anxious questions that had formed in her subconscious slipped through the caffeine gate—like what was it that Jason had to tell her? There were several things he might want to confess, each more scary than the last, but why to *her*, why had Daisy called *her*? Simply because she was a relatively benign authority figure?

Just in time she wrenched the wheel, making the hard eastward turn toward the reservation on two tires. The folded grass-covered hills beyond the river were luminous in the early light; the sky was a pale transparent blue except for a few gold-hemmed clouds in the east; a hawk caught a thermal and floated above her, claiming the valley with his high falling call. Claire was oblivious.

The car bumped and shuddered, and she blinked in panic, thinking the loose horses had materialized again, and that she had plowed right into them. But no, it was the cattle guard, and there was the deserted plaza: somehow she had arrived at the reservation.

She drove up the dirt road to the church, at which point the road became too rutted for the Toyota, and she parked and walked. She passed the corral, where three white horses grazed placidly, and passed the furled umbrella of the sawmill's incinerator. There was Daisy's white trailer, but no blue Pinto, and Claire had an uncertain moment. Maybe Daisy had said they were supposed to meet outside the reservation, back at Uncle Robert's?

But then the trailer door swung open, and the aroma of bacon and coffee flowed into the morning. If she feeds me, thought Claire, I'll forgive her.

"Thank God!" Daisy said. "I wasn't sure if he'd change his mind!" And in fact Jason made a break for the door as soon as Claire slipped in. Daisy interposed her considerable bulk, and he backed away and stood with clenched fists and lowered eyes in the doorway of the kitchen.

"You wanted her. Here she is," Daisy said.

Jason touched his upper lip, and his eyebrows, and his ponytail, and the stubble below the ponytail, in an inventory of identity. Again Claire was struck by how big he was, and this morning that reality was unpleasant. She kept thinking of him as a little boy, as Shannon or Terry, and he was boy-faced, but he was almost man-shaped: tall, already taller than his uncle Dustin, she would guess; way taller and stronger than Marcy and probably even Andy. The morning's fear revisited her as a sensation, like heat or cold or lust.

Was this how other people experienced emotions? she wondered, her weary mind skidding like a hockey puck—physically, the way she felt fear? Was that why they seemed to know so easily what they were feeling? Daisy's face was white beneath her straw-colored hair.

White and gold, like her namesake. What had Robert called her? Petunia . . .

And in that moment she had it.

"It's the flowers, isn't it?" she said to Jason. "You picked the mariposa tulips."

Chapter 34

There was a charged silence. Then, "Mariposa tulips," Jason said. "Is that what they were?"

Claire's legs nearly gave way with relief. Daisy's did; she sat down hard on the brown-and-beige plaid sofa. She too had expected something else. A liquor store, at least.

Only Jason stood at attention, big-eyed and miserable.

"So," she said, "that was *you* Marcy and I heard that afternoon! I thought it was a deer." She had an image of Jason bounding down the hill the other day; in a way she had been right. Adolescents were half deer, like centaurs.

He stroked his ponytail. "I was out walking. I go up to that hollow sequoia a lot; it's only a few miles from the res, straight overland. I just sit in there and . . . and think."

Smoke a joint and think, she thought, remembering the stained cigarette papers.

"See, that's the thing," he continued urgently. "I wasn't

following you guys or anything. I just saw you and figured you found that flower you were talking about at the
meeting. So that night . . ." He trailed off, miserable again.
"Were those the only ones in the world?" he asked,
sounding exactly like Terry.

"No!" Claire cried, wanting to comfort him. "No," she
repeated, appropriately stern. "But they're very rare.
There's only one other group that we've found so far."

Jason touched the corners of his mouth.

She remembered something: Gene Senior sweeping
past her in his tricked-out pickup. "Did Gene put you up
to this?" she said in a hard voice, hoping to catch him off-
balance.

"Gene? You mean the guy from the sawmill? No," he
said, scornful, gathering himself up. "This was all my
idea."

"But why, Jase?" asked his bewildered mother. "Why
did you pick these—these things?"

"Well, you know, Ma, everybody—I mean Dustin and
Kyle and Kyle's dad and Uncle Billy and Nacho an'
maybe me this summer"—he stole a look at his mother—
"they all get work on the logging crews, and these flowers . . . I thought maybe these flowers would mean there
wouldn't be any work."

This was a bright boy, thought Claire. And a nice boy,
basically. Anyone so obviously distraught over a few
flowers couldn't have committed any real violence, right?

Unless he was a sociopath and a brilliant actor. Things
weren't always what they seemed: skim milk masquer-
ades as cream, and sweet-faced kids with little wire-
rimmed glasses are soulless killers. Sometimes. "The
flowers won't stop the logging," she said. "How did you
know to dig up the bulbs?"

"I heard you call them tulips. I used to help my mom plant tulips, in Galena."

Even gardeners were killers sometimes, she told herself dutifully. But she didn't believe it. Maybe she and Ramón should make a special effort to involve Jason in his mother's farm, and maybe in some 4-H—

"Will I go to jail?" he was asking anxiously.

"No, I'm afraid not," Claire said, then added hastily, "I mean, I don't want you to go to jail, but it's too bad the law doesn't take these things very seriously."

Jason wasn't listening. "'Cause there's this farmer down in Bakersfield," he was saying, "and he killed this little rat, and Fish and Wildlife dragged him off his tractor and *he* went to jail!"

"That was under the Federal Endangered Species Act, which protects animals a lot more vigorously than plants, and a kangaroo rat isn't really a rat, and they didn't drag the farmer off his tractor; they just warned him. Three times," she told him, correcting point by point the disinformation of the wise-users. "Anyway, in the end he was only fined."

Jason relaxed for the first time that morning, but Daisy sat erect and said, "Fined!" in tones of panicky outrage.

"I think they even suspended the fine." Claire was suddenly very hungry. "How about some breakfast?" she said, shameless.

"Oh. Sure. We ate, but there's more bacon and eggs if you want. Jase, I suppose you want some more."

Jason nodded happily.

Replete, Claire walked back toward the plaza. The thin, pure light of early morning had coarsened, and already the day teetered on the cusp of too hot. Someone was sitting on the corral fence watching the horses—

broad back, bare, the color of acorn; thick knot of black hair; Dustin Gomez.

"Hi," she said. His only reaction was to turn his head five degrees in her direction, so she walked past.

"Gene would know," came that unexpectedly deep voice from behind her.

"What?"

"Gene Doughty. He would know there ain't no way you can take a quarter-million board feet out of Mint Meadow." He jumped lightly down from the top rail and began a slow walk back up the road toward his sister-in-law's.

"So was Pringle—"

Pressuring Gene into the deal? she was going to say, but Dustin just kept walking. Motes of dust swirled around his feet like smoke, so that his legs seemed to disappear a few feet above the ground. "What is this, Deep Throat?" she called in frustration, then started back to the car.

Driving back along the river, she was as blind to the landscape as she had been earlier. Only once a sprinkling of gray boulders off to her left intruded into her consciousness because she took them for a flock of sheep, which made her think of Andy, which made her think, for some reason, of Will.

Will. She hadn't had time to review last night, and as soon as she did, that strange queasiness revisited her. It was like an inner-ear problem, as if the information of her senses contradicted some internal gyroscope. Was it the sex? Simple morning-after regret?

She did feel some chagrin, she decided, but only at having deferred to Will's urgency. She had felt lucky just to have this beautiful man in her arms and had not asserted her own desires.

Not the sex, then. Something Will had said? She re-
viewed events, conversations, thoughts, and remembered
when the vertigo had occurred, but not why.

She called Marie from the lab to tell her about Jason.

"Jason?" Marie exclaimed. "That baby-faced kid? He
seemed so sweet!" A pause. "Claire, it *was* just the flowers, right? I mean, not . . . not Marcy, or Andy? You believe him?"

"Yeah. But then I want to believe him. He's a sweet
kid, like you said. I mean, I even believe that Gene didn't
put him up to it, which is *really* naive."

"I wonder— Oh, Claire," said Marie, "Tom's waving at
me. He's got something to tell you."

Tom got on the phone. "Forgot to tell you. I got that
info from Pacific Bell about the calls," he said.

"Oh! Andy's calls?"

"Yep. Six of 'em. Starting at eight thirty-two, one every
two minutes."

"Just long enough to leave a message."

"Right." Silence.

Claire sighed. "Who did he call?" she enunciated
slowly, as if to a non-English-speaker.

"Batts, Hazel; Martelli, Marie; Preuss, Cheryl; Sharples,
Claire; Weissberg, Paul."

"That's only five. Who's the sixth?"

Another pause. "Well, that one's kinda weird, under
the circumstances: Hobbes. Marcy Hobbes."

"Oh," Claire said. Then, "Oh!" She stared out her window at the dead hills.

"Claire?" Tom's voice said, from far away. She looked
blankly at the phone in her hand. Then, very softly, she
hung up.

*   *   *

She worked late, not returning home till after nightfall. Her house creaked and snapped like a schooner as it cooled from the day. She flicked the still useless light switch, a habit she did not seem able to break.

The house popped loudly and she jumped and stopped dead in the dark hall.

Then she sniffed like a fox. Sour skunk as usual, but there was something else, some other overtone. . . .

If she hadn't been half expecting him she wouldn't have reacted fast enough, but her hand darted to the top of the refrigerator, felt for the heavy long-handled flashlight, and found something else.

The butt of her CO_2 pistol.

At that moment an arm swept up out of the shadow and the moon showed silvery flesh and a glint of something in an upraised fist. She fired wildly. Someone cried out, probably scrabbled for a wall where there was no wall, and with a terrible clatter fell backwards down her basement stairs.

Chapter 35

Claire staggered against the kitchen counter and doubled over it, blood roaring in her ears. Terror dimmed her eyes and made the darkness absolute. But then someone moaned from the cellar, and she managed to straighten and again feel for the flashlight on top of her refrigerator.

Popgun in one hand and flashlight in the other, she advanced cautiously toward the stairs. At the last possible moment she switched on the torch.

He was sprawled on his back halfway down the steep flight. He moaned again, and because she couldn't help herself she said, "Are you all right?"

"Oh, God, I think . . . I think I managed to sort of catch myself with my heels as I was going down."

"But are you bleeding?" She scanned him with the light, saw no dark spreading stain.

"Bleeding?" He felt his head and winced. "No, I think the carpet—"

"I mean, from the bullet! I shot you!" she said with a kind of indignation.

"Is that what that noise was?"

"Yeah!" she exclaimed, brandishing the pistol. This was beginning to be farcical.

"Well, I guess you missed me. Um, can I get down from here?" he said in a voice pinched with pain.

"You can move down to the bottom of the stairs. Slowly."

"Oh, it'll be slow." He groaned, struggled up to his elbows, then pulled himself upright and moved down the stairs. When he tried to put weight on his right leg he collapsed, but Claire didn't know whether to trust him.

She perched on the top step, leaned forward, and switched on the only working light in this quadrant of the house. Will sat slumped against the far wall, next to a stack of paneling. About two feet to his left, where it had rolled to a stop in the ancient shag carpet, was the heavy glass insulator from the lightning board; he must have pocketed it last night. And a foot in front of that was the small pellet that had sailed from her gun in an unobstructed arc.

She had missed him.

At point-blank range.

"Were you going to hit me with that?" She motioned toward the insulator.

"I'm not sure." He seemed surprised. His eyes were shadowed to purple in the dim light. "I mean, it wasn't exactly a plan."

"How about Marcy?" she said, daring. "Was that a plan?"

Don't answer me, she wanted to scream. Don't say what you're going to say. Don't have done what you did. As long as he didn't answer, anything was possible.

"No," he said finally, "not a plan. I followed her." He lowered his head and muttered, "I did that a lot. And I saw her and this guy."

"Dustin," she said, on an exhalation that was an expulsion of hope.

"Who?" he repeated. "That Indian kid? Oh, man, no. No. The other guy."

Other guy? She waited.

Finally he said, "'It's nothing, Will,'—that's what she always used to say. 'It's nothing.' Meaning *I* was nothing, meaning she didn't respect me enough to talk to me. . . . 'Nothing,' she said, even after I *saw* his skinny butt down there, in *my* meadow, and I saw him give her the flowers—*my* flowers, that *I* used to give her." By now his voice was loud and high, entirely unlike his beach-boy drawl. "And I saw her stick her tongue halfway down his throat!"

Skinny butt. *"Andy?"* Claire squeaked in disbelief. It was so close to, yet so different from, the scenario she had imagined at the ridge the other day that she was breathless. Andy *had* given the monkshood to Marcy, but Marcy hadn't laughed in his face. She had accepted the flowers and had rewarded Andy with a particularly enthusiastic kiss—

"See," Will was saying almost inaudibly, "sometimes you get addicted to people—"

"Jealous!" She smacked the bottom of the flashlight against her thigh. "The word is 'jealous!'" Then, realizing that exasperation was ludicrous at this moment, "It's a perfectly good word and a perfectly natural human emotion—"

She stopped suddenly, remembering where this perfectly natural human emotion had led. Suddenly she saw that the new mealymouthed Will had certain advantages over the old authentic Will.

"So," she said, "you followed her, you saw them . . ."

"I watched them for a while, until he took off up the hill." Will dipped his head. "And then I . . . and then my—"

His voice broke, garbling the last word, but "my arm" was what she heard, and she looked at his right arm, at the blue-and-red wreath tattooed below the sleeve of his T-shirt.

Images of that right arm came to her: curling in anger at Casey's that night, so long ago; pulling the maul through the air outside in the driveway. It was as if all of his native rage had retreated to his right arm and now he had no control over it. Like Dr. Strangelove. It's the tattoo, she thought. "Semper Fi." It's a vaccine against good intentions.

But "My ego-mind" was what he actually said, finally. "I let it throw me out of a loving space. I always do that."

I hit her with a rock, Claire translated numbly. "And when Andy left that message . . ."

"I thought he'd seen me! Of course!" He slapped the wall in agitation. "I thought he'd seen me and was threatening me. I mean, when he says, 'Some things can't be discussed over the phone, call me right away,' what else am I going to think? Then at the meeting I realized that it was just something about the forest—" His voice gave way again in the middle of the last word, turning it to "farthest." "But by then . . ."

She had known most of this, just as she had known Marcy was going to die. But it wasn't any easier to accept. This was just *Will,* after all, sweet-mouthed Will, who loved bats and owls and had kissed her and consoled her and come in her arms, and this was just another of Will's silly stories, like potlatch and the Indian shaman and the crystal.

"And Andy," she said patiently, really trying to understand, "was that a . . . an ego-mind thing, too?"

"No, that was more of a marine thing." The wiseass redneck kid surfaced for a minute.

Presently he said, "I didn't plan it, you know. I mean, I didn't plan to hit Marcy, and I sure didn't plan to k—" His mouth worked, hoping for one of those new, clean words. "To kill her," he finished in defeat. "I can't even believe she died. I mean, it seems impossible that anyone as alive as Marcy could . . . go, you know? But even this guy, this Andy, I didn't plan nothing. I was just out walking, 'cause I didn't know what else to do—this was before I started climbing—and I wound up by the hollow tree where Marcy and I used to . . . Well, anyway, he— Andy, I mean—was sitting there, just like I figured he'd been sitting, watching me and Marcy that day, after he and Marcy . . . I got real pissed off and grabbed him without thinking. Seems as how I barely touched him, but he must've had bones like a bird. 'Cause next thing I know I hear this sound like a branch cracking. *Snap.*"

Snap. Claire jerked upright as if she had fallen asleep, and in truth, lulled by Will's boyish voice, she had passed into a warm, milky empathy, seeing the encounters with Marcy and Andy through Will's eyes and feelings, understanding their inevitability. Understanding.

But *snap*, and she remembered Andy staring up into blackness. And his cap, placed perkily on his forehead. That was cold, not hot, Tom would say. And impertinent. And unforgiv—

"I covered his eyes," Will was saying softly. "I had to." He covered his own. "Sweet Jesus," he said, harking back to a *really* early Will, "what am I going to do?" He seemed surprised, as if he literally hadn't thought about it.

You? thought Claire. What am *I* going to do? Half of her wanted to call in the marines—no, not the marines— and half of her wanted to run downstairs and cradle Will's poor battered head.

She compromised: she descended to the lowest step, careful to keep out of range of his wild right arm, careful to lay her popgun across her lap so he could see the butt but not the barrel. The room was damp and cool, and the smell of skunk/septic tank seeped through the uphill wall. If she had entered this room, she never would have noticed the light sweat that was eau de Will.

He looked up at her quizzically. "You're smart. Like Stewart. Way smarter than me. Marcy was, too. I knew you'd figure it out."

"But I *hadn't* figured it out!" she cried. "Not really, I mean, I realized you must have lied about not getting Andy's message, because you heard *my* message that same night, and you just about fainted when I used the word 'blackmail' last night. I realized the message Andy left made you think he was trying to blackmail you. And I finally understood just how jealous you were of Marcy." He opened his mouth to protest the word "jealous," then closed it again. "But the truth is," she went on, her voice expanding in anger and frustration, "if you hadn't shown up here ready to kill me—"

"You know," he said absently, "your front door doesn't latch too good. I could fix—" He stopped. "I wasn't going to kill you. I couldn't have."

The idea did seem absurd as they sat in her basement and held a near-normal conversation. "I don't think you know what you can do, Will. Anyway, until now you could have just left town and I probably wouldn't have said anything."

"And now?"

"Now?" She started to rub the too-big barrel of her pistol thoughtfully against her cheek, saw Will's eyes follow it, and buried it in her lap again. "Well," she said, "what can I do? I mean, if it was just Marcy . . . not that killing Marcy was—"

"I never meant to—" he began.

"*Meaning to* doesn't seem to be your strong point, Will. But you do manage to look out for number one. I just don't think you're safe on the streets." Safe where, then? In the state prison at Corcoran? She thought about prison. About Will in prison. No blue Sierra sky, no women, even women who broke his heart. Lots of suitors, though, for such a pretty boy.

More suffering, more pain, and it wouldn't restore Marcy or Andy. Her loyalty to the dead and to the idea of justice began to fray like an old beach towel.

"What can I do?" she said again, resting her head in her hands.

He was rubbing his medicine bag between thumb and forefinger. "I have my climbing gear in the car."

She looked at him, uncomprehending.

"One last climb."

"Now? In the dark? With a bad leg?"

"One last climb," he repeated.

Chapter 36

"Well, I'll be damned," Tom said at the other end of the line. "Guess I better have J.T. stake out the Needles, huh?"

"Actually, I think the . . . the problem, is going to solve itself." *Solve itself. Collateral damage. Uplevel to preference.*

"Oh." A long pause. "Well, I'll tell J.T. to send somebody over at first light."

"Call me as soon as you know something," she said, and went to the sofa, which felt like less of a commitment than bed, where she finally dropped over and fell asleep in spite of herself.

The call came at dawn.

"Where?" she said on an intake of breath, half hoping she'd misunderstood and that Will had just kept going, skipping over the tops of those peaks, higher and higher—

"At the bottom," Tom replied. Pause. "You want any more details?"

"No. Shit," she said inadequately, her eyes starting to leak again. Will had given away what he had, after all. Potlatch.

"Marie's calling your crowd, telling 'em to meet at Ma's Donuts at nine. They need to know. Set everyone's mind at rest."

Mind most definitely not at rest, she drove into work, where she found a message from Ramón Covarrubias on her desk: "Lunch? Wednesday?"

If he weren't a married man, thought Claire dully, I'd think . . . But as it is, I think, business. Codling moths and parasitic wasps and ladybird beetles and other winged creatures.

And creatures without wings, dropping like lumps of glass to shatter on the stones below.

She shuffled the note to the bottom of her pile.

Ma's Donuts was a reprise of two weeks ago, except that Paul and Naomi now sat under We Support Loggers. Even the total attendance was the same: Marcy and Will had been subtracted, but Dustin had been added, for real, and Tom was present, for the moment.

By the time Claire staggered in and slid into the corner booth next to Naomi the communal shell shock was beginning to pass and the postmortem was well under way.

"I can't believe it had nothing to do with the loggers," Paul said with disappointment.

"I can't believe it's really over," Naomi said, with no disappointment whatsoever.

"I can't believe all that stuff about Gene's deal with Pringle didn't mean nothing after all," Tom said.

"What stuff?" Paul said, "Oh, what you"—he nodded toward Dustin—"said about Mint Meadow. That's still strange. Why *would* Gene bid on more timber than he could get? Not much of a deal."

"Well, I was thinking," Claire said. "Maybe that *was* the deal." Everyone looked at her blankly. "That conversation Andy overheard," she explained. "It sort of sounds like Nelson was *forcing* Gene to bid on this sale. And I heard the two of them arguing, too. I mean, maybe Gene was sort of . . . of repaying Nelson."

"Repaying?" Paul said. "For what?"

"Maybe for all the extra salvage he's taken out," Naomi suggested.

"No way," Hazel said. "Nelson's been looking the other way for years! Why should he suddenly start making Gene pay for it?"

Cheryl nodded vigorously. "It'd be like the town whore suddenly doubling her rate to her best customer!" and they all laughed, Paul and Naomi leaning toward each other so that their heads touched.

"But," said Marie, "this district is really in the red this year. They really need revenue. Remember what Nelson said about the budget at the public hearing?"

Cheryl stared at her. "You followed all that accounting bullshit?" she said.

"Sure. It was pretty interesting." She blushed. "I've always been better at numbers than words."

Claire, meanwhile, was looking at Paul and Naomi settled against each other and remembering the CCC kids, sleeping in this very booth. The fire. Suspicious origin, the kid had said, and Will—her mind skittered away from Will like spit on a griddle—*someone* had mentioned a mysterious, ill-advised backfire—

"The fire," she blurted out. Everyone looked at her expectantly, but it turned out to be all she had to say.

Tom, of all people, picked it up. "I heard that fire was

kinda suspect. And it spread a little more than neces-
sary," he said thoughtfully. "You thinking arson?"

She nodded mutely.

"You thinking maybe Gene paid somebody to start it?"
She nodded again. "For the salvage?" She could have answered, but was enjoying too much the spectacle of Tom
prying information out of *her*.

"And Nelson knew!" Paul said, "and decided to call in
his chips!" Then, forehead plummeting, "Gonna be hard
to prove."

Claire looked over at Dustin. He wore a little Mona
Lisa smile, and she remembered Gene Doughty sweeping
past her over the cattle guard at the reservation.

"Dustin, did Gene ask you? To set the fire, I mean?"
she asked.

"Sure," he said in that surprising voice. "Everybody
asks us to do their dirty work. Thought Gene was gonna
have a stroke when I turned him down."

"Why didn't you say anything?" asked Paul, and Dustin
looked at him with mild contempt.

"I don't look for trouble. It finds me anyway."

"Well, nevertheless, somebody must have said yes,"
Paul pressed, and Dustin's mouth snapped shut. Okay,
thought Claire, a friend, a family member, please God,
not Jason.

"Howdy," said a familiar, incongruous voice, and a
storklike shape was silhouetted against the open door.
She studied the figure with detachment. Ichabod Crane.
Hatchet face, heavy glasses, sharp Adam's apple like
a . . . a *querdlying* . . .

It was several seconds before she realized the unattrac-
tive newcomer was Sam.

He slid in at the end of the booth next to Claire. "I
heard about what happened," he said in a rapid whisper.

"I'm really sorry. I wouldn't have left you if I'd had any idea . . . I guess I was a little miffed."

Miffed? thought Claire. Try "jealous." Why did everybody recoil from that word?

"Anyway," he said in a louder, public voice. "I hope it's all right if I sit in. I was in the neighborhood, and I thought I'd stop by." He paused. "I want there to be sequoias left for my kids." He wouldn't meet Claire's eye.

"Welcome," Marie said, and grinned at Claire.

Paul ignored him. "Tom?" he said. "Maybe we can look into this fire thing?"

Tom inclined his head.

"Because," said Hazel, "if we could prove it"—she looked uncertainly at Dustin, meaning, *if* he would go on record, *if* people would believe him, an Indian—"Gene Doughty, Nelson Pringle, arson, blackmail . . . What a great trial this could be!" she ended ecstatically.

"Yeah," said Marie. "The worm's on the other foot now!"

Once again it was after dark when Claire pushed open her door. The house creaked and popped—it was all she could do to walk past the yawning emptiness of the basement stairs on her left—and through the high triangular window the moon laid sails of light on the carpet. She sat in the light for a while, then tipped over and curled into a tight ball on the floor.

Eventually she actually fell asleep.

And woke again at two or three. Something was scraping under the house. Her heart bumped, and she lay clenched, listening, possessed by nameless fear, or fear of the nameless, the impossible—Marcy's stubbled skull. Andy's head lolling like a doll's. Will, back from the rock.

The scraping modulated into knocking, and she marshaled herself for some action: a dash for the phone or her popgun or a cross and a clove of garlic. But after a while, as the surreptitious shuffling continued, the rational part of her developed a hypothesis. And there was only one way to test it.

Outside and down the front steps she crept, hefting the long flashlight that would make a good weapon. She opened the door to the crawl space, peered over the water heater, and aimed her light.

From the circle of radiance a startled little black-and-white face looked back at her.

She jumped straight back, scrambled for the door, and slammed it. An intense sensation of astonished delight suffused her for a moment: it was like love, like a jolt of the purest love she'd felt since adolescence. She laughed out loud and sat down hard on the steps. And then she began to cry. *Really* cry, not merely choking up and overflowing in silence, but sobbing and rocking, nose and eyes streaming. It was rare and wonderful and exhausting.

When, drained, she looked up at the blank-faced moon, an idea came into her empty head. This was it, she thought. This was her life. She'd be one of those self-sufficient, solitary women she'd always imagined herself becoming—women like Hazel Batts and Kate Dolmovic—and she'd love her work, and grow old up here in her little pointed witch's house with the trees and the animals.

And no men. A dog, maybe, but no men. They robbed her of completeness. They left her confused, they left her disappointed, they left her sad beyond telling, they left her. Definitely no men.

From over her shoulder the moon seemed to wink at her with the broad features of Ramón Covarrubias, but when she whirled to look, it was round and dumb as a hubcap. She stood and dusted off her hands, then examined them with her flashlight.

A half-dozen sticky gray pellets adhered to her palms.

The bats were back.